[**O u r   A r c a d i a**]

Our Arcadia

[An American Watercolor]

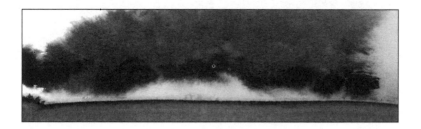

ROBIN LIPPINCOTT

Viking

VIKING
Published by the Penguin Group
Penguin Putnam Inc., 375 Hudson Street,
New York, New York 10014, U.S.A.
Penguin Books Ltd, 27 Wrights Lane,
London W8 5TZ, England
Penguin Books Australia Ltd, Ringwood,
Victoria, Australia
Penguin Books Canada Ltd, 10 Alcorn Avenue,
Toronto, Ontario, Canada M4V 3B2
Penguin Books (N.Z.) Ltd, 182–190 Wairau Road,
Auckland 10, New Zealand

Penguin Books Ltd, Registered Offices:
Harmondsworth, Middlesex, England

First published in 2001 by Viking Penguin,
a member of Penguin Putnam Inc.

10 9 8 7 6 5 4 3 2 1

PUBLISHER'S NOTE
This is a work of fiction. Names, characters, places, and incidents either are the product of the author's imagination or are used fictitiously, and any resemblance to actual persons, living or dead, business establishments, events, or locales is entirely coincidental.

LIBRARY OF CONGRESS CATALOGING IN PUBLICATION DATA
Lippincott, Robin.
    Our Arcadia : an American watercolor / Robin Lippincott.
        p.   cm.
    ISBN 0-670-89273-4
    1. Cape Cod (Mass.)—Fiction.   I. Title.
    PS3562.I583   O96   2001
    813'.54—dc21   00-032474

This book is printed on acid-free paper. ♾

Printed in the United States of America
Set in Figural with Anglophile and Nieman and Altemus Borders
Designed and illustrated by Carla Bolte

4-09

While friendships are at the heart of this book,
I dedicate it to my family—

my sisters

Marcia Kay Lippincott
Cindy Lippincott Brown

and my parents

Robert W. Lippincott
Marcia L. Lippincott

Contents

■\\\\\\\\\■

II *Specimen Days*

IV *The Swept Azure*

[O u r A r c a d i a]

I *Arcady*

I have desired to go
Where springs not fail
To fields where flies no sharp and sided hail
And a few lilies blow.

Gerard Manley Hopkins, "Heaven-Haven"

How to Live?

▪⟍⟍⟍⟍⟍⟍⟍▪

Lark hovers in the little rowboat: it is just past dawn and the lake is still cast in fog. Obscured and surrounded by what might as well be masses of gas, he could be anywhere—on the moon, even. The thought makes him shiver; he tucks his hands into the sleeves of his red jacket and then tosses out the question he has been pondering, imagines it as a solid object that hits the water's surface, causing first ripples, then concentric circles to form and float. *That is where I live,* he thinks, *within those circles; with my friends.* But the thing that formed the circle, the question itself? It is *the* question, the question of the day and, as Nora would remind him, of the great Russian novel: *How to live?* He still does not know. But does anyone? It has long seemed to him that Nora knows, but he guesses, too, that the answer is not really something one person can impart to or share with another; it is ineffable, personal, individual: one has to answer it for oneself. He has been searching, casting about, even flailing for the answer for years— to no avail.

Where? Who? What? When?

■⟍⟍⟍⟍⟍⟍⟍■

15 May 1928
Truro, Mass.

Dear Nora,

I am now safely *ensconced* in the house (our house!) in Truro, & it is beautiful & big & everything we expected: I just know you & Schuyler & Emily & I—& whomever else we eventually choose—will be happy here. We are on something of a hill & there are several lilac bushes around (& others—a couple of forsythia, & I think I spotted an apple tree) & the grasses are long & deep green (almost blue) & lush. Pilgrim Lake is not too far (nor is a graveyard), but even closer still is the ocean, merely a few hundred yards away—it can be seen from some of the upstairs rooms & heard from anywhere (it sings now, as I write). I understand from a local I met coming up the road (who eyed me rather suspiciously at first) that there is also a lighthouse not too distant from here—Highland Light it is called (also Cape Cod Light)—but I have not seen it yet. All in all this is a far cry from Manhattan, and just where I want to be.

I am tired & dusty at present as I wound up having to hitch a ride (several rides, actually) from Hyannis (damned train!—perhaps the Old Colony Railroad is *too* old!—a long story) & so I arrived only a few hours ago, & there is much to be done today before I can rest, but

I could not *not* write immediately. Soon I will begin stocking the cupboards & the icebox, & I hope to find a used bicycle for cheap. & of course we will want a little boat of some kind, but then I know you would tell me that there is plenty of time for all that. (So perhaps I will do none of the above & instead lie under a tree or on the beach & read my beloved Hopkins or, as you would prefer, Tolstoy, Dostoyevski, or one of the other Russians.)

Oh, & speaking of "whomever else": when I got here there was already a note attached to the front door from one Hortense Stone, who has a most unusual & distinctive handwriting—very blocky, practically like furniture (& speaking of furniture, she says she has lots of it!). She lives presently in Provincetown Center but wants to get out of there and into the countryside; she asked that we call her & schedule an interview as soon as possible: my, news does travel fast! She said she had heard about us from a Boston friend of yours (friend unnamed). I suppose tomorrow I will try to find a telephone & call & tell her that she must wait for your arrival—Do you know yet when that will be? Please make it soon as already I am missing you & the children very much, & I look forward to setting up house (& *to naming it!*) & living together for the rest of our natural & *unnatural* lives (Ha!).

X Lark

P.S. Can you smell the lilac & the fresh, sea-salted air on the paper (& the apple trees & the surrounding dunes & the wood of the house & *my hands?*).

Our Arcadia

That was how it all began, with Boston-born Lark, twenty-four, his good friend Nora, thirty-three, and her two children, Schuyler, eight, and Emily, six, buying—cash down—a house on Cape Cod together with money Nora got from her divorce combined with a small inheritance Lark received from an uncle who had loved him. The house paid for, their ultimate goal (or one of them) was simple: to be able to pursue their own interests, and not to have to take on meaningless jobs. A happy solution to that was to rent out rooms, not only because they would need the money, but also because it was something they wanted to do, part of their philosophy. For what they wanted in this new life was to surround themselves, in the most immediate sense, with interesting people, to form an enclave of like-minded friends. But they knew no one else, or at least no one whom either of them would have considered living with: Nora, born and raised in Charleston, South Carolina, had moved to Boston to live when she married her husband, Ben Croft, and he had succeeded in isolating her for a time; and Lark, though originally from Boston, had lived in Manhattan for the past three years and had, before he left, more or less severed all ties with anyone and everyone he had ever known in both places.

It had been a dark time for Lark: the move to Manhattan had been prompted by a break with his parents, and he hadn't spoken with them since. They didn't understand him, was what he told Nora. Or listen to him. *Or* respect him. Knowing no one in Manhattan, lonely and scared, he had reached out to strangers; it was a world in which Lark had been way over his head.

Then, fortunately, he had met Nora. *How* they met was a story unto itself, a story both of them loved to tell *and told* whenever they could. Best was when they happened to find themselves together in a situation with someone who, recognizing their closeness, posed the question "How did you two meet?" The conspiratorial glance exchanged, each would then ask the other, Who should tell it? Lark liked Nora's version better, and Nora, Lark's. Not that their stories were all that different; it was more a question of *narrative stance.* But it is a story that deserves a chapter all its own—perhaps even two chapters.

That Cup of Tea
(Nora's Version)

⦁⟍⟍⟍⟍⟍⟍⦁

"Lark and I met at the Museum of Fine Arts in Boston. Do you know the painting by Mary Cassatt called *A Cup of Tea*?" (Nora waits for the answer.) "Well, we were entire strangers to one another still at this point, though I think we had exchanged a smile or two." (At this point in the telling Nora always glances Lark's way—if he is present—and smiles.) "Lark and I both happened to be standing directly in front of the Cassatt, examining the brushstrokes and the overall, moving closer and then stepping back, generally admiring the work, when a well-dressed man and woman, presumably husband and wife—poor woman—walked between us and the painting. To make matters worse" (here Nora rolls her eyes), "he smelled of cigar. And as if all of that weren't rude enough, the next thing I knew, my concentration— not to mention my enjoyment—was completely broken when I over- heard the man pronounce, in a loud, booming voice, 'Isn't that a trivial and ridiculous subject for a painting! *"A cup of tea"*?' Then he paused, looked the Cassatt up and down, and sniffed, 'Too femi- nine!'" (Here Nora always pauses, giving the moment the dramatic weight she feels it should have.) "To which I responded, in a scathing whisper, 'Do you mind? I am trying to enjoy this marvelous *feminine* painting.'" Well, Lark did the best he could to stifle his snickering, and the Mr. and Mrs. skulked off into the next room. It was then that

Lark turned to me and whispered, 'Thank you.' So we got to talking, and the next thing we both knew, there we were—out on snow-covered Huntington Avenue together in the middle of February, searching for a teashop."

Whispering Before the Cassatt
(Lark's Version)

■◥◣◥◣◥◣◥■

"It was a cold and snowy Sunday in February," Lark always begins, almost shivering and drawing an imaginary coat close as he emphasizes the words *cold* and *snowy*. "I was in Boston only for the weekend and had decided to take in the Museum of Fine Arts. I remember I was studying Mary Cassatt's wonderful painting *A Cup of Tea,* which I had never seen before, when I noticed a fair, handsome woman in a brown cloak enter the room. She seemed to glide," he usually adds, sometimes going even further (depending on his audience), "like a swan on water. Before long, she, too, was admiring the Cassatt, and I believe she may have smiled at me, so of course I smiled back; she had such a pleasing mien." (Here, and throughout his spiel, Lark often pauses for effect.) "She moved close, right up to the painting, then stepped back, across the room; in short, she looked as if she knew what she was doing. (Of course I did not know at the time that Nora had taken her degree in art history from Vassar College.) Then, just as she was moving in close again, a man and a woman—dressed to the nines, I might add—entered the uncrowded room and began crossing directly in front, *between us and the painting!* In addition to noticing the woman's fox collar, I remember thinking how rude and inconsiderate it was, but I didn't say a word. The couple stopped in their tracks, directly in front of where Nora and I were standing, and looked up at the Cassatt.

What *pearls* would issue forth? I wondered. It was as if we weren't even there! And just as I was about to say something—'Are we invisible, or is it simply that you have no manners whatsoever?'—the man made some ludicrous remark about a cup of tea being a ridiculous subject for a painting: 'Too feminine,' I remember he said. Well, that was too much! All this time I had been keeping my eye on Nora, of course, to gauge her response, and I noticed her face turning redder and redder. Clearly, it was just a matter of time before she exploded; I knew this was going to be good. Then it happened—but it wasn't an explosion so much as it was one very carefully placed lob, much more subtle and effective than anything I could have carried off. 'Do you mind?' Nora asked the man sternly but politely, grinding the word *mind* between her teeth. 'I am trying to enjoy this marvelous *feminine* painting'—the repetition of and emphasis on 'feminine' being the *pièce de résistance*. At which point the man grabbed his lapels, huffed, said, 'Come on, Olive!' (yes, *Olive*), and dragged his poor wife off into the next room. I immediately lit upon Nora and thanked her, and as we stood there laughing and whispering before the Cassatt, we realized we had much more to say to one another, so much so that we took it outside those hallowed halls and, eventually, into a teashop on Huntington Avenue. And it was then and there that we became fast friends."

A Cup of Tea
The Painting Speaks

▸▚▚▚▚▚▚▚▪

A parlor, it could be in Paris or Philadelphia, late in the nineteenth century. Two women, close friends—like sisters—are sharing tea, exchanging confidences. The women, call them Lydia and Mary, sit on a rose-patterned sofa, and the parlor is rather grand, with red and white striped wallpaper and an ornate white marble fireplace; in front of them, on a red table, is the silver tea service. Still wearing her hat and gloves, Mary—who has just come in from out of doors (where it is snowing; the month is February) and sat down in front of the fire—is visiting. Lydia, however, wears neither hat nor gloves, as she has been indoors all day; this is her ancestral home. A terrible gossip, Mary is already delivering her latest goodie. As the servant puts down the tea tray and exits the room, Mary lowers her voice a decibel and drops her little treasure, plop, just as the sugar cube lands in her teacup; she then lifts the cup to her lips and, as it obscures half her face, looks askance, mischievously, relishing the moment, the impact of her little pearl as it washes across Lydia's face. Within a moment's time Mary will lower her teacup and look over at Lydia, and the two will begin laughing.

But Lydia, she of the high forehead, furrowed brow, and pensive look, is obviously an intelligent, deep-thinking, and contemplative woman, and it is clear that she has very much on her mind also to discuss ideas; and today the subject at hand, because of her reading of late, is transcendentalism. She will mention Emerson, Thoreau, and a woman named Margaret Fuller, and the two will talk late into the winter afternoon, when the sun is but a wish. . . .

"I Cannot Smell the Lilac"

◼◟◟◟◟◟◟◟◟◼

18 May 1928

Boston

My dear Lark,

The house sounds lovely, perfect, just what we wanted: shall we call it "True House"; what do you think? But I can't possibly make it to Truro until the twenty-eighth, as the children and I won't be ready before then with all we still have left to do here. I don't want to rush Schuy and Em too much or they will become resentful, as would I or any human being: please remember that for the small this is a *very* big move.

I would guess that you have spoken with Hortense Stone by now—how is her voice? I suppose I could meet with her the day after we arrive, on the twenty-ninth.

You'll excuse the brevity of this letter, dear, but in fact I *cannot* smell the lilac, sea-salt, and apples of your letter, for the dusty, musty smell of packing a house for moving (there is still so much to be done). At night, somewhere between falling into bed exhausted and dreamland, I read about Margaret Fuller, a most remarkable woman.

See you soon!

Love,

Nora

P.S. I am excited about the lighthouse.

Truro: A Brief History

■\\\\\\\■

"The original name for the settlement of Truro was Payomet or Pamet, named after the Indian tribe that lived there. But in 1709, Pamet formally separated itself from Eastham and was incorporated as 'a township to be called Truroe.' The name undoubtedly comes from Truro, in Cornwall, England—many of the oldest Christian names of Truro have their counterparts in the Cornwall Truro. And the landscape of Cape Cod's Truro, with its rolling hills and moors, its valleys sheltering snug cottages from the winds and storms, bears an obvious resemblance to its English namesake. . . . A quaint village hugging a crescent shore for three miles, Truro has throughout its history always been closely tied to the sea. . . ."

The Furniture Cometh

23 May 1928
Truro

Dear Nora,

Yesterday I met the furniture (aka Hortense Stone)—she simply showed up here out of the blue! She is a large, compact woman, & yet she's wonderfully graceful. Her auburn hair is cut very short (& seemingly with a razor so that it stands on end) & she wears big, full, dark-colored dresses & expensive Italian leather sandals. She says she is thirty-five (but looks younger) and describes herself as wanting to be to painting what Gertrude Stein is to writing (whatever that would be—a cubist, perhaps, or, more appropriate, *Gertrude Stein:* a Stein is a Stein is a Stein . . . ?). But the similarities don't end there (whispered: *I think she prefers women*). Also, money is no object for her as she comes from a wealthy Philadelphia family (& she went to Bryn Mawr). Her voice (you asked) is like a mouthful of apples & honey, & her countenance is forceful & sure: there is something very solid & clear & likable about her. I would say that she is an *enthusiast, &* I think she will do just fine; in short, she is her own woman. But I told her that she must wait to meet with you & the children until the twenty-ninth (she says she has nieces & nephews & is not at all averse to children & in fact values them). A most interesting person, really, & I look forward to getting to know her better.

After that, I poked my head about Truro Square and found there the post office, Cobb Library, Ebsen Paine's general store, and, across the way, Charlie Myrick's confectionery, which I overheard competes with Austin Rose's tiny, lamp-lit ice cream parlor. About all we could ask for in a town square, wouldn't you agree?

Tomorrow I think I will go into Provincetown to try to buy a bicycle. After which, assuming I am successful, I may also search for the lighthouse (or should I wait for you?).

As for remembering big moves for small people, of course I understand that it is all a matter of perspective.

You will have to tell me about Margaret Fuller once you are here—I must confess to never having heard of her, uneducated & uncultured ignoramus that I am. As for me, when I can I indulge, luxuriating in Hopkins & nothing else (no Russians), because I am lonely & counting the days until I see you & yours walking up the drive.

X Lark

P.S. True House it is!

A Walk into Provincetown

The following day Lark walked to Provincetown, taking the winding route along the shore; the town lies at the end of what—from above or on a map—appears to be an outstretched arm that curves inward where the wrist, Truro, meets the (right) hand, as if beckoning the traveler. Starting out early, with the ocean on his right and the bay on his left, he used the towering Provincetown Monument as his guide and got there shortly before ten.

Walking into the center of town, he was immediately struck by the industriousness of the people who lived on Commercial Street, most of whom seemed to be out working on their houses or in their gardens, his walk thus accompanied by an orchestra of banging hammers, buzzing saws, and whirring lawn-mower blades, and a gallery of men and women in blue jeans, overalls, and shirts in a variety of colors (some of the women with their hair wrapped in red bandannas), standing on ladders, holding paintbrushes, or down on their knees with their hands in the soil; one man was painting the whale vertebrae that ornamented his front yard! It was a beautiful late-spring morning, and the houses and gardens, for the most part, were pretty and well kept—perhaps a little *too* pretty and well kept for Lark's taste, since what he preferred was a wilder, *truer,* more ramshackle appearance: weather-beaten houses and gardens run riot. Yes, True

House was just perfect for him and Nora and the children and whomever else they collected.

There were quite a number of art galleries, he noticed, just as he'd heard there were, and which he took as a good sign; he would investigate them later, another day: his mission today was to buy a bicycle. And now, as he walked past Town Hall, and then the library, he noticed a little kiosk outside on which community notices had been posted: a play by Eugene O'Neill being performed at the Wharf Theater; a flier for an upcoming exhibition at the Provincetown Art Association; a lost cat who answered to "Gracie"; a poster advertising Charles W. Hawthorne's Cape Cod School of Art, $50 for the summer, scholarships available; Mrs. Angus Matheson of 368 Commercial Street offering 3 square meals a day/7 days a week, for artists: $6; a boat for sale (Lark wrote down the address, as no telephone number was given); and then, just what he had been looking for: "Bicycle—man's Columbia. Good condition: $10," and a telephone number.

———

Leaving Provincetown on his red Columbia an hour later, riding against the light stream of traffic coming down Commercial Street, Lark thought about the man from whom he had made the purchase. All smiles, he'd said his name was Austin Park; Lark guessed he must be around Nora's age, and he was tall and rangy and good-looking in an unusual way. But what had particularly interested Lark was the fact that he and this Austin Park each seemed to be amid moves that mirrored the other's; for whereas he, Lark, had left Manhattan and moved to the Cape, Austin Park was preparing to leave the Cape and move to

Manhattan. (Lark rang the bell on his bicycle now just to make sure it was in working order; it jingled.) The roads were winding and hilly, treacherously so in some places. There, to his left, was Pilgrim Lake; he would stop another time. There were other places he had either heard or read about that he wanted to investigate, too, such as Corn Hill, which was to the south, near Wellfleet. Also the Pamet River. And of course there was still the lighthouse. "Perhaps tomorrow," he whispered aloud, for now the comforts and the solitude of True House called him home; but first he would stop off in Truro Center and pick up as much as he could carry—for the cupboards—on his way.

Later that evening, Lark again wrote to Nora:

24 May 1928
True House

Dear Nora,

The end of a busy day here—I have dined on fresh cod, cheese, tomatoes, & bread, & am now sitting on our front porch with a cup of tea. The sky is cool calm shades of orange & blue as I write & I am feeling equally pacific—it has been a good, long day. I promise this will be my last letter to you before you arrive—I don't mean to keep interrupting, but it just seems so right to commune with you daily, particularly at day's end, & especially amid the very new & beginning stages of this great project we are undertaking together.

Today I ventured into Provincetown—an interesting place, just as we had been led to believe; it seems to be full of artists & other industrious types. But not only that: it also appears to support & appreciate its artists. I didn't spend too much time poking around, as very early on in my visit I saw an ad for a used bicycle for sale & soon thereafter met the man & bought the bike. His name is Austin Park & he is leaving the Cape to move to Manhattan—can you imagine?

Tomorrow—weather permitting—I hope to take the bicycle in the opposite direction, but I can't tarry too long as I've still much to do here to prepare for your arrival, only four days away now!

Love to Schuyler, Emily, & to you.

X Lark

P.S. & then there is still the lighthouse, but perhaps I should save that search for when you're here?

Rainy Day at True House

The house had been built in 1883, Lark discovered, though he had been able to learn nothing whatsoever about who had built it or lived in it over the years, excepting the last, most recent owners, the Bakers, who were selling it, they said, so as "to move on," to California—*if you can call that progress,* Lark thought. Forty-five years old it was then— True House, painted white, a fine Victorian more or less in good shape. Pretty on the outside: multigabled, with tall windows, scalloped trimmings, latticework along the eaves, a cupola at the top and a long, deep front porch at the bottom, as well as another, smaller porch in the back; typically, it had three floors. Inside, there were six bedrooms, two baths (one of which had obviously been added on), a parlor on the first floor, a large kitchen and pantry, a dining room, and, of course, a drawing room.

Already Lark had claimed his room at the top of the house; there were three bedrooms on each of the top two floors, and he imagined Nora and the children occupying the other two on *his* floor. Which would leave (he figured now) the second floor for Hortense Stone and the two other yet-to-be-found new friends. But who would those new friends be? And what would they be like? He hoped at least one of them would be another man, not only so that he wouldn't have the responsibility of being the sole man in the house, but also for the sort of brotherly companionship that only another man could offer and that Lark, as an only child, had always longed for. It would all work out in time, he supposed; meanwhile, he had things to do.

Heavy rain tomorrow.

It was early morning and already raining, a fact he had heard forecast by a voice somewhere along the way between Provincetown and home the previous day. "All day, they say," the man's voice had called out to his neighbor. But Lark was prepared: he had plenty to do, the first task being to make a sign to post at the top of the road.

The coffee ready, Lark poured himself a large mugful and took it out onto the front porch. He walked the porch slowly; the horizon was now a mist of blue and green, his favorite colors: moody colors. And the sounds? Gently falling rain and, further in the background, the plush splash of the waves rolling in, one after the other, over and over, again and again. Lark closed his eyes and breathed deeply, in, out, in, out. . . . At such moments of *taking it all in* he could scarcely believe that this was his life now (he had escaped the past!), that it had really come to this: he was living his dream; it was only beginning to unfold.

Shutting his eyes and musing, dreaming: this very thing, or so he guessed, was his downfall. Reading Hopkins, for example. His mother had called him shiftless, and his father, worse—it was no wonder he was estranged from them. He had never been able to hold down a full-time job for very long. Nor had he even managed to earn a college degree, though he *had* attended university for four years. Having wavered back and forth between art and literature courses (not to mention the occasional philosophy course), unsure about which field he most wanted to concentrate on, at the end of four years' time he simply hadn't done enough in either discipline to be able to graduate. And so he had quit, thinking then—as he thought still to this day, the coffee cup still warm in his hands, staring into the blue-green mist—that his life would be makeshift, patched together from many and various experiences (degrees be damned!); but of course the question of whether or not it would ever add up, ever amount to anything, haunted him. He listened to the waves.

This line of thinking would lead him nowhere, he soon realized, and he had work to do, but first he would need to feel better, inspired. He looked up through the rain at the sky. He stood like that until—yes, he had it, he knew what he would do next; in fact the very instant he thought of it, he wondered why he hadn't done it before now (he supposed he had simply forgotten). He went inside and quickly climbed to the third floor. There, the staircase continued up, and Lark followed it. The higher he got, the lower the ceiling became, so that he had to crouch. Then, there it was, a square cut in the ceiling above him: the floor of the cupola. He pushed at it, could feel it giving, slowly; he could see cracks of light limning its edges. Who knew how long it had been since anyone was up there? He continued to work the square of wood gently until, suddenly, he felt it give, then pushed it into the little room and climbed in on a small rope ladder.

The first thing he noticed was the shape of the room: octagonal; it was also very small, maybe an eight-foot diameter; the air was warm and the windows were steamed over. He rubbed his shirt sleeve on the panes until he could see all around him, three hundred and sixty degrees! The visibility wasn't very good because of the weather, but there was the ocean; there, Pilgrim Lake and the Provincetown Monument; and there, well, the road—at least—to Wellfleet. Lark was all sensation. He looked about, thinking: they would fill the cupola with cushions. And he wondered if it would be possible to replace these glass panes with the kind of windows that could actually be opened? It was a project. Which only served to remind him of the task at hand.

He lowered himself back onto the third floor, went to his room, and got his work satchel. From there he returned to the first floor and the kitchen: now he was ready. In the satchel were his paints, pens, pencils, charcoal, his notebook, a textbook on anatomy, and other supplies; he laid them out on the large kitchen table that had come with the house. He had found the perfect-sized board—approximately eight by twenty-four inches—and he had already decided on the design. First he would paint the board white; then, once it was dry, using black paint, he would stencil in the letters, all upper-case: TRUE HOUSE. And after that, perhaps—he wasn't as sure about this—some sort of a small flourish at one end or the other (definitely *not* at both ends!); he had a sprig of lilacs in mind.

As Lark set to work, he let his mind roam free. Nora and the children would be arriving in three days. Would it be *then* that their great project, their new life, began? Or had it begun when he arrived (or even earlier, when he and Nora had planned it and bought the house)? Surely she would have an opinion about this; he would ask her. And then he thought how it would be good to have a radio, so as to have music, especially when they were working. (He watched his wrist, as if disembodied, rhythmically, evenly, as it brought the brush back and forth across the board, each time leaving more and more white paint in its wake.) Then he began humming. And the happy thought of music, for some reason, led him to remember his encounter with Austin Park: Lark pictured him smiling as he stood in the doorway of his house saying good-bye.

There, the board was white! Now to let it dry.

A Postcard from Nora

....

[Undated]

Boston

Dearest,

By all means save the lighthouse for me!

L/N

Leaving Boston

Nora walked out the front door of her redbrick townhouse on Joy Street
and closed it behind her for what would be the last time. It was near
dusk; the lamps were just being lit, and she could see across the Common to the lights of busy Tremont Street. The children were already
there, in the hotel—the Parker House—with their nanny, dear Mrs.
O'Connell, who had been with them for five years, yet whom they would
be saying good-bye to in the morning when they left for the Cape.

Nora turned to look back at the house one last time and, as she did
so, gave her mind free rein. She had lived in that house on Beacon Hill
for almost ten years, and mostly, excepting the bad years with Ben, she
had loved it—the history, the redbrick and ivy, and the proximity to
everything else in Boston. Would she be able to do without the stimulation of the city? she wondered now. Without the Museum of Fine
Arts? Without Mrs. Gardner's museum-house? Without the galleries
on Newbury Street and the shops on Charles Street? Yes, she thought
so. And she felt even surer that it was the right thing to do for
Schuyler and Emily—to bring them up in a household of friends, outside of the city, in the country, amid the natural world. But then she
bumped into a lamppost! She had been walking backward, away from
the house, looking at it and musing; she was thinking how she would
have liked to have a photograph of it.

She turned left at the corner of Joy and Beacon Streets and began walking up the hill; a light stream of traffic ran in the road alongside her. Although walking a diagonal through the Common would have been quicker and more direct, she was not so sure that it was safe at this hour, especially for a woman; and besides, this was her last day as a resident of Boston, and she wanted to take in as much of it as she possibly could on this short walk. It was her favorite time of day in the city, with the sun coming down and igniting the redbrick buildings, making them glow, and illuminating, however briefly, whatever was white. There was a calm, a peace, a solemnity, and a beauty to it, something about the quality of the light that reminded her of a Vermeer painting, such as *View of Delft* (though that was most obviously set at sun*rise*). And here she thought of Lark, for how many people in the world would have understood why Vermeer had come to mind? Not many, in her experience. But Lark . . . her dear friend (his image came into her mind: tall and thin, pale, with fine, tawny-colored hair, light-blue eyes, and his distinguishing birthmark, a slightly raised, mocha-colored crescent moon arching over his left eyebrow, like a rainbow). She admired the quickness of his mind, his sensitivity and sensibility, the fact that he valued and did not disparage (or worse, as so many men did, *despise*) what was feminine. That he understood the importance of Mary Cassatt, for example: there was the whole history of art in which, for the most part, women had served as objects; but then with Cassatt, women became *subjects*. It was that simple.

And then, walking along, looking at the Common and thinking of Lark, Nora entered a painting, Sargent's *In the Luxembourg Gardens;*

she imagined the man and woman in the painting as Lark and herself. . . .

Around the turn of the century a man and a woman stroll through a public park, arm in arm, amid statuary, urns filled with flowers, and a small reflecting pond. The quality of the light, twilight, is extraordinary because it is lavender; it could very well be the magic hour. A buttery evening sun hangs low on the horizon. . . .

Now at the corner of Beacon and West Streets, which would take her to Tremont Street and the Parker House, she turned back to look down the hill one last time, and the beauty of it all—the lampposts in a line, now illuminated—took her breath away. "Good-bye, Boston," she mouthed silently. Then she almost waved.

The Dunes

■⟍⟍⟍⟍⟍⟍■

Nora and the children would arrive sometime tomorrow: it was Lark's first thought upon awakening; he imagined the idea lying in wait, hovering in his forebrain, anticipating consciousness. The cupboards were now well stocked with the basics: he had spent almost all of the previous day gathering supplies, and the house was more or less ready. Of course much was still needed in the way of furniture, but that would come, he assumed, would accumulate in time (he sat up in bed). Nora, of course, would be bringing *some* ("though not much," she had said); and then Hortense Stone, he knew, also had furniture: the house would gradually be filled and grow, as it should. Yesterday, he had nailed the sign for True House onto a sturdy post, chosen its placement at the end of the drive, then dug a hole two feet deep into the ground. Cement would have been a helpful thing to have at such a time, but Lark had realized this only too late. And then at the last minute he had decided in favor of the sprig of lilacs, and so he had painted it, small but with a flourish, just before, and curving around, the *T*.

A pattern of leaves from one of the trees outside Lark's window danced in sunlight on the wall. Lying in bed stretching and yawning, he could think of a hundred things that *still* needed doing, but the past several days had been taken up with fulfilling just such tasks, and what he wanted today was a jaunt, a reprieve. Never in his life, not as far back as he could remember, had he been able to go for a long stretch at a time without some sort of alleviation or respite from the day-to-day, whether it was art or play of some kind. . . . He simply could not manage the drudgery of daily life and constant tasks; he needed an escape.

He put on water for coffee, then opened the kitchen door and walked out, barefoot, onto the back porch. The sky was cloudless, and the air cool: it was perfect. He would take his coffee on the porch—he had put a chair out for just such purposes—and then what? Read? Or write, maybe? He went back up the stairs and into his room (the smell of brewing coffee permeating the house), where he picked up his notebook and descended into the kitchen once again. It was really more of an artist's sketchbook, his little notebook was, with its heavy sheets of bound paper (Lark opened it). Inside were sketches, a few watercolors, passages of prose and poetry, some copied out from others—Hopkins, for example:

Myself unholy, from myself unholy
To the sweet living of my friends I look—

Other entries were original, the prose passages most often diaristic. Lark thought of it as an all-purpose notebook. He had already filled seven such notebooks since he started keeping them, on his twenty-first birthday in 1925, and he had three blank versions of the very same kind in his room so that he would be sure always to have one at hand when he needed it. (The coffee was ready; Lark poured it into the large blue and green ceramic mug he'd bought at the Boston Society of Arts and Crafts store on Park Street, then returned to his chair on the back porch.) He opened the notebook: he'd scarcely recorded anything since arriving in Truro twelve days before. Just one entry, in fact, and those lines of Hopkins.

He propped his bare feet on the railing that surrounded the porch, sipped his coffee, and looked out over the yard. He could see a scrap of the sea; he could smell it, too, fresh and salty and wafting in a breezy mix with the coffee and the sweet lilac blossoms: he recorded these observations in the notebook. "Remember this moment," he wrote, as it seemed to him as close to bliss as one could ever get. But there were many kinds of bliss, not all of which were solitary. The company and conversation of good friends, for example. Experiencing a sublime work of art, of course: a great painting, a book, or a piece of sculpture. And touch, the touch of another—that, too, *could* be bliss (*if one could trust the other*).

Perhaps instead of riding the bicycle in the direction of Wellfleet today (he imagined it as a snugger, daintier version of Provincetown), he thought, he might return to Provincetown and go to some of the galleries, to the bookstore, and see, in general, more of what the place had to offer. And who knew, he might even run into Austin Park in his travels; he would like that.

———

Lark was on King's Highway, riding his bicycle, his satchel on his back in case he felt inspired one way or another; it was late morning, and the sky remained clear. Stretching parallel to him, on his left, was the bay, sparkling with morning sunlight; and in the distance, always a landmark, a touchstone, was the Pilgrim Monument—the tallest all-granite building in the United States, he'd read, and modeled after a tower in Siena, Italy.

Nearing Provincetown now, he remembered that the road forked: to his left was Commercial Street, which he'd walked down on his first visit, and to his right was Bradford Street, which seemed slightly elevated, above the town. Lark turned right, enjoying the view on his left as he rode along: the houses and yards of Provincetown rolling downhill; there was Commercial Street, running parallel, and then—the bay! On his right he saw a sign for New Beach; he turned away from Provincetown Center and continued on the open road.

Before long, the shining beach lay ahead of him, narrow and flat in front and to his right, invisible because obscured by hilly sand dunes to the left. Lark parked his bicycle and headed off into the dunes, thinking he would first view the ocean from above. As he walked, looking up into the cloudless sky, he almost bumped into another man lumbering down the trail; he excused himself and said hello. Looking down and ahead now at the glistening, rippled white sand—which was perhaps like the surface of the moon—Lark noticed that there seemed to be definite trails. He also observed that he was walking slightly uphill, and that the higher he got, the more trees and bushes there were. He passed a few other men on the trail until he was in something of a duney forest. There he came upon several men just standing about, leaning against trees, some shirtless, smoking cigarettes, a few in small groups of three or four, talking together; a strange, slightly eerie, even predatory feeling pervaded the air, immediately reminding him of certain bars in Manhattan. He continued walking, following the trail in its twists and turns, ascensions and descensions, until at one point he found himself standing very high up at the edge of the dunes and looking out over the beach, where, below, men, women, and children, most without a scrap of clothing, lay on blankets, walked along the shore—some of the women with parasols—and frolicked in the water. . . . Lark had heard of such places but had never been to one. Instantly he hoped that he and Nora and their friends could join in at some point, as it seemed to him something beautiful and free, something to aspire to.

He turned and headed back into the dunes again and soon entered the most densely forested area yet. Rounding a corner, he happened upon two men locked in an embrace: they were kissing, open-mouthed, deeply and intensely, so much so that they didn't even stop to look up; and their trousers, too, were open, and they were fondling each other! Lark felt—what? excited? frightened? Confused. This, in broad daylight! He resumed walking, his heart pounding hard against the wall of his chest, his breathing shortened. He passed a man who stood with his arms crossed, wearing only the barest of European-style swimming trunks and with a red bandanna around his neck. Lark felt tense as he continued along, looking down at the path yet furtively glancing about. A part of him was teased, invited, and wanted to stop and join in, but the more dominant part simply wanted to flee. He was headed back in the direction of his bicycle now, walking faster but still looking about, hoping he might spot Austin Park.

The next thing Lark knew, he was on the open road again, flying toward Bradford Street on his bicycle and looking forward to the place where the road forked. *And so that is there,* was what he thought about what he had just seen in the dunes. It was there, and he would always know it was there. He wondered if he still had Austin Park's telephone number—he had written it down on a scrap of newspaper after seeing the bicycle-for-sale advertisement on the kiosk. So what if Park was moving to Manhattan, they could still meet for coffee, couldn't they? Or a drink? Maybe even tonight? He would look for the telephone number once he got home; he *was* lonely.

Back on King's Highway at last, he felt calmer, with the bay stretching out to his right and the dunes to his left; it was such a peaceful, simple, blue and beige landscape. And then turning off the highway and winding along and around the bumpier dirt roads that led home, he found it especially pleasing, finally, to see his sign for the first time as he approached the hilly drive, and he could just imagine how glorious it might feel for Nora and the children when they arrived the next day.

A Gift and a Disappointment

▪◟◟◟◟◟◟▪

The following morning, the very day of Nora's arrival, Lark slept in late; his dreams during the night had been prodigious, and in fact he was awakened just past nine only by a loud knocking at the front door. His first thought was that it was Nora and the children—in which case it would be very bad form for him to have slept so late, and not at all the message that he wanted to convey, or felt. Damn! He slipped into a pair of pants, threw on a shirt, and scurried down the stairs. He opened the door expectantly, if also somewhat sheepishly.

"Package for Lark Marin," a delivery man announced impatiently.

"That's me," Lark said, taking the box and thanking him. Then he shut the door and began searching for a clue as to whom the package was from. He opened the box slowly and carefully so as not to break or destroy anything in the process. Inside was a wicker basket filled with cheeses and crackers, some fruit, and a bottle of red wine, all wrapped in a red-and-white-checked tablecloth. And there was a note: "A housewarming gift for Lark, Nora, and the children. All the best, Hortense Stone."

Wonderful! he thought. *That must have cost her some money.* But he needed coffee. He padded into the kitchen, filled the coffeepot with water and coffee, and then set it on the stove and turned on the gas. Now, he must think: what was the earliest that Nora and the children could possibly arrive? Certainly not before noon, he reasoned, which gave him at the very least two and a half hours to get done what he wanted to do. Which was what? he asked himself. Go out and pick flowers for them, for one thing—branches of lilac, a few of the lilies that lined the perimeter of the house, and bunches of those wild daisies just opening up in the field behind their backyard. He still needed to take a bath; he would do that. And he never had found Austin Park's telephone number the night before, so he would look again.

Once the coffee was ready, Lark poured his cup, took it out onto the front porch, and sat down on the steps. As was typical, for him, of first thing in the morning, his mind was blank, fresh, and receptive, recording impressions: the feel of the wood, pliant and textured, rough, under his bare feet; the blowing grasses (like so much hair, he thought); the cool breeze (he had goosebumps); and the pearly gray sky. He hoped it wouldn't rain. And then from that one thought, a myriad of other thoughts began to invade his mind: he pictured singular drops falling slowly on the sand in the dunes (*he saw a drop hit the sand, flattening it, then spreading into a dark stain*). Which only led him to remember what he had experienced in the dunes on the previous day. He supposed he had known all along, at least subconsciously; and of course he *had* heard about similar things on Long Island when he was living in Manhattan. But actually to see it, to witness it, to come upon it firsthand as something real and existing in this world, was—what? Was it really shocking? Yes, for him it was. And he was not at all sure what he thought of it. It seemed, alternately, wonderful and terrible; he couldn't quite sort out his feelings. And what would Nora think? Nora, whose largesse and understanding of all human vagaries seemed expansive and generous to him. She would probably not be surprised, that was his guess; and then even if she said nothing, her expression would have revealed her to think, *Yes, there is that, too.* No horror or judgment or disapproval, just *observation.*

Lark noticed that his cup was empty, and he walked back into the kitchen to refill it. But before he did that, he thought now, he would go upstairs and look around, once again, for Austin Park's telephone number.

Back in his room, Lark paused in the middle of the floor to think, *What was I wearing that day?* He looked around the room at the clothes strewn about and tried to remember. Then he spotted them: his oldest pair of khakis, with the cuffs rolled up so as not to get caught in the spokes while he was bicycling. He picked them up and checked the pockets—no, nothing. The shirt then, and unable to remember which shirt he'd worn, he began to go through them all, thinking at the same time that he must clean up his room before Nora and the children . . . when his hand came upon a scrap of paper in the front pocket of his denim shirt. He pulled it out. "Bicycle—man's Columbia. Good condition: $10," followed by a telephone number. That was it!

At which moment there came another knock at the front door.

"Nora?" Lark called out, scrambling down the stairs. "Nora, is that you?"

He reached the door breathless and full of anticipation. "Who is it?" he asked, opening the door.

"Western Union. Telegram for Mr. Lark Marin." A uniformed man handed him an envelope.

Bad news, Lark thought. *Someone has died.* He thanked the man solemnly and closed the door. Then he braced himself (his mind ticked off the possibilities: Nora, or one of the children) as he slowly opened the envelope. He read: "Delayed one day but for good reason. I'll explain tomorrow! Love, Nora."

And though Lark was immediately relieved that the news was not what he had at first feared it might be, he also felt keenly disappointed. He missed Nora. He missed the children. And he did not want to have to spend yet another day alone; he felt he had done all he could do by himself.

Now in something of a trancelike state, and slightly shaken, Lark walked back into the kitchen to refill his coffee cup. He let the telegram slide onto the kitchen table while still clutching the scrap of newspaper with Austin Park's telephone number. He looked at it again. And then he made the decision to try to turn the situation on its head, to flip the coin: he would ride down to the store in Truro Center to use the telephone there, it was only a mile or so; he would call Park and try to see him later in the day.

"I Felt Just Like *Madame Gautreau Drinking a Toast!*"

▪▚▚▚▚▚▚▪

The previous night, after a late dinner at the Parker House alone, walking through the grand lobby to return to her room, where Mrs. O'Connell and the children were already tucked in for the night, Nora had seen a colorfully dressed, pretty young woman with wheat-blond hair and high cheekbones talking on the telephone. *How modern!* Nora thought, admiring the woman's bobbed hair and general sense of ease and style. *She must be around Lark's age,* Nora continued thinking, *if not a year or two younger.* And then, just as she was passing the telephone booth, Nora overheard the young woman say, "I felt *just* like *Madame Gautreau Drinking a Toast!*" Nora slowed her gait considerably: *Madame Gautreau Drinking a Toast* was one of her favorite paintings by John Singer Sargent; it was hanging in Mrs. Gardner's house just a few miles away; and she had upon occasion felt very much that same way herself! Nora stopped, feigning interest in an assortment of travel brochures on a table beside the public telephone, hoping that she might overhear more. But then the woman hung up.

Nora decided to be bold: "Excuse me, miss."

The colorful young woman turned; Nora could see that she was heavily painted.

"I couldn't help but overhear your saying on the telephone just now that you felt like *Madame Gautreau Drinking a Toast.*"

The young woman blushed, then nodded.

"I'm sorry," Nora apologized, extending her hand: "Nora Hartley."

"Molly Harrison," the young woman responded, taking Nora's hand.

"I know this is awfully impertinent of me, but *Madame Gautreau Drinking a Toast* is one of my favorite Sargent paintings—I go to Mrs. Gardner's house frequently to see it, and what's more, I have sometimes felt that way myself."

Molly was speechless.

"Oh dear, I hope I'm not frightening you. . . ."

"No." Molly shook her head. "No, no, not at all. I'm just . . . it's been a dazzling evening. I mean, I think it's wonderful; it's so amazing that we've met this way and that I said what I said when I said it and that you just happened to walk by at that very same moment; because looking at you now, within the span of the minute or so that's passed, I feel like I've known you for a long time. Or in another lifetime, or something. Anyway"—she began fanning herself; she was flushed, flustered—"I go to Mrs. Gardner's house to study all the time."

"Oh." Nora smiled. "Are you a painter?"

"Yes," Molly whispered. "Trying to be, anyway. In fact, that's what I was referring to just now"—she gestured toward the telephone— "when I told Sally that I felt like Madame Gautreau." She took in a deep breath of air, looked around, and continued. "I was at a gallery earlier this evening, at the opening of a show in which a painting of mine is being exhibited. My first, really. Officially. And it was such a heady experience. Or maybe it was just the champagne gone to my head!"

"Oh!" Nora exclaimed, startled by the intensity of her feelings. "How wonderful—I would *so* love to see this painting! Where is this gallery? Is it still open?" She looked at her watch. "You see, I'm leaving town—moving, actually, to Cape Cod, Truro, tomorrow morning. And my children are upstairs asleep. . . ."

"Oh," Molly responded, downcast, "that's too bad. Not that you're moving to Cape Cod, I mean"—and then she laughed—"well, I guess that *is* what I mean, because I was thinking that you would be able to come to the show . . ." (. . . *and that we might become friends,* Molly finished the sentence silently).

Nora's head was swimming. The children were upstairs, presumably asleep. They were supposed to make an early start for Truro in the morning. It was well past nine now. Lark was waiting for them. And yet she'd just met this young woman painter who'd said she felt like Madame Gautreau, and that seemed significant to her, important in ways she couldn't fully understand at the moment.

"Will you tell me what you love about *Madame Gautreau?*" Nora asked now, testing the waters.

"Oh my!" Molly exclaimed, closing her eyes so as to picture the painting. "Well, let me see"—she was stalling until she had it in her mind's eye (there it was!)—"I love the movement, the extension of Madame Gautreau's arm, and how the eye follows it; there's a kind of exuberance and grace there" (she opened her eyes again). "And the colors—I think of it as a very feminine painting; oh, and I love that it seems, to me, very much to be a moment captured, like a photograph."

"That's *exactly* what I would have said had you asked me," Nora cried, beaming at Molly. Then she decided to dive right in: "Would you like to have a cup of tea?"

"Now?" Molly asked, looking about the hotel lobby. "I'd love to; why not?" She shrugged.

And so Nora took Molly's arm and escorted her back into the hotel dining room, where, for the next two hours, over tea, the women got to know one another better. Nora asked where Molly had studied, and if she knew that Virginie Gautreau was also the subject of Sargent's infamous *Madame X,* as well as the mistress of another of Sargent's subjects, the prominent Parisian gynecologist Dr. Pozzi, of *Dr. Pozzi at Home.*

The Museum School, Molly said, and no, she had never seen *Dr. Pozzi at Home,* nor had she known that Madame Gautreau and Madame X were one and the same person, though now that she thought about the resemblance . . .

And Molly asked about Nora's children, and why was she moving to Truro, so Nora told Molly about Schuyler and Emily (yes, she *was* named after Emily Dickinson), and about Lark and their idea for a new kind of life, and enough about her marriage to fill in the blanks.

And by the end of the evening Nora had made up her mind that this encounter was significant enough to justify postponing her journey to Truro by one day so that she might see Molly's painting and get to know her a little better, for she had something in mind. She sent Lark a wire to that effect later that same night.

But before parting, walking back through the lobby from which Nora could go upstairs to her room and Molly could exit, the two women stopped to say good-bye. "Do you mind my asking what you were doing in the hotel in the first place?" Nora asked.

"I just stopped in to use the telephone," Molly said, laughing. "I do it all the time. I use the one at the Ritz, too," and she gestured toward the hotel that stood on the other side of the Public Garden.

Nora laughed, too, then looked around at the burnished oak, high ceilings, and chandeliers: "Great things happen here, you know," she said, her eyes aglitter. "Dickens stayed here on his second visit to Boston, in eighteen sixty-seven, I think it was. And Emerson, Longfellow, and Holmes all came here to meet him."

Molly shook her head: "I didn't know."

The two women arranged when and where to meet in the morning, and then they hugged good-night.

The Following Morning . . .

■ヽヽヽヽヽヽヽヽ■

. . . Molly knocked on Nora's door at the Parker House at ten o'clock. Inside, everyone was up and dressed and had breakfasted; Nora hastily introduced Molly to Schuyler and Emily, who would be spending an unexpected, final day with Mrs. O'Connell ("indisposed at the moment," Nora said) while the two women went off together.

Molly turned her attention to Nora's children: Schuyler was an oversized, round-faced boy with light-brown hair cut in a bowl shape; and Emily, whose white-blond hair flew through the air in twin braids, appeared feline and girlish. Together the children danced around her, this new person, crawling about the floor and brushing up against her legs like cats, thus getting to know her better. Emily herself must have noticed this likeness to cats, for she even meowed at Molly, which caught her off guard and made her giggle. And then, because Emily had meowed, Schuyler, of course, had to bark.

As soon as Mrs. O'Connell reentered the room (she was a plump, red-faced woman with a pleasing countenance), Nora introduced her to Molly, and then made a point of promising her animal-like children that all five of them could, assuming the children had reassumed human form by then, have dinner together in the Parker House dining room that very night, news that was greeted first by giggles, then by cheers.

And so the two women said their good-byes and were off—out of Nora's room they walked, proceeding down the stairs, through the lobby, out the front doors of the Parker House, and onto Tremont Street, where Nora took Molly's arm. "To Newbury Street?" she asked.

"To Newbury Street!" Molly responded, clutching Nora's arm and smiling at her, for it was there that her painting hung in a gallery.

"Your children are beautiful," Molly said as they crossed Tremont and entered the Common, through which they could connect first with the Public Garden and then with Newbury Street. It was a sunny May day.

"Thank you," Nora said. "Yes, they are, aren't they? They get it from their father." She paused for effect: "His one redeeming quality," she added. And then she laughed.

The Public Garden was blooming with flowers, but the women were too engaged in conversation to notice much more than the bright and colorful tulips, which Molly said looked so good she should like to bite their heads off.

Boys in the Grass
(Molly's Painting)

⸿⸿⸿⸿⸿⸿⸿⸿

Two figures, male figures, whether teenage boys or young men in their early twenties it is not clear, lie in the grass. It is a pastoral scene: a deep, lush field of grass dominates the bottom two thirds of the canvas, with only an occasional tree here and there and the figures to disturb it; of course it could just be a park in a city, Boston even—the Common or the Public Garden. The top third of the painting is predominantly blue, blue sky and billowing white clouds. It is a sunny day, late spring, summer, or even, just, pre-autumn. The color of the grass is bright green in the sunlight and darker green in the shade given off by the trees that immediately surround and thus, along with the color, delineate the figures in the grass.

The brushstrokes are bold and vivid, almost violent in some places, controlled and delicate in others—each blade of grass individuated here, all of it a blurred rush there (perhaps where the wind blew?). The figures, the boys— probably workers, manual laborers of some kind, maybe farm hands—are on a break. Resting after lunch. Taking a siesta. They are not side by side; the figure on the left is half a body higher than the figure on the right. Their torsos are bare, and both are well muscled. One lies face down, head on his crossed arms; the other is in just the opposite position, face up, his hands crossed behind his head, his eyes closed. Both of them might very well be daydreaming. . . .

Invitations

. . . And daydreaming *is* encouraged in the viewer, Nora thought. The scene is disturbingly sexual (she continued musing), in the sense that the very air, the molecules around the painting, are disturbed, bothered. . . . And Nora herself felt this now, felt *bothered*. The painting owed something to Eakins, of course (she went on), and perhaps even to Homer (a lesser painter, she thought), but there was also something new about it, something individual that was only Molly's, and Nora wanted to put her finger on just what that something was. . . . She looked at it again, moving in close, then stepping back. Those boys, or young men—that was it, she'd got it! It was right there in front of her face: it was the simple *fact* of Molly, a woman, painting and posing men in this way, a way that women had been painted and posed for centuries, as sexual objects.

After the gallery, the two women stopped for tea.

"I just came upon them like that," Molly was saying, "and did a quick sketch. Well, actually, they were there—like that—for over half an hour. So I just took advantage of the situation, sketching fast and furiously, unobserved, for as long as I could."

"You didn't pose them?" Nora asked.

"No, not at all," Molly shook her head. "The way I look at it is, I was just lucky to happen onto the scene, to recognize something in it, and then I was fortunate enough to be able to get it down."

"It's so . . . *inviting*," Nora exclaimed.

From there, the two walked to Mrs. Gardner's house—which seemed only fitting. Once inside, they went directly to *Madame Gautreau Drinking a Toast* and admired it for a time ("How I wish we could see *Madame X* now, too," Nora said). There was another Sargent masterpiece at hand, however—*El Jaleo*, which, Nora told Molly, roughly translated meant "the ruckus"—and Molly pointed out how the extension of the dancer's arm echoed that of Madame Gautreau's.

Then Nora showed Molly another of her favorites, the little gem by Matisse called *The Terrace, Saint Tropez,* saying that she loved the blues and greens in it (*Lark loved blues and greens*), with the sea just visible in the left-hand corner.

"Oh, and there is the Vermeer!" Molly cried.

And so the day passed. And much later, after dinner back at the Parker House, after the children had said their good-nights to Molly (of whom they had already grown quite fond) and gone up to the room with Mrs. O'Connell, by the end of the evening, not only had Nora invited Molly to join them at True House, but Molly, after some thought, had said yes, she thought she was ready for a move.

A Page from Molly's Diary

[Undated]

I have met the most wonderful woman! Nora Hartley is her name. Maybe ten years older than I am, she is very smart, she is pretty, she is sophisticated (she knows a lot about art), and she is to me like a mother, a sister, and a best friend all rolled into one. She is what I have been waiting for for as long as I can remember—to be noticed, to be recognized for myself and for my work, something that always seemed impossible at home, what with Sally and Meg and Todd and John and Sam and Susan and Kathy and Laura, and me being neither the oldest nor the youngest but lost in the middle. Of course I've had attention from men for years—the wrong kind of attention. Nora likes me for *me,* and she loves my work (I took her to the gallery). And best of all, she has invited me to live with her and her children and friends— other artists—in a house on Cape Cod, and I have accepted! I am deliriously happy—and exhausted. . . .

Packing and Unpacking

Sitting on the floor underneath his drafting table, because precious little floor space was available now, Austin Park was packing up his books—*Fundamentals of Architecture;* Kandinsky's *The Art of Spiritual Harmony;* essays, manifestos, by Gropius, Wright, Mies van der Rohe, Le Corbusier—when the telephone rang. Thinking about the contents of each book as he put it in the box, he got so caught up in remembering the Wright and the first time he'd read it that he almost didn't answer the telephone; but then on the fifth ring he picked it up. It was that young fellow who'd bought his bicycle, Lark Marin, asking if they might meet for a drink that night. Austin was amused. Sure, he said, he'd like that. He was amused because he *just knew* about this Lark Marin and had thought that he *would* call; amused, too, because here he was packing up to move to Manhattan, and yet he felt certain that this intense young fellow would want him to *unpack* his entire life story for him. But Austin had felt freer ever since he'd made the decision to move, so what the hell! He hadn't met anybody special in a long time. He liked practically everybody, just nobody well enough. And he could probably help Lark, being new to the area, and he liked to help people when he could.

Lark and Austin Park, at Sunset

The sunset at New Beach spread across the horizon in front of them through the windshield of Austin Park's automobile. The sky was pale and seemingly watered down in layers of orange and pink in gradually lighter shades. Austin had picked up Lark at seven-thirty and driven straight there. He was smoking a cigarette, the burning orange tip of which Lark watched circle about the air with Austin's gestures as he talked.

"Do you want to go for a walk on the beach?" Austin asked.

Lark said he did, and so the two got out of the car and descended onto the strip of white sand, walking to the left where the dunes rose up opposite the shore in the near distance; Lark immediately took off his shoes. They walked along in silence for a while, occasionally bumping shoulders, Austin continuing to smoke; the sea was calm, and the waves were lulling.

"I read somewhere," Lark said now—he remembered it because he'd written it down in his notebook—"that sunset is the time of day when the world appears least structured, when forms dissolve and are replaced by new colors."

Austin was silent for a long moment, seemingly deep in thought, and then he responded. "True enough," he said. "It makes me wonder if the mad feel even madder at dusk."

Lark found this to be an interesting observation—something he hadn't thought of—and for some reason he now found himself studying Austin's high forehead, noting his gentle speaking voice: "I see what you mean," he said slowly, realizing that he himself felt slightly unsettled, unnerved in Austin's presence.

"Too bad we missed magic hour," Austin added.

"Yes," Lark answered distractedly. And then he turned to face Austin as they continued walking, the light growing dimmer by the moment. "Do you mind if I ask why you're moving to Manhattan?"

"No, I don't mind," Austin said with a laugh, "but nor am I sure I can give you a satisfactory answer. The truth is, I don't really know. It's just that I have lived in Provincetown for almost ten years now; I came here when I was twenty-five." He sighed. "The winters are hard; it's very isolated and can be terribly lonely sometimes. I guess I just want a change, want the stimulation of the city—for now. It seems the right time."

Lark was silent; he liked the fact that Austin laughed so readily. But while listening to him, he had suddenly noticed that the dunes were now to their immediate left—the very dunes he had walked through on the previous day. Did Austin know about them, and if so, what did he think? Was Austin leading him there now? *Something* seemed to be in the air between them.

"What's wrong?" Austin asked, half laughing, having received no response. "Was there something wrong with my answer? I don't mean to discourage you—it's a wonderful place to live."

"Oh no, no," Lark responded, smiling. "I'm sorry. No, I was just thinking. I mean, I understand. I'm just sorry because I'd like to get to know you better."

"I'll be back," Austin said enthusiastically. "And who's to say you can't visit me in Manhattan?"

"You could move into True House," Lark suddenly blurted out. "I'm sure Nora would like you, and you wouldn't get as lonely." But then he immediately hated himself. *That was a stupid thing to say. Frighten the poor man away.*

"What's True House? Who's Nora?" Austin asked.

"Didn't you see the sign when you picked me up?" Lark joked; then he proceeded to tell Austin about Nora and Schuyler and Emily, and about their plan.

"That's very generous of you," Austin said, giving Lark an affectionate pat on the shoulder, "but I'm afraid it won't do: I've got to get out of here." Then he shrugged. "Who knows? I might come back. Maybe even soon. All I know is that I have to leave first to be able to get from here to there."

Lark nodded.

"But I admire your plan," Austin added. "And I *would* like to meet your friends before I leave, if that's possible."

"Yes," Lark said, "we'll all have dinner."

The two men continued walking, sometimes in conversation, sometimes not, until they reached the breakwater that stretched out at what was the very tip of Cape Cod. Austin pointed out the Red Inn, where President Roosevelt had stayed when he came to town to commemorate the Pilgrim Monument, then he suggested that maybe they should turn around.

Walking back, with the tide gurgling at their feet, Austin told Lark that he was an architect (Lark might have guessed as much) who worked only occasionally, by choice—"mostly the painstaking but often pleasurable and rewarding—to me—work of restoring old houses." He'd been independently wealthy since he was twenty-four, Austin said, when his parents had died together in a house fire; that was just after the Great War—he'd been stationed in France. He had grown up in Greenwich, Connecticut, not far from Manhattan, so he knew it well; and he'd been traveling back and forth into the city from Provincetown for work for many years.

Lark deprecatingly described himself as a misfit.

There were the dunes again, he noticed, now to his right. But already he felt safe with Austin and knew he wouldn't lead him there without first asking if he wanted to go. Austin didn't ask, and before long they had reached the car.

"It's getting late," Lark said, checking his watch—it was after ten.

"Yes," Austin said, stretching and yawning. "I'll drive you home."

Now they were silent, driving along, as a palpable tension cut through the cool night air and settled in between them. Lark enjoyed watching the yellow path of the auto's headlights as they illuminated the lonely, winding roads; Austin smoked cigarette after cigarette, until they reached the drive to True House.

"There's the sign!" Lark pointed. "Made it myself."

Austin smiled and nodded his head in acknowledgment as he pulled up to the house.

"Would you like to come in?" Lark asked suddenly, surprising even himself. "You could see the place. I've got a bottle of brandy. . . ."

"Sure," Austin said. "It's a handsome place."

They went into every room of the house, and they shared the warm brandy while touring; the cupola was the last stop. The night sky was so clear and clean that a glittering of stars was visible, and the white-caps of the waves seemed to match them far off below. Contemplating the stomach-dropping distance between stars and sea, Lark began to feel slightly dizzy when Austin made the first move. Leaning over, he took Lark's face in his hands and kissed him gently but fully and at some length on the lips. This was what he had wanted, Lark realized now, was what he had been waiting for—it had been so long, and he responded tenderly, and appreciatively, returning the kiss and slipping one hand inside Austin's shirt.

Eventually they made it back down inside the house and into Lark's bed, where, throughout the night, they were explorers on the terrain of their bodies, which rose and fell in shapes that, for Lark at least, brought to mind the dunes of New Beach. Austin was gentle, and for that Lark was grateful.

They didn't get to sleep until just before dawn, and the light of the morning sun found them both sans bedclothes, with Lark lying on his back and Austin on his stomach, one arm thrown across Lark's chest.

Raining Daisies

Lark turned onto his side and propped himself up on one elbow so as to study Austin, who after mumbling "Good morning" had closed his eyes again. Was his a beautiful face? Lark asked himself now. Yes. Or it was to him, at least, though he realized some people might think Austin looked odd, or silly even—or that he resembled Ichabod Crane. But to him it was a beautiful, an *interesting* face, with its keen green eyes and many planes and angles: the high forehead and prominent brow, the pronounced cheekbones, the slightly jutting chin, all distinctive, even exaggerated. *The architecture of Austin's face,* Lark thought. And Austin's body? He supposed it was what people called a swimmer's body, broad-shouldered, long, and rangy: just what he liked. *Austin Park, Austin Park,* Lark repeated to himself inside his head. *If I were to marry him and take his name I would be Lark Park.* And then he caught himself: now wasn't that ridiculous—he didn't even believe in marriage between a man and a woman! But between two men—it was impossible; it would never happen. Now Austin opened his eyes again and turned over to face Lark, then kissed him on the lips.

"What time is it?" Austin asked.

Lark looked at his watch on the bedside table and gasped: "After eleven!" He got up from the bed and announced, sighing, as if it were the ultimate sacrifice, that he would go downstairs and make coffee. Austin grunted approval, a sly smile creeping across his face. Still naked and enjoying the feeling of the fresh, cool breezes that were blowing through the house on his bare skin, Lark descended the stairs.

There was a knock at the front door. More deliveries? he thought. Or was Nora postponing *again?*

"Be there in a minute," he called, then ran back upstairs, found his clothes from the previous night on the floor, and slipped into his trousers. He kissed Austin, who was in the process of dressing, on the top of his head, and quickly went down the stairs again, pulling on his shirt as he went. He reached the landing in a state of breathlessness and was still fumbling with the buttons of his shirt as he opened the front door.

"*Good* morning!" Hortense Stone said, filling the doorway and then walking into the room as if she owned the place. She was again wearing a loose, dark-colored dress, this one forest green, and the same simple but expensive-looking Italian leather sandals. She turned her head sideways to examine his shirt, which he immediately noticed was buttoned wrong, so that one side hung down longer than the other. "I've come to meet Nora and the children," she said cheerfully.

"Nora postponed their arrival," Lark told her, still catching his breath. "Sorry, I ran down," he said, gesturing with a thumb toward the stairs. "But just by one day—I'm expecting them later today." He was trying to smooth down his hair with one hand; he knew his cowlick must be sticking up.

Now Austin descended the staircase, walked into the room, and stood beside Lark.

Appraising the scene, Hortense Stone chuckled. "Well, well, well— I hope I didn't wake you boys."

Lark blushed. "Hortense, this is Austin Park. Austin, Hortense Stone: she may be living here with us."

The two shook hands. "So do you live here, too, Mr. Park?"

"No, no," Austin assured her. "Just passing through."

Lark winced. "Actually, Austin is moving to Manhattan."

"What on earth for?" Hortense chortled.

Lark had to laugh. "That's just what I said."

Austin shook his head and waved one hand dismissively: "It's too early in the morning to explain."

"Too early? I've been up since six," Hortense said. "Painting. Gotta catch the light. For me it's almost lunchtime."

Hortense's energy was too much for the two men, neither of whom was at his best first thing in the morning. And so there briefly fell over the three of them that uncomfortable silence which almost inevitably happens among strangers forced together.

Lark broke it by snapping his fingers: "Coffee, I'll make coffee."

"Mmm," Austin muttered.

"Hortense, coffee?" Lark asked.

"Sounds good to me. Mind if I look around while I'm here?"

"Help yourself," Lark told her, already halfway into the kitchen.

And so Hortense set off on a tour of the house, while Austin followed Lark into the kitchen.

"I like her," Austin whispered.

"Me, too," Lark responded, giving Austin a quick peck on the cheek while measuring out the coffee.

"I see you received my gift," Hortense called out from the dining room.

"Yes, thank you," Lark answered as he walked in her direction. He arrived in time to find her polishing one of the apples on her dress. "Do you mind?" she asked, laughing. "I'm *starving.*"

Lark shook his head. "Help yourself."

Hortense bit into the apple, quickly applied her wrist to her chin to catch the ensuing juice, then proceeded on her self-guided tour, climbing the stairs to the second floor. Lark returned to Austin and the kitchen to wait for the coffee.

"I've found my room!" Hortense called out before long; it was the one under his, with a view of the ocean.

Once Hortense had seen the entire house and rejoined them for coffee, she and Austin discussed their years in Provincetown (Hortense had five to Austin's nine-plus), discovering that they had both been at the ice harvest on Shank Painter Road just that winter. Conversation flowed and became easy, and after a time it became apparent to Lark that neither Hortense nor Austin seemed inclined to leave anytime soon, which was fine by him; but noticing that it was already past noon, he suggested that the three of them go out and collect flowers for Nora's arrival, which could come at any time now.

And so out the front door the party of three went. Lark would tackle the lilac bushes, he said, if Austin and Hortense could gather some of the lilies and what was left of the forsythia; after that, perhaps together they could walk out back into the field for the daisies.

The three worked diligently for the next forty-five minutes; though there was not much left of the forsythia, the lilies and the lilacs were in full flower, and thus armloads were taken into the house and stood in water-filled jars that Lark had collected for just such a purpose. Out the back door and into the field behind the house, they now began picking the wild daisies.

"The daisies are early this year," Austin said as the three of them traipsed about the field gathering flowers; it was another clear, beautiful day in late spring. "Does either of you know where the word *daisy* comes from?"

Hortense said that she did not, and Lark shook his head.

Austin held one in his hand, spinning it about as he examined it: "Day's eye."

"The eye of the day," Hortense exclaimed. "Of course!"

"Just imagine all that these day's eyes have seen!" Lark said, laughing.

"So you think the golden center represents the sun?" Hortense asked.

"And the white petals are—what? Hours, maybe?" Lark added.

"That sounds about right," Austin said.

By now each of them had a substantial handful, and Lark said he thought it would be enough.

As they headed back toward the house, Lark heard the sound of an automobile coming up the hill. He immediately began running toward it; Austin and Hortense followed, walking behind. Lark paused once he reached the side of the house: a taxicab had stopped in front, and there, emerging from it, were first Nora, then Schuyler, and finally Emily.

"Nora!" Lark called, just as Hortense and Austin caught up with him.

Nora turned.

Lark threw his daisies into the air and took off running toward them. Austin and Hortense were running now, too, and they also threw their daisies into the air, laughing.

"It's raining daisies!" Emily cried.

Lark finally reached Nora, and the two of them embraced tightly for a full minute, then stepped back and looked into each other's eyes. Momentarily, time seemed to stop.

"It is *so* good to see you," Nora said.

"You, too," Lark said, beaming.

A cacophony of voices replaced the near silence as Lark greeted both Schuyler and Emily, crouching down on his knees and hugging them properly while the adults introduced themselves to one another; then Lark introduced Austin and Hortense to the children.

"So this is our house," Nora said now, stepping back and looking it over. "It's beautiful!" she exclaimed, moved by the sight of Lark, his two new friends, and Schuyler and Emily standing in front of it. "And so are all of you."

Later the Same Day

Framed inside the parlor window now, Nora and Lark were up late and finally alone, sitting on the floor, both wrapped in oversized sweaters of Lark's, a half-empty bottle of red wine between them, deeply and intensely engaged in conversation—a tableau. To the casual passerby looking in, it might have appeared a picture of marital bliss.

It had been a long day, for after the daisies rained there had to be a tour of the house, of course—a tour guided by Lark and featuring the cupola, everyone's favorite room. And after Nora and Emily and Schuyler and Austin and Hortense had become better acquainted (the party of six had quickly helped the movers unpack the van when it arrived, and then spent the rest of the afternoon walking alongside the ocean, surf pounding), it was decided to be only natural that they should dine together, which they did, all four adults chipping in to help prepare the food. And then during dinner, to no one's surprise, Nora—her glass raised (inevitably she thought of Madame Gautreau and Molly)—welcomed Hortense as a member of True House, and she also invited Austin to join them, which brought laughter from Lark, Austin, and Hortense; yes, it had been a long day. But now the children were tucked into their beds; Austin and Hortense had driven back to Provincetown together; and Nora and Lark—at last—were alone.

"I've invited someone else, someone wonderful, to join us," Nora said. "She'll be here by the end of July."

The eyebrow below Lark's birthmark shot up.

"Molly Harrison—a painter I met the night before we were supposed to come here, which is why I was delayed."

And so Nora told Lark the story of their meeting, of her having overheard Molly say she felt like Madame Gautreau, and then their going together the following day to see Molly's painting (which she did *not* describe, since she had bought the painting for him as a surprise: it would be sent once the show closed). Lark replied that it all sounded good to him, adding that they now had but one room left to fill, for which he hoped they could find another man: "Just so that I'm not the only man in the house."

Nora agreed, saying that she thought that would be a nice balance. And then, as they exchanged glances, Nora let a little silence settle in between them, since both of them seemed to know what was coming; it was inevitable. "And what about this Austin Park?" Nora finally asked, smiling mischievously.

"What about him?" Lark shrugged, trying to suppress his own smile. "He's the fellow I bought the bicycle from."

"I remember his name," Nora said ironically. And then she decided that perhaps it was too soon; Lark didn't seem to want to talk about his feelings for Austin Park, which were obvious to her.

"I *like* Hortense very much," she said, changing the subject.

"So do I," Lark responded overenthusiastically. "She has a way about her."

"Yes, she interests me," Nora said distractedly, taking a sip of wine. "And she's wonderful with the children. . . ."

But Lark couldn't go on, because it was clear that neither of them was talking about what they wanted to be talking about, which was ultimately unfair both to them and to Hortense. "OK," he blurted out, "I can't hide anything from you, Nora: I'm smitten; I guess I've fallen in love with him. I know it's fast. . . ."

Nora smiled and briefly cupped the side of her friend's face with one hand: "Oh, Lark, I know that; it's written all over you. You know I understand, and I can certainly see what you see. I just worry for you, because he does seem so resolved on moving to New York City."

"Yes, there is *that*." Lark chuckled, swirling around in his glass what was left of the wine and then tossing it back, as if in desperation. "Well, we will see what we will see," he added. "A lot can happen in two days."

"Yes, it's true," Nora said, summoning her energy, "a lot can. And people do carry on relationships across the miles," she added, wanting to help him, to prepare him, if necessary. "After all, New York is not all that far."

"Now *there's* a sad thought." Lark was thrumming on the floor with one hand. "I don't want to live that way, Nora; I need Austin *here*." He felt himself beginning to well up, so he wrapped his arms around his knees and looked down at the floor. "I'm sorry. Let's talk about something else. I want to know about leaving Boston—how it was for you."

And so, sensing that Lark was feeling bogged down and eager to change the subject, she recounted for him, in detail, what had happened in the moments after she closed the door of the house on Joy Street: How she had seen then, as if afresh, the beauty of Boston, had even felt a tug of sadness about leaving it, but then had thought about the future and about him, Lark, waiting for her and the children; how she had noticed the line of illuminated lampposts on Beacon Street, which suddenly had seemed to represent the future, bright and shining and stretching out before her; and how she had felt, somehow, that she was walking to greet that future. "And meeting Molly later that evening only seemed to confirm all of that," Nora added. "You will like her, Lark, I'm sure of it."

But Lark was gone, somewhere else.

"It is all right, isn't it?"

"What?" he snapped to. "Oh, *of course*. Sorry, I was just thinking, wondering, do you ever get scared, Nora?"

"Sure, but about what? What do you mean specifically?"

"That's just it," he said. "About everything; the future. . . ."

"No," she responded. And though Nora smiled when she said it, Lark heard a cold, hard resoluteness in her voice. "No," she repeated. "I'm not afraid of the future at all. Not now. Because we're *here*, you and I and the children; and now Hortense and Molly and even Austin are here in some sense, too. I *refuse* to be afraid of the future." She paused. "I know it will have its hardships, but this is what we wanted. How many people actually have what they want, Lark? Not many. We're lucky!" She looked at him when she'd finished speaking. She was thinking that she knew two Larks, and this was that other one, the one who was frightened and small and negative. She loved them both, and though she understood this other one, she didn't always know quite what to do with him. She took Lark's hand. She said, "Let's be happy."

Lark smiled, then apologized. "Maybe I've had too much wine," he offered by way of explanation.

"Yes," Nora said. "We need food—something good!" And suddenly she was off in the direction of the kitchen.

Which left Lark feeling guilty, guilty and grateful, for he was lucky to have Nora, he knew that; and especially now, to be living with Nora and the children. There was no excuse for this sort of behavior. But he had met a man who treated him well, and he felt he *needed* him. . . . And Austin? Austin was moving away. Which meant what, that Austin did not need him? And then Lark literally shook his entire body: *You were fine before you met him,* he told himself. *Everything was looking up—you had the future, here, with Nora and the children, and you were happy about that. Why should meeting Austin change anything?* And then he felt himself growing angry at Austin, but immediately he realized how wrong and ridiculous that was. It was himself he should be mad at—himself, for falling apart like this and letting it spoil Nora's first night at True House, all because someone, a man, had been kind to him. He would pull himself up; he would apologize to Nora.

And then she reentered the room. She placed a plate of cheese and crackers on the floor between them and sat down.

"I'm sorry," Lark said, rubbing Nora's shoulder.

Nibbling on the sharp cheddar, she shook her head.

And then Lark sighed, long and deep. "How to live, Nora?" It was a question each of them had asked the other time and again. "How to live?" he repeated. He paused to take a sip of air. "Dying is easy," he went on. "It's how most people live their lives, don't you think? Slowly dying; it's living, living *fully*, that's hard."

"You haven't been reading your Russians, have you, Lark?" Nora said, and then she gave a little laugh. But once she saw that Lark was not laughing, she repeated the question and then answered it seriously: "'How to live?' you ask," she said. "Then let me answer, firmly and with conviction: *Together. Together and well.*"

Lark raised his glass of wine in a toast. "Amen!" he said. "I'll drink to that."

A Day at the Beach

For the next two days the spotlight falls almost exclusively on Lark and Austin, for these were all the days they had left, just a few, before Austin was to depart for Manhattan. But around the edges of the spotlight, in the dark periphery, Hortense moved into True House, with an army of women trudging behind her, and Nora settled in, unpacking, rearranging furniture, hanging pictures, and frequently looking through the window screen at the children, who ran outside. There they played, first, at Emily's insistence, "raining daisies," and then at Schuyler's instigation lying on the ground, hugging their bodies tightly, and rolling down the hill in back, acquiring leaves and brambles in their hair as they went, happy together in their new life. But Lark knew nothing of these goings-on since he spent the entire day and night at Austin's house on Pearl Street in Provincetown.

On the morning following the group dinner he had awakened early and ridden his bicycle into Provincetown; rabbits scurried along the side of the road and a thick, white mist lifted off Pilgrim Lake. Arriving at Austin's just after eight, Lark woke him up and, while Austin, wearing only his undershorts, was still yawning and scratching and making coffee, sat down at Austin's kitchen table and declared his undying love. Tomorrow that kitchen table, and indeed all of the furniture, would be gone, packed up and hauled away by movers, on its way to Manhattan, and the day after that Austin would follow it; but today Lark rested his elbows on the table and, crying, told Austin that he loved him and came *this close* to asking him not to leave, but didn't.

Standing beside him, Austin cradled Lark's head against his bare chest and said that he cared for him, too, but that to be honest, so much emotion so quickly frightened him; it seemed a bit excessive.

"That's me," Lark said, laughing and sniffling at the same time, "excessive!" But he also understood what Austin was saying. It was a warning; he would try to pull himself together. "Sorry."

Austin put up a hand: "Don't apologize."

And then the coffee was ready, which gave Austin something to do, a distraction, a chance for the two to normalize things and start over. "Want some?" he asked.

Lark nodded. "I think it's going to be hot today," he said, doing his best. "I saw a thermometer in somebody's yard on my way over that read eighty degrees, already—before nine in the morning."

"Maybe we should spend the day at the beach," Austin said.

"Mmm," Lark murmured. "I think so."

————

They arrived at New Beach shortly after noon. Although hot, the day was overcast and gray, with the sun putting in only an occasional appearance. Because of this the beach was not as crowded as it might otherwise have been. Since they'd put on their suits back at Austin's (or what would be serving as suits, for Lark had only a pair of shorts), as soon as their shirts were off they were ready to go into the water.

"Race you!" Austin said, and the two immediately took off running toward the water, Austin always one stride ahead. They ran until they could run no more, until the seasonally cold water—by now at their waists—had swallowed them. Both men submerged themselves completely, then came up laughing. "Doesn't this feel great?" Austin called.

Lark smiled and nodded. He was so happy; and yet so sad. He went under again. His one-man struggle between now and when Austin left would be to fight off that sadness and keep it at bay until *after* Austin was gone. And he had to continually remind himself that though Austin was going, he had not gone, and that he—Lark—should seize the moment, the present of Austin's presence, and enjoy it. Reemerging, Lark swam over to Austin and then, just before reaching him, went underwater again and pulled down Austin's swimming trunks.

"Hungry shark," Austin said, once Lark had resurfaced.

"I *am* hungry," Lark said. "Let's eat!"

"Me, too."

Austin had packed a picnic, and it was here that Lark got to know him better, as this was no ordinary picnic. For one thing, Austin had a proper wicker picnic basket; inside it was, first (packed in order), a sheet for them to lie on, then a red-and-white-checked gingham tablecloth and, for food, two ripe avocados (which Austin served by cutting each in half, removing the seed, and sprinkling the flesh with olive oil, salt, and pepper, to be eaten with a spoon), a freshly baked loaf of sourdough bread from one of the bakeries in town, no meat—Austin was a vegetarian (for the simple reason that it was healthier, he'd said)—but a couple of kinds of cheeses, ripe tomatoes, apples, plenty of water, and, later, for dessert, a linzer torte from the same bakery, and coffee in a thermos. (Lark watched, completely rapt, as Austin slowly and methodically peeled an apple, one hand holding it and the other deftly pushing the knife around and around until the red peel came off whole, in a corkscrew shape, revealing the naked white skin of the fruit. Then he generously handed the apple to Lark and started to peel another. And to Lark at that moment the action of Austin's peeling the apple seemed to define who Austin was, his very character.)

After lunch, the two rested; Austin even fell asleep for half an hour. And then it was back into the water again, boisterously. Jumping up and down, in and out of the spray, or catching waves and riding them in to shore, Lark was doing his best, giving it his all, and Austin was grateful.

"When are you coming to see me in Manhattan?" he said now. "Let's plan your first visit."

Lark smiled, and his eyes stung: he was moved. For in that one question was both the *fact* of Austin's leaving and also the evidence of his love. "Next weekend, the weekend after, *yesterday*—you name it and I'll be there," he replied.

"Next weekend I will have been there all of a few days," Austin said with a laugh. "The weekend after it is!" he called out over the waves, which had become rougher as the afternoon passed.

Lark swam over to where Austin was treading water. With his hair wet and flat against his head, Austin's features appeared a bit severe, but they were softened by the love Lark felt for him. He looked around to make sure it was safe, then kissed him on the lips. "Thank you."

Austin shook his head: "No, thank *you*."

"OK." Lark laughed. "That's enough of *that*—let's don't go getting soft."

"Let's have dessert instead," Austin responded.

It was late in the afternoon by now, and the sea was growing rougher and the sky grayer and more troubled-looking; the beach was almost deserted.

Over coffee and linzer torte, Lark told Austin the story of his birthmark, or rather the version that he had overheard his mother tell one of her friends. When he was a newborn, she'd said—just brought home from the hospital, in fact—his cradle in the nursery was directly under a window. That first night at home, his mother said she'd nursed him and then put him to bed. Sometime between then and when he woke up in the middle of the night, the crescent moon must have shined through his window so brightly, *for him,* that it somehow etched itself onto his brow. She said after that she became convinced that if she had left the cradle there another night, he would have awakened the next day with a star on the other side—he was that special. *I wish she had maintained that feeling,* Lark thought to himself.

"Hey, where does 'Lark' come from?" Austin asked now. "It's so unusual; is it a family name?"

"Do you know that I don't really know?" Lark said. "I never thought to ask, though I've always been aware that it's not your ordinary, run-of-the-mill name. And of course I got teased about it constantly as a child. But I don't think it *is* a family name. It must just be after the songbird; it would figure that my parents would do something like that, since I'm afraid of birds."

Austin was surprised: "Why afraid of birds, of all things?"

"Because they seem so delicate and nervous," Lark said, his brow furrowed and knitted. "So breakable. And the smaller they are, the more afraid I am. Like hummingbirds: such tiny bones"—he shuddered—"and all that constant movement and fluttering about. I read somewhere that their wings beat something like five hundred times per minute."

"Oh, Lark." They were lying next to each other on the bedsheet; Austin leaned over now and embraced him.

"And what about 'Austin'?" Lark asked, recovering.

"It's a family name; it was my father's name, and his father's name. So officially I'm Austin Park the Third."

A thunderbolt slammed across the horizon. Lark shivered and looked around: the beach was completely deserted now except for the two of them, and the sun was going down.

"Cold?" Austin asked.

Lark nodded.

"Want to leave?" Austin asked.

Lark shook his head.

"Good, neither do I." He shook the thermos. "Coffee's gone," he announced. And then he rolled over on top of Lark (who lay on his stomach). "Here, I'll keep you warm."

"No!" Lark said emphatically, shaking him off.

Austin rolled over onto his side, then sat up. "OK, OK."

Lark turned over and sat up, too, but he was shaking and shivering. He wrapped his arms about himself and lowered his head; he was afraid he was going to cry.

"What is it?" Austin said softly.

Lark shook his head, still not looking up. He knew he would have to explain himself if there was to be any hope at all for him and Austin. He raised his head and looked Austin in the eyes. "The first man I was with," he began, but then his voice broke and tears sprang from his eyes. "This was a few years ago, four years ago, in Manhattan. He"—Lark gulped, took a breath, and steeled himself—"he got me drunk and then . . . I didn't know what he was doing . . . he raped me." And now that he'd said it, at last, instead of dissolving, as he thought he would, he poured forth a torrent of words. "But it wasn't just that one time. It continued. He became my lover. For almost a year. And then even after I got away from him I, . . . I went looking for the same thing. I'd always felt that there was something wrong with me, that I wasn't good enough; my parents had made it clear that they were disappointed in me. And so it was all a confusion of finally feeling loved and at the same time feeling like I was getting what I deserved, that *that* was what I was worth."

There. He had said it; he had finally told someone. And now he completely broke down sobbing. He was relieved, yes, but also certain that he had ruined whatever chance he might have had with Austin. But then Austin took him fully in his arms, held him close, and rocked him, stroked his hair, not saying a word.

———

As they lay warm and dry in Austin's bed later that night, Austin leaned over, kissed Lark's head, and said, "OK, you've convinced me."

Lark had on his glasses and was reading Hopkins. "What?"

"I don't absolutely *have* to be in Manhattan until Thursday; I'll stay a couple of extra days."

Lark smiled.

"But," Austin said, raising a hand, "I'll have to stay *with you,* because all of my things are being carted away tomorrow and I have to be out of the house."

"Forget it," Lark said, suppressing a grin. "Staying with me is out of the question."

With that, Austin turned out the bedside lamp. "Curses upon you, then," he muttered, kissing Lark on the cheek.

"Kisses upon me," Lark murmured.

Falling asleep in Austin's arms that night, he felt a peace he had not known for years: he was loved.

Hortense Takes the Floor

It was all kind of a shock, Nora thought—leaving Boston and arriving in Truro only to find that Lark had fallen in love. And now his being gone all day her first full day at True House . . . She was standing in the middle of her new bedroom late in the afternoon, still unpacking, feeling sorry for herself and thinking, *What* am I doing? She recognized it as a moment of hysteria and knew that she must try to calm herself. The children seemed fine, out of doors all day playing together, and there was plenty to do. Fortunately, just when she thought she might collapse into a heap on the floor, Nora heard Hortense's rich, resonant voice—like apples and honey, as Lark had aptly described it—calling her name, and then her solid, sandaled footsteps mounting the stairs to the third floor.

"Nor-a?"

Apples and honey, Nora thought, collecting herself. "I'm in here, Hortense—in my room."

Arriving in the doorway of Nora's room, Hortense took one look at her face and quickly read its open pages: "You're finding all of this difficult, aren't you?"

Nora's impulse was to shake her head no, but she caught herself, slowly nodded, and then walked over to Hortense and threw her arms around her.

"I know," Hortense said soothingly, stroking Nora's hair. "I understand."

She held Nora like that briefly, for a few moments, and then released her, changed the subject, and moved on: "I thought we might prepare dinner together. It's past time," she added.

"Yes," Nora said, patting her hair and thinking that food probably *would* help. "Just the two of us—I'll let the children stay out and play until it's ready."

And as the women began descending the stairs together, Nora put her hand on Hortense's shoulder and thanked her. Hortense just shook her head and waved one hand dismissively, as if saying, "Don't mention it."

But Nora *was* grateful, and once they'd reached the kitchen she found herself wishing that Hortense would just go on and on talking. She would try to draw her out. "Tell me about your parents—are they still alive?"

Hortense laughed. "Daddy's very much alive," she replied, opening cupboards and banging pots and pans. "But Mother's been half dead ever since I can remember. She's neurasthenic—spends all her time in bed. It's such a waste." Hortense filled a large pot with water, set it on the stove, covered it, and turned on the gas. They had decided on macaroni and cheese.

What a way to sum up one's mother! Nora thought. *Such dispassionate clear-headedness.* "I'm sorry," she said.

Biting into a slice of the cheddar she had removed from the icebox, Hortense waved it off. "Daddy's a pistol. He's sixty-eight years old and still active in the firm—he's a lawyer. He still rides his favorite Arabian mare, still looks forward to fox-hunting season. He swims. Boats. And he travels like you wouldn't believe!" Cubing the cheese, she paused. "Clearly, I take after *him*." Then she laughed.

Tearing lettuce, Nora felt better already. *This is normal,* she thought. And she liked Hortense immensely for it.

"And what about *your* parents?" Hortense asked.

"My father died when I was eight," Nora said. "My mother still lives in Charleston, South Carolina, which is where I'm from. She's kept herself busy—she teaches piano. And I have a twin brother, Michael—he's also in Charleston. I've sometimes thought that he might like to join us here, *if* he could leave Mother." But thinking of Michael made her think, too, of Lark, and suddenly Nora began withdrawing again and grew sad.

Hortense watched, could see all of this happening. She felt she *had* to say something, to speak up. "Look, Nora," she said at last, "this is about Lark, isn't it?"

Nora nodded, and Hortense paused so as to better collect her thoughts, all of which Nora tried to watch play across her face.

"You know him much better than I do," Hortense said carefully. "However, it's important, no matter what, for him to follow this through, wouldn't you agree?" She tasted the macaroni. It was ready; she would drain it.

Feeling slightly ashamed of herself, Nora whispered, "Yes."

Then Hortense continued, "Austin Park will be leaving soon— tomorrow, in fact—and then Lark will be here most all of the time. Oh, he'll probably be a mess for a few days"—she chuckled—"but he'll be here." She carried the heavy pot over to the sink and slowly poured the boiling water and macaroni into the strainer, steam rising to color her face. "You're not actually worried that he'll take off for Manhattan with Austin, are you?" She shook the strainer vigorously, and without even waiting for an answer she added, "I don't think so. I don't think he'd give up all this just yet." And then she poured the drained macaroni into a large bowl and began adding the cheese, along with milk, butter, and eggs; then she stirred. "Besides," she went on, "I'm not at all sure Austin would let him do that even if he wanted to. He seems to have a good head on his shoulders, and I think he knows what a mistake it would be at this point, so early on." Now she spooned the macaroni mixture into a greased baking dish.

Astonished at Hortense's levelheadedness and insight, Nora shook her head. "Of course you're right," she said. And then she began cutting up the tomato.

With the macaroni and cheese in the oven, Hortense moved on to washing out the large pot for corn. Nora watched her. "Thank you," Nora said.

Hortense shrugged, then laughed. "We'd best get to shucking that corn. And we're going to need a dressing for the salad."

Nora laughed, too. "Yes, ma'am!"

"Meanwhile," Hortense said, lifting a bottle of red wine, "I'm going to have a glass of wine before dinner. Will you join me?"

"Yes, indeed," Nora cried. "I think I need it."

"I do, too!" Hortense laughed. Then she poured two glasses, handed one to Nora, and lifted hers in a toast. "To sisterhood!" she exclaimed.

"To sisterhood!" Nora echoed her. And then there followed a long conversation, which saw them through the rest of dinner preparations, about how much both of them loved women and their company, Hortense carnally and otherwise, and Nora just otherwise, which gave her the opportunity to tell Hortense about their future housemate Molly.

Animal Cracks

Over dinner, Nora could not help but step back and watch her children as they ate and talked, wondering how it all was sitting with them—their first day after the big move, with Lark not around. Hortense was asking them about their day, and Schuyler was telling her about how they had pretended that they were felled trees, rolling down the hill out back. Emily was staring at her plate while chewing on one of her braids, seeming to listen intensely.

How she adored them, Nora thought now, equally but differently. Schuyler was her firstborn, and she felt especially protective toward him, probably because he had witnessed the difficulties of the marriage far more than Emily had, and because—as was not uncommon—when living with his mother after the divorce, he had frequently acted out against her, taking his father's side. Emily was another matter; Emily, Nora just sat back and watched, in awe: she had been fiercely independent almost from the beginning, perfectly able and content to go off into a world of her own making. Nora felt certain that Emily would go into the arts—painting or poetry perhaps—whereas she very much doubted that Schuyler would. No, she saw him as having more of a difficult time in the world, and thus her need to protect him rushed in, precisely what he did not want.

But as she studied her children now, eating, talking with Hortense, she realized that they were somewhere else completely.

"I taught Schuyler where we live," Emily was saying. "Didn't I, Schuy?"

Schuyler smirked and said, "Rural Truro," and then both he and Emily broke up laughing.

"Rural Truro," Nora and Hortense said repeatedly, until the table was humming with the tongue-twister.

But Schuyler and Emily were not finished. They had spent the entire day together and they had conspired to join forces. With a storm now raging outside, the children made known their desires, which came out in a barragelike attack of words:

"What this place needs," Schuyler told his mother now, "is a few animals. Pets. Specifically, I should like a dog and a rabbit."

"And I should like a cat," Emily chimed in, "which I shall name *The Bernhard*, after a character in a book not yet written."

"And I wouldn't mind having a cow and a horse; we have all this room," Schuyler added, motioning out the window. "But I suppose those could wait."

"And maybe a pig, too!" Emily said, giggling.

Nora looked at Hortense, who—unable to hold it in any longer—was laughing.

"Oink, oink," was Nora's response, at which point she, Hortense, and the children all roared with laughter.

Molly Writes to Nora

....

May 31, 1928
Boston, Massachusetts

Dear Nora,

How are you? And how are Emily and Schuyler? And Lark? And your new place?

I stopped in at the Parker House again yesterday to use the telephone, only this time you weren't there. But I had the memory of our meeting to comfort me. I still can't quite believe my lucky stars. And just think, in about two months' time I will be there with you: I can't wait!

Thank you again for buying *Boys in the Grass*. I do hope Lark likes it and I wish I were going to be there to see his face when he sees it for the first time. Will you write and tell me about it? And more about him—what is he like?

By the way, there was a review of the show in the *Boston Post* that briefly mentioned *Boys*, referring to it as an "unsettling, feverish dream of a painting with echoes of Eakins by Molly Harrison, a former student of the Museum School whose first exhibited work this is." It's not clear to me whether he (the reviewer) actually liked the painting or not, but all the same I suppose I am glad to have been mentioned.

Also (much going on here!), there is a very rich woman who saw the show and contacted me through the gallery and wants to commission me to do a portrait of her gardener. She thinks $500 a fair price and—gulp—so do I! I am to go to her house in West Newton and meet them both tomorrow—she is sending a car for me!

Who knows what else may come of all this, but whatever, I will greet you in July a (temporarily) rich woman. Oh—also, I ran into one of my former teachers from the Museum School at a party Saturday night, and upon hearing that I was moving to Truro at the end of July he fell into a rhapsody about the light down there and about all of the artists and galleries and possibilities. So you see, everything is pointing in your direction and telling me that it is the right direction.

I have never felt comfortable in my own skin, Nora. The only place I've felt confident, and comfortable, is in my work. But I'm hopeful that's about to change.

Please say hello to everyone for me.

Kisses,
Molly

Men in Love

Unable to bear watching Austin's possessions be removed from his house, Lark left Pearl Street early that morning, returning home on his bicycle with the knowledge that Austin would follow as soon as the work there was done. King's Highway was slick with rain and scattered leaves, remnants of last night's storm, but today was sunny, and Lark greeted it as he rode along, happy in the thought that it was not Austin's last day after all, and that he would be in town for a few more days. *Perhaps in those few days I'll be able to convince him to stay,* Lark found himself thinking, even against his better judgment. He knew such thinking was both wrong and wrongheaded, and yet the fact of Austin's going and leaving him was devastating; in fact he felt desperate when he thought about it, something he was trying not to do.

Arriving at True House, Lark found Nora sitting alone on the front steps with a cup of tea. The children were still asleep, she said, if he could believe that: "They must have completely worn themselves out playing yesterday." And she assumed Hortense was still in her room; she hadn't seen her. She patted the place beside her on the steps, motioning for Lark to sit down, which he did.

"How are you?" she asked, putting her arm around him.

Lark shrugged, then smiled. "Better now; Austin doesn't have to be in Manhattan until Thursday, so he'll stay till then. But he loses his house today, so I told him he could stay here with us—I didn't think you or the children or Hortense would mind."

Nora took a deep breath and shook her head.

And then a tense silence, as if another person, settled in the space between them. Always sensitive, Lark felt the change, and it made him think, brought him out of himself. "I know this must be hard for you, Nora."

There, she thought, *he said it;* he acknowledged her—that was all she needed. But she didn't know what to say in return; in fact she was afraid that if she opened her mouth to say anything at all she would cry, she was so full of disparate feelings. And then she did cry: she broke down and threw her arms around Lark.

"Thank you," she said, tears shining her face. "Thank you."

Lark held her and looked at her, surprised by such an outpouring.

Nora caught his look of dismay out of the corner of her eye and started laughing. "Don't be frightened," she said, still laughing. "It's just—*everything;* I'm so full of feeling: preparing for the move, the move itself and leaving Boston, then meeting Molly, now being here, seeing you, realizing our dream. . . ."

"I know," Lark responded. And she knew that he *did* know, for that was what was between them: the ability to know, to understand the other's feelings without his or her having to articulate them.

"Let's go for a walk!" Nora said suddenly, standing up and wiping her face. "Just the two of us." She looked at Lark for his agreement, which he freely gave. "Good!" she said, smiling. "I'll ask Hortense to tend to the children if they wake up while we're gone." And then she was off. And as Lark sat there waiting for her, he thought about Nora's vulnerability and about what he saw as his responsibility toward her, and he felt torn. What was happening with Austin was a complete surprise, and yet he needed it, wanted it, felt he should be prepared to throw himself into it, to give it his all. But he needed Nora, too; he needed both of them. *That* would be the complete life. Why should he have to choose?

When Nora returned, the two of them set off walking into the field behind the house, the field just days before resplendent with white and gold daisies, now almost completely "eyeless." They walked over the hill in back and then down to the beach. Once there, Lark took off his shoes as he always did; Nora followed suit.

"How happy do you feel at this moment?" he asked Nora now, smiling.

"I'm trying," she responded.

"Me, too."

"I think this is all going to be just fine," she added.

"Yes," Lark said, and then he took off running, sprinting for a hundred yards or so down the beach. When Nora caught up with him, he was still catching his breath. "Sometimes I just need to do that," he said.

Nora laughed and said she understood. This was Lark at his most boyish and ebullient; she had seen him like this before, and she loved it in him.

Walking along, Lark told Nora about the section of New Beach where people bathed and frolicked without any clothes on, and how free and admirable it seemed to him; he said he hoped that she and the children and he and Austin, and whoever else, might go there someday and join the crowd, as it were.

Nora agreed that it sounded ideal and said she thought it was something to aspire to, anyway. But then suddenly, in the distance, up and off to the right, she thought she saw the flashing of a light, though it was difficult, in the sunlight, to know—and trust—the source of such a glinting.

Lark noticed her distraction: "What is it?"

Nora didn't respond, but held her gaze until she had seen the faint flash of light several times and could be sure. Yes, she thought, it was regular, it was rhythmic: "It's the lighthouse!" she called out.

"Where?" Lark asked. His eyesight was not the best.

Nora stood behind him and held him close. She positioned herself so that the flashing light was in her line of vision, extended her arm, and then pointed her finger. "Follow the line of my arm all the way down to my finger," she told Lark. She felt him adjusting his position. "Do you see it?"

He was silent for a moment, then he cried out, "There! Now I see it! It must be Highland Light. Let's go!"

Nora looked at her watch: half an hour had already passed since they left the house. "I should be getting back," she said. "I don't want to leave the children too long too early on. But let's plan to go—soon."

"Just the two of us," Lark said.

"Yes, the first time out, just the two of us. We can take the children with us another time. I'm sure Hortense would agree to watch them."

She took a deep, luxurious breath and spread her arms as if they were wings: "A journey to the lighthouse!"

"You'd think we'd be able to see it from the cupola," Lark said, "but it's impossible—I've looked in every direction, three hundred and sixty degrees."

And now, as they headed back toward True House, Nora said that she hoped they could all do a lot of exploring together in the next few days; she was interested in going to Provincetown, she said, and to Wellfleet, and of course, closer to home, she looked forward to venturing out and about in Truro and seeing what was around them. "That is," she added, "unless you and Austin want to spend time alone together."

"I don't see why we can't do some of both." Lark smiled. "I mean, for example, Austin—and Hortense, too, for that matter—would be excellent guides in Provincetown. Maybe we could do that tomorrow, while we still have Austin and his automobile."

And so they wound their way back home, talking and planning all the way. Walking around the side of the house to the front, they spotted Hortense and the children sitting on the porch; they were eating breakfast.

"Good morning!" Nora called.

Lark waved.

"Welcome back," Hortense said. The children waved in unison, their mouths full.

Nora leaned over and kissed each of the children while Lark stood above them, tousling their hair affectionately.

Nora noticed that they were eating eggs and toast. "You didn't have to make them breakfast, Hortense."

But Hortense brushed it off: "I was hungry." Then she quickly covered her mouth, shook her head, and squinted, as if she'd blundered. "I mean, *they* were hungry."

"I'm hungry, too," Lark said. "Want some breakfast, Nora? I'll cook."

Nora nodded and said "Thank you," and Lark headed off to the kitchen.

Nora looked at her boy and girl now; they appeared happy. "Did anybody have any interesting dreams last night?" she asked.

Emily piped right in: "I dreamed about the ocean," she said, gasping. "It was *so* beautiful—green and blue, with rolling waves and white-caps—and I want to see it again!"

"Mmm," Nora mooned. She dared not tell Emily she and Lark had just been there.

"And I dreamed about a monster in the ocean," Schuyler began confabulating, "who rose up out of the ocean and, and was big and black and hairy and caused big waves, too, and who, who ate a lot of people in a boat, and . . ."

"That sounds like a nightmare to me," Nora interrupted. "What about you, Hortense?"

She shook her head. "I can never remember them. I keep promising myself that I'm going to keep a little book by my bed and force myself to write them down as soon as I wake up. But I haven't got the little book yet." She laughed. "Actually, I think maybe I'll just paint them instead," she added.

Nora smiled, then turned to Emily and said that perhaps they could see the ocean that very day. And later in the afternoon that was precisely what they did. Austin arrived shortly after two, and a group decision was quickly made to assemble a picnic and then hike down to the beach and spend the rest of the day there.

It was warm but not hot as the six of them set out in the direction of the ocean, the afternoon sun on their shoulders. Across the field they went, essentially retracing the steps Nora and Lark had taken earlier in the day; in fact Lark was leading the way, with Austin at his side. All of them had their bathing suits on under their clothes, except for Lark, whose shorts of the previous day had dried in time for him to put them on again.

As they walked, Nora could not help but notice that the group was not one: Lark and Austin seemed to be alone together, followed by the children, off in their imaginary worlds, playing as they went, with Hortense and her bringing up the rear. But she so wanted the group to be united, to be one. *Perhaps it will happen once we reach the beach,* she thought.

In the meantime, amid conversation with Hortense, she would try to observe Austin Park and sort out her feelings about him. Was she jealous? Yes, she had to admit, perhaps a little. But she also liked him. He seemed like a genuinely good man, and good to Lark; and she could see that the children liked him. As for his appearance . . . she supposed he was attractive, in an unconventional way. All in all she found him very appealing, she decided, and she was happy for Lark; she approved.

The group seemed to begin to coalesce once they were all working together to set up camp, laying out the two sheets they'd brought along and tacking them down at the corners with the heavier items of the picnic. And then once that was done, at Austin's suggestion, holding hands they ran into the water *en masse,* one long line of anticipation. And though the water disconnected them physically, broke their hand-holding, they were still one.

———

After dinner, resting before returning to the water, with the sun, an orange ball, beginning to melt into the sea, Austin told them some of what he knew about Truro. "Its original name, or one of them, was Dangerfield—because of the treacherous waters just off the coast" (he gestured out). "In fact, if you go to the Congregational Cemetery you'll see a plain, marble shaft that chronicles what locals called the October Gale, a sudden storm that blew up and took the lives of fifty-seven men from Truro."

Schuyler gasped, and the others all made sympathetic sounds of one kind or another.

"This was in the mid-nineteenth century," Austin added.

But then Nora, noticing that her children were brooding on this mournful fact, suggested that they all sing, and began herself singing, "Way down upon the Sewanee River. . . ." Soon she was accompanied by Austin (who had a fine baritone), then Lark and Hortense joined in, and finally, reluctantly, the children, too, agreed to sing. And now song, melody and harmony, really and completely united them, so that if such a connection could be made visible, Nora thought, it would appear as one long shining silver thread, like a held note, spread on the shore.

"Waiting for You to Blow In"

■\\\\\\\■

2 June 1928

True House

Dear Molly,

It was wonderful to hear from you. In those few days after I left Boston and before I received your letter, I began to think that perhaps I had merely imagined our meeting. It *was* very dreamlike, wasn't it? I was glad to hear all your good news—the mention in the *Post* and, especially, the commission: how is that going?

Here, life is an ocean breeze, and we're waiting for you to blow in and join us. I *do* think that your coming here will make a difference, Molly—that you'll feel more comfortable. Every day the children ask, "When is Molly coming?" Yesterday we spent a whole afternoon at the beach, concluding with a picnic (besides me and the children, "we" is Lark, Austin Park, Lark's new love—he's moving to Manhattan this week—and Hortense Stone, our only other roommate so far, a really good, solid, fun-loving woman I am sure you will enjoy, and vice versa).

"What is Lark like?" you asked. Oh, Molly! He is *so* special, that rare thing . . . a blue flower. . . . I don't know quite how to tell you. There is something hurt about Lark; that's one side of him. And yet he's also full of life. It's his phenomenal sensitivity, I think, that makes him so unique. But probably the best and most encompassing description of Lark actually came from my ex-husband, of all people, and though Ben meant it pejoratively, I think of it as the highest compliment. He once said that Lark is so intense he stands on tiptoes the entire time he's talking to you! Isn't that wonderful? And it's true, too, though not because Lark is short—he isn't—he's just so intense and intent on listening. You'll meet him soon.

Do you still plan to arrive here by the end of July? Please let me know if there is anything we can do to help. And by all means write me again if you have the time.

Love,

Nora

Black Wings

■⟍⟍⟍⟍⟍⟍⟍■

During the following week, as Nora, the children, and Hortense were all settling in, other forces in the house were shifting and becoming unsettled. As was inevitable, Austin left for Manhattan, and just as inevitably, Lark grieved a grief so big it seemed to cast a pall over everything and everyone around him. Once again he was struggling: Was he merely getting what he deserved? Would he ever see Austin again? For several days the house was still and quiet and stifling, but by the end of the week Nora, the children, and Hortense had moved on and out from under the black wing of Lark's sorrow. For Lark, however, time stood still. Any sort of movement was too much effort. He lay in bed *not sleeping.* He skipped meals.

On Friday, Hortense packed up and went off to Boston for the weekend with several of her women friends. Nora at first tried to rouse Lark from his grief and self-pity, to involve him; but when she saw that he was having none of it, she simply told him that she loved him, walked out of his room, and closed the door behind her. *He'll come out when he's ready,* she thought. And she thought, too, how, when hurt by grief or wrongdoing, we are like injured animals who skulk off and curl up in the closest, darkest spot, some hiding place, to lick our wounds.

On Saturday afternoon Nora and the children set out to find Pilgrim Lake, taking a picnic along with them. She left Lark a note saying they probably wouldn't be back until sunset.

Lark slept most of the day, since he had not been able to sleep at night—the darkness both called to *and* frightened him. At around three in the afternoon he woke up and, hearing that the house was quiet, crept downstairs. He made coffee, drank two cups, then went back upstairs, took a bath, and dressed. Somewhere between sleep and waking he had dreamed his next move: he was going to the dunes.

As he dressed, he noticed that his clothes now hung loosely on his body, his pants falling low over his hips; there was a dissoluteness to it that, while not exactly pleasing, felt right.

The bicycling was strenuous for him in his weakened state, but he had the will—he knew that. And because he was so much inside of his mind, thinking *Austin, Austin, Austin* (and the *sound* of that thought seemingly merging with the sound of the tires hissing on the pavement: *st . . . st . . . st . . .*), the ride seemed to pass within minutes, so that almost before he knew it, he found himself walking up the path that led to the dunes. He wanted nothing less than to throw himself away.

The day was warm, and there was a fine breeze blowing off the ocean. The gaunt Lark unbuttoned his shirt as he climbed the duney path, letting it flap in the wind, exposing his taut stomach. But once he'd reached the forested, hilly section of the dunes, he was unsure of what to do next. *Just find a tree to lean against,* he supposed. And then he found himself wondering what Austin was doing at exactly that same moment, in Manhattan.

At first it seemed that he was the only one there, and he found his mind wandering back to the first time he and Austin were together, walking along New Beach just below where he was now—how safe he had felt. But before long other men began to come onto the scene and mill about, interrupting his reverie. Some of them seemed to look him up and down and try to catch his eyes, while others merely filed past; Lark wasn't always sure, since he was mostly looking down. But then suddenly there was a man's face less than a foot away from his own. At the same moment, as if on cue, anyone else who might have been around at the time seemed to disappear, and Lark and this man were alone together. All of that took place in less than a minute, at the end of which this stranger got even closer and began kissing Lark, tongue and all. Lark was passive at first, leaning against the tree, hands at his side—the receptor. But because this man's kisses were so intense and *involving,* before long Lark found himself responding, pushing against and into this stranger with all of his being, with the hope that he might be swallowed up, become one with him, and, ultimately, disappear.

Now the man's hands were traveling over his body, pressing against his chest, caressing his hips, and then moving down, inside his pants, grabbing between his legs and gently rubbing the insides of his thighs. Lark half collapsed from weakness, and the stranger picked him up and carried him. He closed his eyes and went with it; the blue sky spun above him weaving cotton clouds.

———

By the time Lark came to, it was dark and he was alone and cold. Shivering, he found his clothes thrown over a nearby bush and put them on. Everything ached when he moved—every muscle, joint, tendon, and bone. Bicycling home would be impossible; he would have to walk. And so he set out, under an almost black, moonless sky and at a very slow pace.

When he reached True House a couple of hours later, the children were clearly in bed asleep, and Nora at the very least was in her room, with the door closed. He badly wanted to take a hot bath, but he feared the sound of running water might rouse her, and he did not want to have to see her (or for her to see him, especially as he was), and so he decided against it. Instead he went straight to his room and, without even turning on the light or undressing, climbed into his bed, pulled the covers up to his chin, and hugged himself until he fell asleep.

The Lighthouse

Standing in the golden glow of the porch light, Hortense watched as Nora and Lark disappeared into the gradually darkening field behind the house. Lark had been so pitiful in the week since Austin left that this seemed an especially important mission, and she wanted to see them off. Now she caught a brief, final glimpse of their silhouettes against the still-blue sky, Nora leading Lark by the hand; and because in silhouette they were completely featureless, mere stock figures, she thought of scenes from the old morality plays—where the blind man is being led by the wise man, say, or where, at night, so as to escape public ridicule, the unrepentant sinner is led out of the decadent city and into the countryside.

A warm summer wind suddenly blew the screen door shut behind her as she returned to the children at the dining room table, finishing up their dinner.

As Nora and Lark walked across the backyard and down the hill toward the beach, they were connected by flesh, his hand in hers as she led him, but they were not joined in mind. For though Lark was trying, he could think of nothing but *Austin*. And Nora was thinking only about *Lark*.

The beach, glistening with high tide, was now swept in the darkness of a moonless night. But regularly, rhythmically, there it was, a source of light, their destination: the lighthouse itself. Nora so wanted to speak, to say something comforting to Lark, to tell him that they were almost there; but one look at his face told her to wait, that he would not hear her. For when the light came around and illuminated his face, what she saw, briefly, but again and again, what she read on his face, was always and essentially the same thing: *Austin Park.*

"Lark?" she said now. And she thought she might have felt a slight jerk of his hand in hers in response, but then she left it at that, and they walked on. She must distract him from thinking so much about himself. He was being terribly selfish. Her feelings *were* hurt, yes, but she also understood. And yet he must be set right. Because he was making a terrible mistake; he was wasting precious time. She knew, since she had made the *same* mistake and had lived with it for many years (she had fallen in love with her piano teacher, Anton, while still married to Ben; but instead of allowing anything to happen between them, she had broken off the lessons). It was the mistake of Romance, of believing that there was a one someone out there for whom it was worth giving it all up—including oneself. It was a killing myth: she had almost lost herself in it, and she didn't want to see anyone she loved caught in its web; nor was it a model she wanted her children to witness.

Park, Lark thought. *I wish Austin were here.* And as he thought it, he thought he heard . . . had Nora, too, just said *Park?* Or had she said *his* name? He couldn't be sure. Oh, this was so unfair to her, he knew that. He should let go of her hand right then and there and give it up, give up the pretense, because he wasn't really there; or if he was there, then it was not Nora but Austin who was with him, leading him by the hand. He despised himself for feeling this way, and yet it was how he felt; it was who he was.

And so Lark and Nora walked along the beach in silence, thinking; he was darkness, she was light. And though the two friends were separated in thought, they continued walking toward the lighthouse, still holding hands.

But then . . . neither of them had realized it would end up this way, though it made perfect sense, with them down on the beach and the lighthouse high up on the edge of a cliff; and yet there it was, foreshortened, but still tall and white, majestic. The light swept around and flooded them and then, just as quickly, they were lost in darkness again.

"We're here!" Nora exclaimed, throwing her arms around the skeletal Lark. "Almost," she added sardonically.

"Thank you," Lark managed. It was a start.

They stood in silence for several moments, not touching, not talking, just taking it all in—feeling the night wind, hearing the singing of the ocean waters, and experiencing the regular, rhythmic plunge and flash of dark and light, over and over. It immediately brought each of them little snapshots of the other: Nora saw Lark, so thin he looked lit from within; his frightened face. And Lark saw . . . the luminous whitecaps of the waves far below. But he saw, too, Nora's face, swept with her hair, and her eyes, he saw her eyes; and in her eyes he saw a reflection of himself.

Nora took his hand once again. "Let's find a way up"—she pointed—"so that we can see it better, and stand under it."

Lark consented by starting to walk, and so the two continued on down the beach, looking for a way up.

And Nora thought *Good,* because it did seem to matter to Lark; he seemed to want to get there as much as she did, and that *was* a good sign.

And though Lark didn't quite understand why, getting to the lighthouse, actually reaching it and touching it—the real, material thing—suddenly had some sort of abstract meaning for him, felt important, became something he wanted, desired, cared about, as if he were fulfilling the equation *If we can just reach the lighthouse, then.* . . . But *then* what?

Suddenly he saw a way up, a gradually ascending trail burrowed into the cliff. "There!" he called to Nora, pointing.

She was surprised, taken aback even, by the passion in his voice. *It matters to him,* she thought. *He cares!* She was so happy that she could have cried, and now, for a moment, the flooding of the light and the swelling of her heart coincided. *This* was the sign she had been hoping and waiting for: he was getting better.

And so together, with Lark leading the way, they began climbing the steep path, which was somewhat arduous because of the incline, the rough terrain, and the darkness. But Lark was determined now, and as they climbed he turned to look back at Nora. "Ha!" He laughed at the exertion of it. He was exhilarated.

What is he thinking? Nora wondered, watching Lark. What had changed? And then she thought that because Lark had clearly been stuck, something, some obstacle to his thinking, had simply needed to be dislodged, and that perhaps the lighthouse, for whatever reason, had served that purpose; maybe he had needed something that big and powerful to do the trick. Whatever it was, she was grateful, as before her eyes now she saw him slowly, gradually returning to himself.

He took her hand, pulling her along as they neared the top, the steepest part of the climb: "Isn't this fun?" he called out. Nora laughed and hugged him from behind, and they stumbled onto level ground at last. At that same moment the light swept around and washed them, bleached them, so that a spectral visitor would have seen through their skin and behind their eyes, perhaps to their very cores.

Once the powerful light had moved on, they could see the source of it, the lighthouse itself, standing in the distance about a hundred yards away.

"There it is!" Lark cried. He took Nora's hand and together they began walking toward it; below them the ocean noisily rushed the shore.

Nora laughed, still somewhat amazed by the transformation in her friend. She wanted so badly to know, to understand: What had changed? What had made the difference? Then Lark began talking.

"Architecturally," he said, then paused briefly, thinking of Austin. He took a deep breath and began again: "Architecturally, lighthouses are such odd structures, don't you think? Particularly when you remember that people actually live in them. I've never been inside of one, but I've always wanted to be—have you?" Nora shook her head. "And yet they're beautiful," he continued. "Form serving function and all that."

They were nearing it now; its flash of lightness was brighter, its flood of darkness less dark.

"There's something *comforting* in the rhythmic flashing of the light,"

Lark was almost whispering now. "You know it will always come around again."

"I would add one more thing," Nora said. "That it has a presence."

"A *presence*, yes," Lark said. "Good word."

"A weighty, fundamental presence, especially amid the ephemera of so much sea and sky," Nora went on abstractly. And then she had a thought; an analogy had come to her quicksilver mind: "Like the Russian novel in relation to most other novels," she said, "in the way that they are concerned with the most basic questions, such as 'How to Live?'" Nora paused and looked at Lark: "The question we're answering at True House."

The light from the lighthouse pitched them alternately into darkness and light as the wind blew around them and the ocean surf ebbed and flowed far below.

"Lighthouse as Russian novel." Lark chuckled.

"Yes," Nora said, smiling. "For Chekhov," she went on, wanting to teach him, "the great question, and subject, are humanity." She paused. "Which, because of the spiritual aspect, is more fully, though some would say less subtly, explored in Dostoyevski. Whereas Tolstoy simply does it all." But then Nora saw her friend seemingly beginning to wither before her very eyes, folding, disassembling. . . . She was determined that he should not go back to where he had been, and thinking fast, she nudged him in the darkness: "What do you say tomorrow morning we go to Cobb Library to see what we can find out about the lighthouse?"

Lark brightened a little and nodded. And then, arm in arm, the two began the long walk home.

The Fruits of Their Research

"Highland Light, Cape Cod's oldest lighthouse, sits one hundred twenty feet above the ocean; its beam elevation is one hundred eighty-three feet above the sea. Ships can see the light from thirty miles away.

"The first light was established in 1797, five hundred ten feet from the cliff's edge. It was rebuilt in 1857 and replaced by the current structure on a ten-acre plot of land, but today less than seven acres remain: the sea is a relentless neighbor."

Molly and the Gardener

■〰〰〰〰■

By the end of July when Molly arrived she was not alone, for she had fallen in love with her subject, Mrs. Rothstein's gardener, and he with her. While painting him Molly had at first marveled at the way his skin shone in certain kinds of light, and finally she had coveted him. His name was Davis Munroe, and he was so black he was almost blue, like a dusky plum or, at other times, like an eggplant. As for Mrs. Rothstein, she now had a strong and vivid portrait of her handsome gardener, but she had lost the man himself.

Of course Molly had asked Nora if it would be all right for Davis to join them, and naturally Nora had said yes. But because of an uncertainty on Molly's part as to when, exactly, she and Davis would arrive, it turned out that Lark had gone to Manhattan for the weekend to be with Austin, and Hortense was in Provincetown for the day; the welcoming party was therefore small.

It was a sunny Saturday, and Nora and the children were in the front yard playing catch. But simply tossing the ball back and forth wasn't enough for Schuyler (it was "too slow," he complained), so when the ball wasn't in his hands or on its way to him, he had to be engaged in some other activity, such as somersaults or attempted handstands, the latter of which he was actually too heavy for. Emily, however, just stood there when she didn't have the ball, looking up and down and around, seeming to take it all in; it was as if, Nora thought, she were beginning to ponder the great questions.

Nora was intensely interested in her children's characters, and she had studied the differences between them, disbelieving that those differences were based on their sex. She saw Schuyler, for example, as having been heavily influenced by his father, as well as reacting against what some might call the *feminine* atmosphere in which he had been raised (though perhaps those things were one and the same). But Emily was another matter: she had seemed very much her own person from the beginning. (Unlike Emily, Nora herself was not, nor had she ever been, ethereal; while extremely bright, she had also always been fundamentally down-to-earth. Was ethereality inherently feminine? Nora wondered now, the sun in her eyes as she awaited the toss from Emily. No, she answered; and then she thought, *Lark is often ethereal.*)

Distracted and blinded, Nora did not see the ball as it approached her, and it hit her head-on, smack in the face. Fortunately, it was a big, soft ball, and Emily's toss was light, but nevertheless Nora did experience a brief moment of blackness, of blankness; and when she recovered and could see again, what she saw was Molly and Davis walking up the drive, as if in a vision.

"Hello!" Nora called, waving so as to test reality.

Molly was wearing a large sun hat, and upon seeing Nora she dropped her bags and ran toward her, holding on to the hat with one hand and waving back with the other: "Hello, Nora!"

The two women met at the end of the yard and embraced. Davis and the children caught up with them, and Molly introduced everyone.

Schuyler and Emily were especially happy to see Molly again, and they were intrigued by Davis. Having grown up on Beacon Hill in Boston, they had not seen many Negroes, but because they were children, Davis's skin color was a difference that aroused their *curiosity* and not, as was so often the case with adults, their *animosity*. In fact, all Emily could think of (she would tell Nora later) while staring at Davis's massive biceps—he was wearing a sleeveless, faded denim shirt—was that she should like to apply her tongue to his skin. Of course in her innocence Emily understood nothing sexual in her desire, but when Nora told Molly later what Emily had said, and translated it to mean that Davis looked good enough to eat, Molly laughingly replied, "He is!"

But now Davis was down on the ground, wrestling with Schuyler while Emily looked on. Then, up on his feet again in a mere jump, he took Emily's twin braids in his hands and, pretending she was a horse, shook them and said, "Giddyap!" And so Emily ran in circles around the yard, with Davis holding on to the reins of her braids. Schuyler followed, sometimes charging at Emily as if he were a bull, wanting Davis's attention.

"You're glowing!" Nora said to Molly as they watched the threesome play.

"Am I?" Molly blushed. "I feel like I am, but I didn't know it showed." And then, gesturing toward Davis, she added, "Well, wouldn't you?" and laughed.

Nora gave her a knowing look and laughed in response. "He is beautiful! Tell me about him."

"Mmm." Molly took a deep breath: "Where to begin?" She looked around as if expecting the sky to answer, then she jumped in. "Well, Davis isn't an artist, at least not in the traditional sense of the word, since, being a Negro, he hasn't been afforded that luxury." She paused, pawing the ground with one foot in anger. "But I like to think that he *is* an artist of sorts, and maybe of a more important kind, Nora . . . because . . . it's in the way he lives—slowing things down, examining them, appraising and appreciating them. You should have seen his garden; it was exquisite!" Molly looked at Nora quizzically, wanting to know that she understood. (Nora was nodding.) "He's very quiet and doesn't talk much, though he has a great voice," Molly went on, "but when he does talk . . . I think what he says has a beautiful simplicity. He seems to understand things in a profound but very instinctive way; and I think it's *there*—in the instincts—that we meet, because I'm that way, too." Molly paused again, embarrassed at having gone on so. Then she concluded, "It's all about the quality of life for Davis. About the day-to-day, the beauty of the moment."

"I understand," Nora replied. "And I identify with it, too"—she laughed—"since I have no artistic ability whatsoever, and yet all of the inclination." She looked around, then heard the children's laughter coming from the field in back of the house.

"You know I painted Davis as something of a king." Now Molly laughed. "Which is probably not quite what Mrs. Rothstein had in mind."

Nora looked at Molly with anticipation; she was waiting for more.

"The very instant I met him, I just felt aware of a certain—I don't know what else to call it—*regality* about him, a *kingliness:* he has this incredible *presence.* So as I was painting him—and he sat for me for almost two weeks; we extended it" (she winked)—"as I was painting him and noticing his beautiful skin and how it appeared to change colors in certain lights, I began, almost subconsciously, to change the colors of the clothes he was wearing, adding new colors and then new and finer clothes. First, it was a bright white silk shirt; then a red satin vest. I couldn't help but paint in two small gold hoop earrings in each ear, and then" (Molly laughed) "I added a royal-blue turban, with a pear-shaped ruby hanging down in the middle of his forehead!"

Nora was fascinated. "Oh, I would *so* like to see it!"

"That might be difficult," Molly said. "Mrs. Rothstein *loved* the painting, or at least she said she did—and she did pay me in full. But she was not at all happy about the fact that Davis was leaving her, and of course she blamed me for that. I think she had an eye for him herself." Molly laughed again.

"Well, certainly you can understand *that,*" Nora said with a wry smile.

"Yes," Molly said. And then for the first time she really noticed True House. "It's wonderful," she said to Nora. But then something else suddenly came into her head: caught up in the excitement of arrival, she had almost forgotten the fact that *Boys in the Grass* was here, in Lark's room; could she see it immediately?

"Sure," Nora replied, and then she repeated it, with emphasis, because *of course* Molly would want to see her painting in its home and context as soon as possible.

The two women walked around to the back of the house to tell Davis and the children where they would be, and found Schuyler atop Davis's shoulders and Emily standing and watching, perfectly content. *Perhaps she is inventing a story about it,* Nora thought. Then she and Molly disappeared into the house.

Boys in the Grass Revisited

There it was, on the wall directly opposite Lark's bed so that he might best view it from that position; otherwise the white walls were unadorned. Behind the bed were the two windows, one on each side, and Nora looked out now, briefly, at the children and Davis below; the scene, one of three people enjoying themselves and one another, appeared more or less unchanged.

The room was in disarray. Molly stood at the foot of the unmade bed and silently examined her painting, her arms crossed. Then she asked Nora if she thought Lark would mind if she lay in his bed for a moment, to view it from that perspective. Having Nora's permission, she lay down: yes, she immediately thought, it had been hung well, and in a good location. She studied her painting now, crossing her eyes, interested more in its composition—the relation of sky to grass to figures, and the proportions and shapes of each, *of planes*—than in its mere representation. And she was pleased with what she saw; she thought it achieved an *overall* effect, which was both what she had been taught to strive for at the Museum School and what she herself believed in.

"And what does Lark think of it?" Molly asked.

"He *adores* it!" Nora exclaimed. "Didn't you get my postcard?"

Molly shook her head.

"Oh!" Nora cried. "I wrote you all about his immediate response; I can't believe you didn't get it," she continued. "Well, let's see: we un-packed it together, and as soon as we had it out of the crate, Lark propped it up in the chair over there" (she pointed) "studied it for a few minutes, and then said, 'It's gorgeous!'"

Molly beamed.

"He *loves* it," Nora repeated. "Of course after a few minutes of look-ing at it and enjoying it and thanking me profusely and deciding where he was going to hang it, he added that he wished you could do something like it of him and Austin." Nora grinned.

"Mmm, how's that going?" Molly asked.

"Fine," Nora said. "Lark seems to have settled down, to have ac-cepted Austin's living in Manhattan. . . . I think he has gone there probably every other weekend since Austin left."

Molly grimaced. And then the two women were silent as they both meditated on the painting. Molly wondered what a version with Lark and Austin Park would look like, but since she had met neither of them, her imagination halted at the one image she did have of Lark: him standing on tiptoes, listening intently.

Nora, for her part, was picturing Lark and Austin on the beach, pos-sibly naked, in poses similar to those of the figures in *Boys in the Grass. Boys on the Beach,* perhaps? And just as she thought of that she re-membered a Sargent painting she'd once seen; it was called something like *Neapolitan Children Bathing* and depicted four children on the beach, all naked and pink.

Nora Puts the Children to Bed

■﹨﹨﹨﹨﹨﹨﹨■

It was a Saturday night, though it could have been any night of the week, since putting the children to bed was a ritual that for the most part went unchanged. Nora and the children had left Molly and Davis downstairs with Hortense, who had returned from Provincetown after dinner, to get better acquainted, and climbed the stairs to the children's room on the third floor.

Emily had insisted that her summer pajamas be the same as Schuyler's, and so instead of a nightgown, she, like her brother, wore a short-sleeved top and short bottoms made of simple white cotton.

While Nora was brushing Emily's hair, Schuyler looked out the window.

"Tell us what you see, Schuy," she said to him now softly. She always tried to help the children calm down before they went to bed.

"Nothing!" Schuyler said impudently.

"That's impossible." Nora chuckled. "You have to see something."

"Blackness," Schuyler said. "Or maybe blue-blackness. And outlines of things, like trees, in black."

"You mean *silhouettes?*" Nora asked, supplying him with the word.

"Mmm." He nodded. "And far off in the distance maybe it gets a little lighter."

"Are there any stars?" Nora asked.

He looked up; no, he said, it was too cloudy.

Nora finished with Emily's hair, kissed her on the forehead and told her she loved her, then tucked her into bed.

"OK, Schuy," she called to him at the window. "Bedtime."

He moseyed across the room to his bed. He also got a kiss on the forehead and an "I love you," both of which caused him to bristle a bit; then Nora tucked him in.

Settling back into the chair between her children's beds now, Nora picked up the book she was reading to them, the story of mythology, sighed deeply, and said, "Now, where were we?"

"Pegasus," Emily said—she always knew.

And so Nora read to them the myth of the white horse that could fly. Schuyler always had to ask a series of questions at first, and occasionally Emily would ask one or two, but after a while both children settled into a silent listening until either one or both of them had fallen asleep, or until Nora had finished reading, at which point she always closed the book, placed it on the night table, and stealthily walked out of the room.

"It was Pegasus who brought thunder and lightning to Zeus," Nora concluded, almost whispering.

But tonight, for some reason, she wanted to linger. She looked at each of her children in turn, both safe in their chambers of sleep. And then she quietly got up and walked over to Schuyler's window, the same one he had been looking out about half an hour earlier. She crouched down, resting her elbows on the sill; she peered out. It was dark, yes, but not completely black, not impenetrable. Schuyler's increasing resistance toward her made her sad. She looked up at the night sky as she considered this; he was right about the stars, though—there were none visible tonight. But then suddenly something passed over her—a terror, a premonition of something horrible. Nothing in the landscape or on the horizon had changed, and yet Nora was completely spooked. She shuddered. She stood up. She hugged herself. She must get control; nothing *real* had happened. She took a last look at the children and slipped out the door. But instead of returning to her friends downstairs in the parlor as she should have done, Nora went directly to her room and, without even turning on the light or taking off her clothes, fell into bed. She was asleep within minutes.

"Independent Suns"

■﹀﹀﹀﹀﹀■

1 September 1928

New York City

Dear Lark,

I am writing this because I love you—I think you know that. I love you and I love being with you—most of the time. But increasingly I feel that your constant insecurity and your mistrust are like a beaver gnawing away at a tree that he'll eventually fell, even though that may not be his intent. You need to know and be responsible for the fact that this sort of behavior is wearing and destructive. For example, when I told you that I wouldn't be able to see you next weekend because I have to go to Chicago on business, you responded, "What's his name?" There have been many other instances, but I won't cite them here; I think you know what I'm talking about.

I want our love to be strong, Lark, and to grow even stronger; I want us to be independent suns orbiting the same galaxy.

I have been tossing these thoughts around in my head since you left yesterday, if not longer. I had to say them, to tell them to you, but please remember and take heart: I say them *because* I love you, *because* I want things to work out between us.

It was a fine weekend in so many ways—I'm remembering our coming back to the apartment late Saturday night after the picture, and getting caught in the rain. . . .

I love you. I miss you. I'll see you in two weeks—would you like me to come there this time?

Austin

P.S. Please don't fret too much over this, and if you feel like it write me back and tell me *your* thoughts.

Hortense on the Lawn

Of all the inhabitants at True House, Hortense alone was up and about early in the morning. Her opening moves were like those of a sleepwalker, she went about them so rotely, so methodically. She got up with the first light, splashed water on her face, dressed, fixed herself a big breakfast, and then marched out onto the front lawn, carrying her easel, canvas, and paints (for she was of the *plein air* school)—all before seven o'clock. The still-dewy grass was cold on her feet, sheathed as usual in only the simplest of leather sandals, which she wore, she had told Nora, because they made her feel solid, grounded, and connected to the earth.

She walked to a point about seventy-five feet in front of the house, which she had marked with a large stone. She had told everyone about the stone and about the importance of its not being moved, and so she always felt sure of its being in the right place. She set down her easel and paints and then positioned the canvas.

A passerby rude or curious enough to look over her shoulder at the canvas would have seen True House against True House; yes, certainly it was recognizable. But would one have known that the painting was of True House if the *real* True House had not been behind it? Well, that was another story. For on the canvas was a house, yes, or parts of a house, but most of it was obscured by the oversized and disembodied heads of its inhabitants, all of which were projecting almost ghost-like out of front windows that, in life, were nonexistent. There they were, Nora and Schuyler and Emily and Lark and Molly and Davis and Hortense herself, all rendered with a childlike naïveté, simplified versions of themselves. It was—what? Surreal? Yes, perhaps. But what was Hortense trying to say? That the house was too crowded? That it was a fun house? That they were all characters and that the house, too, was a character? The chance passerby could not be sure. But that the painting had a charm, a certain *je ne sais quoi,* yes, about *that* there was no doubt—for Hortense's painting was as charming as the woman herself.

"Myself Unholy":
A Postcard from Lark to Austin

▪╲╲╲╲╲╲╲▪

6 September 1928

True House

Dear Austin,

I take to heart all you wrote & I apologize. I will try to do better. Of course I will miss you this weekend, but doing this little charcoal sketch for you has kept me in your company. It is not much, but I send it, & this from Hopkins, with love.

> Myself unholy, from myself unholy
> To the sweet living of my friends I look. . . .

X Lark

Painting the Sky Blue;
or, And Then There Were Eight

▪\\\\\\\▪

It all started one fine, sunny day in mid-September when Molly and Nora were walking up the drive, returning home after picking up a few supplies in Truro Center. Molly's eye happened to catch the top of the house at an angle that, for a moment, made it seem as if it were suspended in, and a part of, the sky. She immediately stopped walking, put down the bag of groceries, and then, almost as if she were in a trance, said, "We should paint True House sky blue."

"Yes!" was Nora's immediate and enthusiastic response, delivered in a tone of voice that suggested nothing could have been more right or obvious, as in *Yes, of course.*

That night at dinner, Molly announced what she called her vision to the group, and while not all of them saw or understood it as clearly as Nora had, everyone readily agreed to it.

It would be quite the job, Molly said, warning them. They would have to act quickly, too, before the weather changed and it grew too cold. (And as she said this, Molly had a brief image of the seven of them standing about out of doors, holding brushes dipped in sky-blue paint, while all around the gold and red and orange and amber leaves swirled through the air and tumbled to the ground. She could feel— and smell—the crisp, fresh air . . . oh, it would be lovely.) When could they start?

Lark offered that he thought Austin was coming for the weekend and that he was sure he'd be glad to help.

"Where's the nearest paint store?" Molly asked.

"Probably Sy Swift's in Provincetown," Hortense piped in.

Molly said she and Davis would go in the next morning to buy the paint—she had strong feelings about just what sky blue looked like and wanted to pick it out herself. "How much paint do you need to cover an entire house?"

Davis said he thought he had a pretty good idea.

"When can we start?" Molly went on. "Friday, weather permitting?"

Friday it was.

"We'll need ladders," Nora threw in.

Hortense came to the rescue: "I think my friend Abigail has a couple we could borrow; I'll ask her."

Not wanting to be left out, Schuyler said that he would like to sit on the very top of the house and paint the cupola, an attention grabber that brought a big laugh from the table; and Emily took the opportunity to add quietly that she should like to apply her brush in one place and then walk around the entire house, making a big blue stripe, never lifting her hand, and watching that stripe gradually grow bigger and bigger as they painted, until the entire house was blue and the stripe had completely disappeared.

The following morning, Molly and Davis left early for Provincetown. Walking across the front lawn, they saw Hortense standing in the middle, painting. They crossed to the far side so as not to disturb her, then waved when she looked up. She waved back, smiling, then returned her focus to the canvas.

"How are you?" Molly asked Davis, tugging on his shirt sleeve as they walked along the winding, hilly roads of Truro. "I mean, how are you liking it here?" They had been there less than two months.

"I'm fine. And I do like it," he answered. "I'm used to being the only Negro in situations, but it's more unusual, or *exaggerated*, when you're the *only* Negro living in a house full of white folks. But don't get me wrong, I like everyone: Nora's a fine woman; the children are a lot of fun; and Hortense is . . . *Hortense*, one of a kind." He chuckled. "Lark can be difficult for me, but I think that's probably me, not him."

Molly looked at her lover with curiosity: "What do you mean?"

Davis shrugged. "He's just so, I don't know . . . so sensitive, and . . . intense." He winced and added, "And kind of girlish; I'm just not used to seeing all those qualities in a man."

"I know what you mean," Molly responded, "but you have most of those qualities, too. Maybe less than Lark does, but you've got them." She looked up at him: "It's one of the things I love about you."

Davis smiled.

"And I actually think Lark is brave," Molly continued, "because he doesn't try to hide those things. . . ."

"Do you think I do?" Davis asked, not defensively.

"No, that's not what I'm saying; but I believe that most men do. All I'm saying"—Molly was struggling for the right words—"is that for whatever reason, those qualities have come to the surface in Lark. Knowing they aren't qualities that most people associate with men, in this *man's world,* I admire him for going forth and for being himself. . . ."

Yes, Davis said, he understood: he could see a kind of courage in that.

"I'm sure Nora would have a lot more to say on the subject and could say it much better than I can," Molly offered now.

Davis laughed: "Yeah," he said. "She's crazy about him."

"As he is about her," Molly replied. "I think it's wonderful."

And then Davis took her hand, as if to say *yes,* he, too, thought it was wonderful.

Once they'd reached the edge of Provincetown, Molly and Davis boarded one of the open-air buses Hortense had told them about—"accommodations," they were called—which ran from one end of Commercial Street to the other, a three-mile trip. As usual, they were glared at.

At Sy Swift's they went about gathering the necessary paint supplies—including two smaller brushes for the children—and ten gallons of sky-blue paint. Davis said he thought that would do it, but if not they could always come back: better less than more. But they would clearly have to take a taxicab home.

A tall, round young man with a shaved head standing beside them at the register laughingly stated the obvious—that it looked as though they were going to be doing some painting.

Molly smiled back. She liked his face: wide and open; friendly. She had read somewhere that the shape of a person's face described his or her character. And a round face, she recalled, suggested that the person was generous, understanding, and a good listener. . . . Well, this man's face was especially welcome and pleasing here and now, being the complete opposite of the mien of the tense clerk, which she suspected had to do with Davis, and particularly Davis's being with her;

this sort of response was something they were getting used to, if not accepting.

"Leo Harmonica," the man said, extending his hand first to Molly and then to Davis.

Molly laughed spontaneously at the man's name, then quickly covered her mouth, not meaning to be rude.

"If you need any help," Leo added, "I have a lot of experience painting houses." He laughed. "I'd just need room and board. I've been staying at Captain John Smith's Atlantic House"—he laughed again—"but it's time for me to move on."

Molly looked at Davis. She had a feeling in her stomach that this was something that mattered, *someone* who mattered. After all, she and Nora had met in the same way—by chance. She looked at Davis again. He smiled at her knowingly. She probably shouldn't commit, she reasoned.

"My father's a contractor in Brooklyn, and I've done a lot of work for him," Leo said.

Molly looked at Davis, then she took the plunge: Could he come to see her and her friends tomorrow morning? she asked (she wrote out the address on a slip of paper). She thought they might be able to help each other. "Say, ten o'clock?"

"Ten it is," Leo said with a smile. He shook their hands again before they left. "See you then."

———

Leo showed up at ten the following morning; everyone had gathered in the parlor for the interview. They all loved him immediately: Emily told Nora she thought she had never seen a face quite so wide and friendly, and a head with so little hair. She and Schuyler both laughed out loud at his name.

There was something infectious about him—a generosity of spirit, Nora said later to Lark. Would he like to join them, Molly had asked by ten-thirty—move in and help paint the house?

"Well, I'll have to think about it . . . ," Leo answered, mock-stroking his chin, a ploy that at first caught the adults by surprise; then they laughed. "Yes!" Leo said, laughing heartily himself. "Yes, of course!"

"I'll show you your room," Lark said, standing up and extending a hand to Leo. "Welcome to True House!"

True Blue House

....

By Friday morning, which was clear and cool but not too cool, the oc-
cupants of True House—except for the children, whom Nora had en-
rolled in the Montessori school in Provincetown—had assembled in
the front yard dressed in various states of painting gear. Wearing overalls, a T-shirt, and work boots, Hortense had been successful in bor-
rowing two ladders from her friend Abigail, a Provincetown native
who had been kind enough to drive them over in her truck that morning. Abigail volunteered that she would have offered to help were it
not for the arthritis that seemed to go along with her sixty-two years.
Abigail was an old salt, Hortense said admiringly as the old woman
drove off.

Nora had on an old shirt of Lark's over an even older dress, and
Molly was wearing a pair of men's pants and a man's shirt that be-
longed to her. All of the men seemed to wear more or less what they
usually wore: their street clothes.

And so they set to work, everyone with his or her own can of paint.
They took turns on the ladders, with Molly and Hortense insisting on
doing their part; Nora half joked that as the mother of two young children, she had no business climbing ladders.

Austin arrived on Saturday afternoon and immediately agreed to
join in. He and Lark worked side by side, catching up: Austin was ex-

cited about the restoration of a Victorian he was currently working on in Westchester County (one not unlike True House, he said). Fortunately, there was no strain between them, after his letter.

Leo hummed as he worked—perhaps an opera? And he once surprised the children by standing in front of them and then, suddenly, painting a sky-blue stripe on his nose.

By Sunday everyone was sore and exhausted—*their shoulders, their arms, their backs.* . . . They agreed to take the day off. With so many people painting, Leo said, he felt sure they could finish by Tuesday.

Sunday passed in a daze, with everyone going his or her own way, unusual for a weekend; but by Monday morning the adults were all hard at work once again. Austin, however, had to return to Manhattan; Lark said he wished they'd had more time alone together.

Were people liking the color? Molly asked when they broke for dinner. She laughed and said she certainly hoped so.

Davis beamed at her; she knew he did.

Leo laughed, thinking about the irony if someone *didn't* like it.

"Yes!" Once again it was Nora who first affirmed Molly's vision.

"It's breathtaking at dusk," Lark said.

"It's certainly bright first thing in the morning," Hortense offered. "Alive and energizing."

"I like it all day," Emily chimed in.

"I think it looks like the sky," Schuyler weighed in.

"Yes!" Molly exclaimed, hugging Schuyler and laughing. "That's exactly the point, Schuy."

And then by Tuesday evening they *had* finished. Perhaps they worked later than they should have done; they would have to examine the house tomorrow in the light of day. It was dusk now, and the house seemed to glow; Emily was fascinated by the vivid blue spots of paint on the green grass. They all gathered together on the front lawn at some distance from the house to admire it. Lark dashed into the house for a bottle of wine and glasses, which they shared, toasting; Nora even let the children have a sip.

"To True Blue House," Molly said now, raising her glass and hugging Davis close to her.

II *Specimen Days*

Now I am minded to take pipe in hand
And yield a song to the decaying year;
Now while the full-leaved hursts unalter'd stand,
   And scarcely does appear
The Autumn yellow feather in the boughs;
   While there is neither sun nor rain;
And a grey heaven does the hush'd earth house,
And bluer gray the flocks of trees look in the plain.

     Gerard Manley Hopkins, "Now I am minded"

First Snow

■◟◟◟◟◟◟◟■

"Was that the Yule log?" Schuyler asked Lark as he added a large log to the fireplace.

"Yep," Lark replied, pushing at the wood with the poker and sending cinders flying. "That was the biggest one."

Emily said that the cinders looked like fireflies, and Nora smiled and said she supposed that was exactly, or *literally*, what they were; then she wondered aloud if that was how fireflies had got their name.

It was a skeletal crew inhabiting True House this Christmas Eve, just Lark, Nora, and the children. The night was especially cold for December, and the moon was full, and the four of them had gathered around the fire after dinner—to eat baked apples and tell stories: a family. There was no tree, and no talk of Santa Claus, but there was a festival atmosphere, and there *would* be gifts in the morning.

Molly and Davis were in Boston, visiting their families, while Hortense was back in Philadelphia, and Leo was in Brooklyn, reluctantly doing the same. Austin had said he needed to stay in the city during the holidays, a fact Lark was unhappy about and wasn't sure he trusted. They had fought about it the previous weekend when Lark was in Manhattan, after which Austin had written him a terse letter:

Dear Lark,

You have got to try to get control of your insecurities or they will destroy us. Please take some time to think about this. I want things to work out between us. Remember: I am on your side, but we are two people, not one. I am trying. I love you.

Austin

But Lark didn't want to think about it, at least not for the moment—it was Christmas Eve. "It's your turn, Emmie," he said to her now.

Emily pulled the sleeves of her wool sweater down over her hands and then propped her head in them. "Sometime in the not-too-distant past," she began, "there was a boat that was bound for Nova Scotia with a cargo of fine horses and cattle. Sadly, the boat was wrecked off the coast of Provincetown during a winter storm and all aboard were drowned except for this one beautiful white stallion, who swam ashore."

"I know this story already," Schuyler said.

Nora *shhh*-ed him.

"For a year, they say, this beautiful white stallion ran wild up and down the dunes, and it was a beautiful sight. Many men saw him and tried to catch him, baiting him with oats. When that didn't work, they tried to trick him by building a corral and putting a mare inside. At first this worked, but then when the men came for him, the white horse realized he had been trapped, and so he jumped the fence. With the men chasing him and no other options, he plunged into the sea. For a while the men could see his white mane tossing in the surf, until they could no longer distinguish it from the whitecaps of the waves." Emily looked down now as she delivered the story's final line: "His body was found on the shore several days later."

Nora took Emily's hand. "That's sad," she said. "And you know, I think it is a *parable* about what men often feel compelled to do to beauty: trap it and kill it."

"If it had been Pegasus, he could have just flown away," Emily said.

Nora smiled and rubbed her daughter's head affectionately. But she was concerned about her son, too. "You knew that story, Schuy?" she said, now turning her warm gaze upon him.

"Yeah, everybody tells it at school," he said. "But nobody tells it as good as Emily just did," he added.

"As *well*," Nora corrected him.

And though Schuyler didn't say so now, he often felt just like that white horse: trapped.

Suddenly Lark looked out the window and noticed the white flakes falling. "Snow!" he cried, and everyone ran to the window; it was the first of the season. (And perhaps because he was thinking of the situation between him and Austin at that very moment, Lark briefly imagined the snow as pieces of the beautiful white horse in Emily's story, then as ashes. Then he let it go.)

Snow it was. And it fell so heavily and constantly throughout the night that by Christmas Day the grounds around True House were covered and glistening with pristine white snow, magic in the morning sun.

Emily's Secret

And in the deep of midwinter, with the region blanketed by a heavy snow, sky-blue True House looked almost obscene and certainly anomalous, standing amid all that whiteness.

One night that winter while lying in bed and looking out her window (Schuyler was already asleep), Emily thought she saw the flash of a light: Was it a shooting star? she wondered. A falling comet? A meteor? She lay completely still, watching, her gaze fixed on the same spot until she saw it again; then she got up and tiptoed over to the window. All of the trees now, save for a few pines scattered here and there, were bare, and because of that (there it was again!), because of that she could now confirm it: it was the beacon from the lighthouse coming around and around. She moved over to Schuyler's window and looked—no, the light was no longer visible; it was too far to the left. And then she recognized the strong likelihood that this was *something only she could see*—if not the lighthouse itself, then at least its light. The room below hers and Schuyler's, Molly and Davis's room, would be too low, she reasoned. And yes, she supposed the light probably would be visible from the cupola now, with most of the trees bare, but no one went up there in the winter; it was much too cold. And so it was that Emily decided she would tell no one else about the light, and that it would be her special secret, a gift to herself. She began talking to it, in a whisper, as she returned to her bed—until she fell asleep.

Almost Lost

Spring came slowly to the Cape that year. But then suddenly it seemed that new green was shooting up everywhere, and the forsythia was just beginning to open.

True House, from another, greater perspective—from above—might have appeared as nothing more than a bluebird on a great, greening lawn. Unfortunately, however, no one and nothing from above, if indeed anyone or anything was there, seemed to be watching.

As for the rest of the house's inhabitants on this fateful day, Hortense was off on one of her weekends with the women; Austin was there visiting Lark; Molly and Davis had had to go to Boston for the weekend; and Leo was in his room. Nora sat by the window reading, regularly looking up and out to check on the children. Thinking about the flowers she would soon plant (she listed them: spirea, phlox, golden glow, lilies of the valley, and bittersweet), she looked up and actually saw it happen: Schuyler, running in ever-widening circles, one arm raised as if he were carrying something (perhaps he was flying an imaginary airplane?). An automobile speeding along the drive at the same time that Schuyler's circling began spilling over into it, and then ... impact! Schuyler scooped up into the air and thrown back into the yard like a toy, and the car just continuing on and disappearing on the horizon. ... And all of it silent from Nora's perspective. Why hadn't Schuyler heard the car? she would ask later. Was he so lost, caught up in flying his imaginary airplane? (He would not be able to answer her; he would remember nothing.)

Nora saw it happen. Watched it happen. Her face exploded—her eyes widened, her mouth opened, her nostrils flared. But there was no freezing, no moment of disbelief or hesitation; immediately, she was merely a wild animal reacting. She screamed, dropped her book, and rushed out the front door. Suspended in the air was a high-pitched sound; it was Emily, mouth open, hands to her face, screaming. Nora took off running across the lawn, screaming, "SCHUY-LER!"

Once the ambulance arrived, Schuyler was carefully placed onto a stretcher and then lifted into the rear of the car; Nora climbed in behind him.

Lark said he and Austin would follow in a taxi, and Leo offered to stay with Emily.

Then the ambulance took off, the siren resumed, and suddenly it seemed to Nora that she had never stopped screaming; she was screaming inside. But she willed herself to focus, to be calm—for Schuyler's sake. She rubbed his hand and then his forehead, alternately, the entire way to the hospital; she told him over and over that everything was going to be all right.

It was a long night, and it wasn't until the following day, well into the afternoon—almost twenty-four hours later—that Nora learned Schuyler had suffered no head injuries. Dr. Barber was old—a wizened sage, so Nora decided; she liked and trusted him at once. The most serious problems, he told her, were the punctured lung and the internal bleeding: "We had to transfuse him with four pints." There were also several broken ribs, a broken arm, and a broken leg. Lark and Austin were at her side, ready to catch her should she fall.

Schuyler lay in his bed awash in the waves of a big sea, sometimes relaxed but at other times flailing just to stay afloat, to keep from going under.

After another twenty-four hours Dr. Barber pronounced Schuyler "out of the woods" but said he would have to remain in the hospital for several weeks.

Nora bought an automobile—a '28 DeSoto—and everyone took turns driving to and from the hospital in Hyannis, watching over Schuyler, and, as he improved, entertaining him. And then once he was sent home, it was another month before he could resume so-called normal activity. But Nora wasn't sure that she knew what normal activity was anymore. Everything had changed.

One Anniversary, Eight People in
Birthday Suits—and One Not

Late May—one year, give or take a few days, at True House. But Schuyler was still recuperating and would not really be able to participate in any celebrations before . . . well, that depended upon his progress. And so it was unanimously decided that to be safe, the official anniversary party should be delayed until the last weekend in August.

How best to celebrate? they asked each other over a typically animated Sunday dinner.

A beach party, was the uniform response, though Leo jokingly suggested something on the top of the Pilgrim Monument.

That got a few laughs, but then the question remained, *what kind of beach party?*

Lark and Nora conferred quietly together on the subject of the area of New Beach that he had once told her about, where people went without clothing: was that a good idea? Was it the right time? Nora said she would ask, but she wanted to phrase the question in a way that would not stigmatize nakedness in the minds of the children, for she had raised them to feel unashamed of and comfortable with their bodies.

"Lark once showed me a section of New Beach where people bathe naturally," she said now, "without any clothes. It seemed so . . . *marvelous:* what about having our party there?"

"That sounds fun!" Schuyler said.

Sticking close to her brother these days, Emily agreed.

"I've been there with friends," Hortense exclaimed, "many times; it's really wonderful—so freeing!"

Nothing Hortense says or does will ever surprise me again, Lark thought, for he never would have guessed. And she was constantly surprising him like that.

Molly smiled at Davis, and he nodded his head. "Davis and I think it's a great idea," she said for both of them. "I always love a party!"

Well, that was everyone, then, except . . . "Leo?" Nora asked.

Leo laughed and said, "OK," but not without a hint of resignation in his voice.

"Austin should be there, too," Nora said, turning to Lark. "Will you find out if he can make it that weekend?"

Lark said that he would. And so plans for the party were put in motion—True House at one year.

June was a busy month: Lark and Austin spent two weeks in Manhattan together, during which time Austin quit smoking. Molly was looking into renting a studio (having learned that all of the studios at Days' lumber yard on Pearl Street in Provincetown were occupied, she heard about the Vinton studios on Commercial Street). And Davis had to go to Boston to visit his ailing father, who died before month's end.

In July, a painting of Hortense's was chosen for the annual exhibition at the Provincetown Art Association (in the new, *separate* Modernist show), and of course they all went to the opening. The *crème de la crème* of the art scene was there (so Hortense told them): Bill and Marguerite Zorach, Ross Moffett, Blanche Lazell, Edwin Dickinson, Ambrose Webster, and so many more. Hortense looked grand in a long, flowing purple dress (and her trademark sandals), a drink in one hand as she greeted well-wishers. That the Modernist exhibition had split off from that of the more conservative artists (called the Regularists), with the latter's now being held in August, was still the talk of the town. Some of the men had even come to fisticuffs over it, Hortense said. "Isn't that ridiculous?" And then she laughed.

At True House that summer, Leo was spending a lot of time in his room, creating *something*—he wouldn't say what, exactly. And Nora? Nora was happy to watch over the children, who were growing so fast: Emily would turn eight in October, and exactly two months later Schuyler would be ten.

By the time that last weekend in August arrived, Schuyler had been declared well enough to resume normal activity, "with caution," his doctor added. Nora vowed to watch him like a hawk. Austin came to town on Friday, and later that same day he, Lark, Nora, and Leo went shopping for food for the party: Nora thought she wanted to make cucumber sandwiches, she said; Leo suggested a pâté; and they also bought a few loaves of bread, several cheeses, fruit—strawberries and grapes—and, of course, several bottles of wine.

The next morning, the day of the party, the sky was clear and the air, if not cool, was not hot, either. But then they were presented with a problem that none of them had considered: how would they all get to the beach? There were nine of them. It would take too long to walk, they reasoned; they would simply have to make two trips in the car, Nora said. Which is what they did.

Finally situated on that section of New Beach well after noon, they set up camp. Somewhat surprisingly, there was only a smattering of other people there, playing in the water, walking, or lying on blankets, bathing in the sun; a few had their clothes on, but most did not. The children took to the scene almost immediately, asking if they could go in and, given permission, innocently shedding their clothes and walking into the surf. Nora joined them so as to watch over pale Schuyler, who had lost weight and looked so vulnerable to her now.

In general, the adults were slower to undress: after Nora, Hortense was the first to take off her clothes, followed by Austin, Lark, and then Molly and Davis. Davis had been lethargic since his father's death, and Molly was worried about him; she hoped the party would do him some good. Leo stripped to his bathing suit and a T-shirt but said that was as far as he was going.

Of course it was awkward at the beginning, with all of them trying *not* to look and so keeping their eyes unnaturally *glued* to one another's face so as to reassure the other that they weren't, in fact, looking; and then their looking, or trying to look, surreptitiously. Austin finally broke the ice by saying that the real obscenity was how pale they all were, excepting Davis, of course. The ensuing laughter was a great relief to them all, a release; and as the afternoon lengthened, most of them grew increasingly comfortable without any clothes: Hortense in particular seemed fearless, a fact that Leo noted and admired.

Did they all know about the Smooleys? she asked, hands on her hips.

They all looked at one another and several of them shook their heads, but no one said yes.

"The Smooleys," Hortense said with a laugh, "are a family of four friends—Edie Foley, Katie Smith, her brother Bill, and Stella Roof—who all live together and combine their last names to make the group name."

Everyone laughed.

"I think *we* should do that!" Leo exclaimed.

"Let's see," Nora began: "Marin, Hartley, Harrison, Stone, Munroe, Harmonica. I can't even begin . . ."

"A lot of *M*'s and *R*'s," Lark said.

"And *N*'s," Davis added.

"Mmmmaaaarrrrrstttoneica!" Schuyler shrieked.

"The Marstones," Emily called out.

"Mmm," Austin responded.

Did people like Blanche Lazell's woodcuts at the Art Association exhibition? Molly suddenly wanted to know—*Those overviews of Provincetown.* She said she had been reminded of them in the car on the way over, looking from Bradford down the side streets, over the houses and yards, across Commercial Street and into the bay.

While several of them asked, "Which were those?" Hortense knew immediately and said yes, she *had* enjoyed them, particularly Lazell's sense of perspective and use of color. Then she told them that Miss Putnam, the town librarian, disparagingly referred to Lazell and the other artists who did woodcuts as the "woodpeckers."

Leo grunted, then asked if anyone else had met that man who was going around saying, "A near Vermeer is a mere veneer."

The group marveled at the clever tongue-twister and tried repeating it.

And so they all settled into the business of celebrating, losing self-consciousness and assuming party consciousness.

The Rocking Chair Winner

Summertime seemed to come and go in a breeze, and by the time September was in full flame, Leo announced that he was ready at last to reveal what he had been working on for so long. He had done all the necessary preparatory sketches. He had ordered the supplies he thought he would need. He had borrowed or rented the tools. And then he had started to build it. But preceding all of that was the dream: this was *his vision,* he told them as they gathered in the parlor, drinking hot apple cider late one Sunday afternoon—just as Molly's vision had been to paint True House sky blue.

In fact it had been not long after they finished painting the house, Leo said, and perhaps even inspired by it. "On one of those crisp, cool fall days," he began, "I was lying on my back out on the grass in the front yard with my head in my hands" (*Boy in the Grass,* Molly thought) "daydreaming and looking up at the house and the sky, which was furrowed with clouds; it was that crystalline blue that seems to go with cool fall days. My eyes went from the sky down to the house again, and suddenly on the left I saw this huge, oversized rocking chair—about twelve feet high! It was so . . . *beckoning.* I thought it was actually there, until I looked again and realized that I had just imagined it. But because I had seen it and because it seemed *so right* to me, the scene now appeared to be missing something, and I felt disappointed. It was then that I decided I would try to construct what I had seen." He laughed.

Oohs and *ahhs* circled the parlor; they were all really dumbstruck, fascinated with Leo and the way his mind worked.

"I see the chair as eventually standing in the middle of a vegetable garden, with vines climbing up, over, and around to anchor it," he went on. "We'll have to plant the garden whenever it is that you plant such things." He laughed again. "You and Davis know all about that, don't you, Nora?"

Nora nodded and said that she did indeed. "That is *my* vision," she said, "a vegetable garden *and* a flower garden."

"I know more about flowers than vegetables," Davis added. Then he turned to Molly and laughed: "Imagine Mrs. Rothstein with a vegetable garden!"

It took Leo a solid month of work, well into October, to build the chair, but he did it and he did it alone, as was his desire—to prove to himself that he *could* do it. And at the end of the month he staged an unveiling. While everyone waited inside, Leo climbed into the rocking chair and, with Hortense's assistance, covered both himself and the chair with a very large piece of white fabric (actually several bedsheets sewn together). Hortense called them all out and then, once they had assembled and Leo was ready, she ceremoniously pulled the covering aside, and there sat Leo, rocking and beaming.

Applause.

An Old, and a New, Leaf

■\\\\\\\\■

Who the hell you think you are, boy?

The words reverberated in Davis's head—especially that *boy*. He'd simply been taking a walk around Truro by himself.

We've seen you around town with that pretty little blond thing. . . .

Piece like that, she don't have no business with a nigger. . . .

And *nigger.*

Rather, shouldn't that be put, he don't have no business with her. . . .

Now you just tell us where we can find her and we'll let you go. . . .

The idea that he would give Molly up to them!

Davis simply shook his head no. And then they were at him, on him, beating and kicking.

But there were only three of them, and Davis was a strong man— strong enough if not to do in all three, then at least to fight his way out of it and take off running. And that was what he did. Of course he was bruised and sore afterward, the kind of muscle and bone soreness that would last for days. But the worse damage was inside.

Always in life, Davis's father had told him, you get something and you give something up. His father had also said that there were two kinds of men in this world, lovers and fighters, and Davis knew that he was not a fighter.

He told the others at True House what had happened, then said he didn't want to hear about it again; it was over. He would have to be more careful in the future, that was all; he probably shouldn't go about alone. (Understanding Davis's pain, Lark took him aside and told him that he would gladly accompany him anywhere he wanted to go. Moved, Davis thanked him.)

But that winter, his second in Truro, was a particularly hard one for Davis. Besides feeling somewhat confined, for some time now he had felt that he had been floundering since he left Boston. As Mrs. Rothstein's gardener, at least he'd had something to occupy his days, something he cared about, and for the most part he had loved the work, because he pretended the garden was his own. Then he had left Mrs. Rothstein's to be with Molly, and that was good, but it wasn't enough: he needed to *do* something, to be of use. Especially now.

And all the while, he told Molly one night in bed, all the while there was the specter of his father hovering over him. He had been a proud, hardworking man all his life, Joseph Munroe had. The last time Davis had seen him alive, his father had asked him what he was doing with himself down there in Truro. Davis hadn't known what to say. He'd shrugged and replied, "I'm with Molly, Pops, you know that." Davis said his father had sat up in bed angrily, almost spitting out that he "sounded like a woman." Then he had paused and looked Davis in the eye. "Work, son, you've got to have work: that's the only salvation there is in this life."

By the end of March Davis was almost desperate, until he talked with Nora one afternoon when Molly was away at her studio, and she happened to mention again that she was intending to start two gardens in the spring, one for vegetables and one for flowers. She certainly didn't want to offend him, she said, because she knew that *that* was what he had done in Newton, but if he was at all interested in joining her, he would be more than welcome; they could plan—and plant—it together. Also, she said, if he did decide to come aboard, he could feel free to make the garden bigger than she'd originally imagined it—as big as he wanted.

Davis smiled at Nora in the late-afternoon light; she was sitting in a chair by the window, out of which, behind her, he could see the still-snow-covered ground.

"Thank you, Nora," he said. He felt better already, lighter; the answer seemed obvious now. But he didn't want to speak too quickly. "I think I *would* like that," he continued, smiling. "But can I think about it for a couple of days, and talk to Molly?"

"Sure," Nora said. "No rush."

"I just want to be sure; I don't want to lead you on. Because once I commit to something, I'm committed."

The zeal Davis felt inside now was real, real enough for him to know that this was just what he had been looking for, waiting for: it was the right thing. Nevertheless, he did take a couple of days, though instead of actually considering whether or not he should do it, he spent the majority of his time pondering which flowers would go where. And of course he talked it over with Molly, who was equally enthusiastic for him.

And then he told Nora that he wanted to do it, that he was ready and sure, and that he would be forever in her debt for suggesting it and for inviting him to join her.

Nora hugged him, shook her head, and said that she was more than glad to have him along, that she looked forward to learning what he knew, to seeing his ideas, *and* to having his company. They would start as soon as the weather permitted, she said. And then she hugged him again.

Four Seasons, One (Short) Chapter

Davis walked backward along the shallow trench, letting seeds from his hand drift down into the shallow gully. Once his hand was empty, he dipped back into the paper bag, pinched up more seeds, and continued sowing. It was rhythmic, meditative work, and that was one of the things Davis liked about it. He also liked the hard feel of the seeds between his fingers. These were carrot. Sometimes he covered the seeds; sometimes Nora did. Together they worked side by side, day after day, until the gardens were planted.

The vegetable garden, on one side of the house, built *around* Leo's oversized rocking chair, or rather with the chair smack in its middle, was highly organized and planted in well-defined rows of carrots, tomatoes, corn, and squash, bordered all around by marigolds, which Davis said naturally repelled pests; but the flower garden, in the front and around to the other side, which now contained all of the flowers Nora had imagined *and then some,* was another story. She had convinced Davis that the flower garden should be wild, wild with color and variety and organization (or the lack thereof)—in short, a garden run riot, though that was not at all what he had been accustomed to at Mrs. Rothstein's. So for himself Davis had added a small herb garden out back as well; it was something he had always wanted, something that was his own, something precise. Then the growing began.

But not *everything* at True House was looking up that summer:

Schuyler was becoming increasingly difficult, picking fights with just about everyone; he'd recently told Nora he thought it was about time he had his own room, which of course she could do nothing about.

Also that summer, Lark and Austin were going their separate ways. *Just temporarily,* Austin said. He needed a break: time away from Lark; time to think; time alone; time he could call his own—*just time.*

That was at the beginning of June, and at first Lark balked; it was not at all what *he* wanted. He was hurt. He hid away for over a week. But then he came out, and he began entreating Austin. . . . Austin had said they couldn't see each other, but he had not said that they could not write. And so Lark wrote to Austin several times a week, sending letters, wildflowers, little collages he'd made, quotes, sketches, and poems.

A deer in the clearing
could never be as dear
to me as a Vermeer—
or as you
are.

Lark was not a poet.

The leaves changed and fell, and Lark began sending those as well.

Austin postponed his and Lark's reunion; he needed more time.

Lark fell into deep despair, but in all of those months he did *not* go to the dunes.

The leaves continued to fall until, again, the trees were bare and Emily could again see the lighthouse's light from her bedroom window. It spoke to her; it seemed to whisper. . . .

"Only Connect"

.╲╲╲╲╲╲╲╲.

1 November 1930

True House

Dear Austin,

I am writing to you not for Lark but for myself and the children (and just as surely for Molly, Davis, Hortense, and Leo as well), simply because we miss seeing you; I think you must know that Schuyler is especially fond of you.

It seems so long since we've seen you, though I can't quite think of what has transpired between then and now—it is the quiet time of year. Autumn has been beautiful, as always.

The only real "news" here is that we have bought a refrigerator (modern life!) for $250. As I imagine you must know, the cost of them just keeps going down.

I am reading a wonderful novel by E. M. Forster, *Howards End,* which I think you would enjoy (its epigraph is simply "Only connect"). There is a character in it, Ruth Wilcox, who is very attached to her ancestral home—Howards End—which I can certainly understand now because of my own feelings about True House (if only there were a novelist among us). I'm sure your houses probably have a similar effect on *their* owners.

Schuyler seems well mended and very much his ornery old self again. I will never forget your sure and comforting presence at the hospital with Lark and me. Emily grows and shines.

How are you and how is your work? I know this must be a hard time for you. Please know that I am here, though I realize you probably don't feel you can comfortably drop me a line just now. If there were some way I could come to Manhattan to see you I would, but it is nearly impossible when the children are in school.

Everyone here says hello and sends you his best. Please know that we are thinking of you and that our love for you goes on no matter what.

Nora

Austin Answers

■\\\\\\\\■

11 November 1930
New York City

Dear Nora,

Thank you for the kindness and generosity of your letter: it was good to hear from you and to know that you and the children are doing well. I am fine most of the time, burying myself in my work, which currently proves quite interesting: I am restoring a house in Castine, Maine, the house of a very rich man on Main Street. It was built in 1805 and is in the Federal style—trim, spare, shingled, sturdy, and with a typical pride of function. Its one touch of ornamentation (covered over by a previous and entirely unaesthetic *and philistine* owner, I might add) is a lovely webbed fan window just above the front door. Because the house is so old, the work has involved no small amount of research, something I very much enjoy doing. When I am not fine, I walk the city, say from here—Seventy-sixth Street—down to the Village and back; this always helps: I *love* walking. I am also reading a good deal and, as a matter of fact, I admire Mr. Forster very much. While I enjoyed *Howards End,* I think his *A Passage to India* a superior work—have you read it?

Next week I am going to Chicago for a meeting, but I will also take in the new Board of Trade Building, now the tallest in the city.

Please give my best to Schuyler, Emily, and the others.

Yrs,

Austin

A Chapter on Love

Late in December, Austin wrote that he was finally ready to see Lark again. Feeling no bitterness whatsoever, only hope, Lark was on the first train. Six months had passed, and now it was winter once again. Reunited, the two men celebrated the New Year together in New York City's Times Square, reveling with the revelers. It was as if the whole world were celebrating *them,* Lark said.

All that summer and fall Leo had watched Lark during his separation from Austin, had sought him out for walks and talks, hoping for an opportunity to make his move, looking for some kind of an opening, but it had not occurred. For unbeknownst to everyone except Hortense, to whom Leo had confided, pouring his heart out time and time again (night after night), Leo was in love with Lark, and had been almost from the beginning. He hid it well, but it had not been easy. It had been especially difficult because he genuinely liked Austin and could see that Lark *adored* him, and he respected their relationship. And yet—he felt what he felt. And so he'd had one long season of hope, a summer and fall of ripeness, that was dashed when, in December, Lark and Austin resumed their relationship. Now what? All that fullness inside of him . . . he felt as though he would burst.

And so here he was in Hortense's room once again singing a love song, as he had done so often during the past six months; after all, their rooms were next to each other on the same floor. Everyone else had gone to his or her quarters for the night, and Lark was in Manhattan.

They sat on Hortense's bed; she was wearing a long flannel night-gown. Leo was still in his street clothes. She had been in a similar situation once, Hortense told him now for the first time. *Not* that she had been living in the same house with the woman, she added, but otherwise it was much the same.

And what had she done? Leo wanted to know.

Hortense laughed bitterly. She'd got her heart broken, that was what she'd done: "Broken so badly that I vowed not to let it happen again. *And I haven't,*" she said proudly. "Now I just have my way with them and move on." She laughed, stiffening her back, yawning, and stretching her hands to the ceiling. "But seriously," she added, "a lot of my friendships are physical. And some are sexual."

Leo raised an eyebrow in mock-shock fashion.

"And I like it that way!" Hortense exclaimed.

But Leo didn't have it in him, he said; he was a Romantic, a "one-man man," and simply not interested in sex without love. He propped up his head in his hands; he was tired. "I don't know what to do. Maybe I should just pounce," he said, rolling his eyes.

Hortense slapped her thigh and hooted, and Leo even laughed a little, too.

Had he thought of talking to Nora about it? Hortense asked once they'd both settled down again.

Leo shook his head and looked at her as though she were crazy. "She and Lark are so close. . . ."

"She wouldn't say anything to him," Hortense cut him off. "Unless you wanted her to." She winked. "Nora knows Lark better than anyone; probably even better than Austin. And she's so wise. . . ."

Leo kissed Hortense on both cheeks and said he would consider it.

And then Hortense asked him a question she had been wanting to ask him for a long time but had been afraid to: was Harmonica his real name?

Leo smiled. "No," he said, "but it is now; I've just made it legal."

Hortense looked at him with genuine interest.

"I'm self-invented," he explained. "Self-made, like most real artists, which is what I want to be—an artist—more than anything in the world."

"I think you are," she said, and then she just *had* to ask; she couldn't resist: "What *is* your real name, just out of curiosity?"

"Leonardo Bonaccio." Leo sighed. "But I'm no longer a member of that family. They don't understand me, don't even try to understand me. And they treat me like some people treat Davis—like a nigger! Having me wait on them hand and foot whenever I'm around." And then Leo was off on a tirade against his family.

Hortense assured him that she understood, hugged him, and said she was glad he was there, at True House.

And Leo eventually went off to his room feeling . . . ? Well, feeling happy about his friendship with Hortense, anyway, for they had grown close over time—he admired her and enjoyed her. In fact, he had told her recently that he thought she was positively *delicious,* at which she had howled, and then responded that if she was positively *delicious,* then he was indubitably *delectable;* and off they had gone on a rich platter of appetizing adjectives, culinary and otherwise, all of which had taken them down into the kitchen late that same night, searching for just the right thing to eat.

———

That same winter, their third together, Molly and Davis decided they wanted to try to have a child. They had been going back and forth about it for quite some time, or rather Molly had; for while Davis had always been absolutely certain that this was something he wanted, Molly was never sure. What would happen to her painting? she asked. She needed to study more, to work harder. . . . And she had recently put down a year's rent—fifty dollars—on one of the Vinton studios.

And then there was the fact of their different skin colors, she went on gingerly; what would life be like for their child? They had to think of that. (Would he, too, be accosted by some small-minded locals?) Molly talked to Nora about it frequently, asking her advice; Davis confided most often in Lark—they had grown closer. But then after a while Davis would back off and tell Molly he was worried that she did not love him enough, and that maybe the real problem was that she wasn't sure she wanted to have a child *with him.* At which point one or both of them would start to cry, and then the reassurances would begin, and they would inevitably end up in bed, holding and caressing each other and then, once again, making love.

But then Molly finally agreed to it; she had thought it over and said she felt ready. Davis promised he would assume a large role in taking care of the child, especially during daylight hours when she needed to be at the studio—how she loved him for that. And everyone told her that Davis would make a wonderful father—as if she didn't know that. And Molly felt, too, that Nora wanted this, and she loved and respected Nora so much; Nora had even offered her help in raising the child. But what ultimately convinced Molly was simply thinking about what a positive thing it would be to do, a leap of faith. Inherent in such a decision, she thought, when it was so carefully considered, was an expression of confidence in herself, in her relationship with Davis, and in the environment of True House, if not the world. . . . Yes, yes, yes, she was ready; it was the right thing to do.

And so all that winter Molly and Davis hunkered down to business: they made love even more than usual over those four months. And though their lovemaking had always been enjoyable, the fact that they were now doing it for a reason other than mere pleasure brought them closer; but by spring Molly was still not pregnant, and she had begun to worry.

———

Lark and Austin's *rapprochement,* meanwhile, was running along smoothly, though they *were* seeing each other slightly less often, a fact Lark couldn't help but notice; and while it nagged at him internally—in the form of *What's wrong with me?*—he said nothing. But *the point,* as Austin told Lark, was that it was working and that they were both happy with the way things were: "That's what it's all about, isn't it?"

———

And Nora? After her disastrous first marriage, she had decided that she would not marry again. In the intervening years, however, of course she'd had urges, needs, the desire for another. . . . But just as she was beginning to feel ready, to reconsider, Schuyler had been hit by a car and almost killed; and once it was clear that he would come out of it all right, she had quickly made another decision: she would not get involved with anyone until *after* Schuyler and Emily were grown, and that was that.

———

As for the children themselves . . . Schuyler was at the age when, for boys, attraction to the opposite sex began to manifest itself by a resentment of that attraction, and thus the female species—at least in school—was treated as the lowliest of the low. And Emily? Emily was simply *in love with the world.*

The Exhilaration of the Moment

Whiteness! Molly exclaimed, spinning about the room with her arms outstretched. *Whiteness and silence*—her own studio at last! Always, in her previous life (which was how she thought of it), whether at home or at the Museum School, she had worked in cramped quarters, in bad light, or against walls painted some dreadful color, and always there had been the possibility of someone's lurking over her shoulder, asking questions, making comments, *interrupting*. . . . Now, finally, here she was in her very own studio, *hers* for as long as she could pay the rent; suddenly she was her own mistress. Here the walls were painted *white* and the sounds were sounds of *silence,* and any interruptions would be of her own making or allowance, and the light was Provincetown's best! It was a lot of responsibility—she would have to earn it.

And so as she went about unpacking and arranging her supplies—canvases (some rolled, some stretched), easel, charcoals, pens, paints, brushes, art books, old coffee cans, bottles of mineral oil, and rags—Molly felt what? She could hardly say, it was all so astonishing. She had plenty of ideas, dreams she'd had and stored up, visions she was anxious to try to execute and realize. . . . *That* was not a problem. What *was* a problem was her feeling unworthy, feeling . . . that she had to take care of everyone else first (a legacy from her large family, she'd always thought). She'd felt so much better about Davis, so *relieved*, ever since he'd had the gardens to tend to, but now there was the possibility of a child who, she feared, would put an end to all this (she looked around the room). Because she knew she would worry, and worry intensely, about being a good mother, so much so that she would be willing to let everything else go for their child. . . .

But, she told herself, continuing to unpack, she was not pregnant yet; also, she reminded herself, hers was not the traditional situation: she lived with, and was literally surrounded by, friends who were more than willing to help. *So just put those thoughts right out of your head, missy,* she instructed herself (she always referred to herself as "missy," just as her mother had). She would talk to Nora. *And* she would talk to Hortense—variations on a theme. *Enough of this, now get to work!*

And so to rid her mind of such thoughts Molly did a mad little dervish of a dance in the middle of her studio, whirling and twirling until she was completely dizzy. Then she immediately lay down on the floor (as the room spun around her); she let herself focus on the novel whiteness and silence until she returned to the exhilaration of the moment, a moment that (she thought now) perhaps someday she would try to paint.

Leo's Reading Notebook

From *The Outermost House: A Year of Life on the Great Beach of Cape Cod,* by Henry Beston (1928):

Artemisia stellerina—the most familiar dune plants. Silvery gray-green in summer, gold in the fall

Here, in a little disturbed and claw-marked space of sand, a flock of *larks* has alighted; here one of the birds has wandered off by himself; here are the deeper tracks of hungry crows; here the webbed impression of a gull. There is always something poetic and mysterious to me about these tracks in the dunes; they begin at nowhere, sometimes with the faint impression of an alighting wing, and vanish as suddenly into the trackless nowhere of the sky. . . .

There is no harshness here in the landscape line, no hard northern brightness or brusque revelation; there is always reserve and mystery, always something beyond, on earth and sea something which nature, honoring, conceals.

Anosa plexippus—Monarch butterflies

Hudsonia tomentosa—poverty grass

Pinus rigida—pitch pine

Circus Hudsonius—marsh hawk

Populus deltoides—western cottonwoods rare in the northeast; transplanted from Kansas

From Monomy Point to Race Point in Provincetown—full fifty miles—twelve coast guard stations watch the beach and the shipping night and day. There are no breaks save natural ones in this keep of the frontier.

Between the stations, at some midway and convenient point, stand huts called halfway houses, and stations, huts and lighthouses are linked together by a special telephone system owned and maintained by the coast guard services.

Every night in the year, when darkness has fallen on the Cape and the sombre thunder of ocean is heard in the pitch pines and the moors, lights are to be seen moving along these fifty miles of sand, some going north, some south, twinkles and points of light solitary and mysterious. These lights gleam from the lanterns and electric torches of the coast guardsmen of the Cape walking the night patrols. When the nights are full of wind and rain, loneliness and the thunder of the sea, these lights along the surf have a quality of romance and beauty that is Elizabethan, that is beyond all stain of present time.

From *Cape Cod,* by Henry David Thoreau (1865):

Every landscape which is dreary enough has a certain beauty to my eyes, and in this instance its permanent qualities were enhanced by the weather. Everything told of the sea, even when we did not see its waste or hear its roar. . . .

Though we have indulged in some placid reflections of late, the reader must not forget that the dash and roar of the waves were incessant. Indeed, it would be well if he were to read with a large conch-shell at his ear. . . .

Nothing remarkable was ever accomplished in a prosaic mood.

Ain't it the truth, H.D., ain't . . . it . . . the truth!

Hortense Organizes a Field Trip

Late in the winter, near the end of March, Hortense announced one wool-gathering Sunday afternoon that she needed to see some great art, a lot of great art, and that she needed it badly. *Or else,* she went on, she feared that her senses would dry up and go dumb forever. And so she was planning to make a trip to the Museum of Fine Arts in Boston; was anyone else interested in joining her?

Leo raised his hand enthusiastically, like a child at school, and blurted out, "Me, me!"

"That's a *marvelous* idea," Nora added. She looked at Schuyler and Emily. "Count me and the children in." Schuyler immediately rolled his eyes.

"Us, too," Molly said for herself and Davis, after getting his agreement by a mere look.

Which left only Lark, who had been brooding all day. Everyone was looking at him, waiting for an answer. He shrugged and said, "I don't know. It depends on when. I could be in Manhattan with Austin. Or he could be here."

"He could come, too," Nora offered.

How would they get there? Leo wondered aloud.

That was one of the reasons she was asking, Hortense said. Already there were too many of them to go in Nora's car, she went on, and so she supposed they would have to take the train. "But let's decide on when."

"Next weekend!" Leo suggested. "Saturday?"

Hortense looked around the room. "Is that good for everybody?"

Assent all around, except from Lark.

"Next weekend it is, then!" Hortense proclaimed.

And so the following Saturday all of the inhabitants of True House but Lark, who had left for Manhattan on Friday, took the train in to Boston for the weekend. Because the trip would be brief, Molly and Davis had decided against even letting their families know they would be in town.

"Well, then, we shall all stay overnight at the Parker House," Nora announced; it would be her treat.

They arrived at the museum by midafternoon on Saturday; the city was white with new-fallen snow. It reminded Nora of the day when she and Lark had first met, and suddenly she missed him intensely.

Emerging from the trolley in front of the museum's entrance on Huntington Avenue, Emily said that the statue of the Indian on horseback had always been one of her favorite things in Boston, that it had a certain "majesty" (pronouncing *majesty* with a particular relish). And Davis confided that he had never even been there before.

Once inside, instead of going their separate ways, the members of the group decided to stick together: "Because seeing both *what* and *how* your friends see, and what they love—*especially if they're painters,*" Nora said, unsubtly nudging both Molly and Hortense "—is part of the fun of museum-going."

Then, as they were climbing the grand staircase, Hortense said, "Besides me and Leo, all the rest of you are *from* Boston—so why don't you lead the way?"

"Mother's not actually *from* Boston," Schuyler said suddenly. "But my father is." And then he added, under his breath, "And I'd much rather be visiting him than looking at all this stuff."

Nora gave him a sharp look, then said that she would happily lead the way.

As they walked through the galleries, Molly announced that they should all pick a favorite work for that day, and then say *why* it was a favorite. Hers today (and today only, she emphasized; it could easily be something different tomorrow), was Mary Cassatt's *At the Opera*. She stopped in front of the painting.

"Because?" Leo asked.

"Oh," Molly gasped, laughing, having forgotten the rules of her own game. "Because . . . because of the sweep of it." She suddenly went animated. "The movement, and the interplay of the colors. Look at the contrast between the black dress of the central figure and the rust-colored background that dominates the painting. And then there's this white-gold color"—she pointed—"along the front of the two balconies that draws the light and the eye to their curving." She paused to take a breath; her fellow housemates appeared rapt. "And just the subject itself," she went on, "the *moment* of this woman, opera glasses to her eyes, seemingly lost in the story and pageantry of the opera. While across the room"—Molly pointed again, laughing now—"there is this man with opera glasses: is he looking at her? Or is he looking at the painter? Or at us? It's very clever."

The group mumbled their opinions as to just *whom* the man was looking at as they walked on.

In that same room, Hortense said that for her it would have to be one of two Monets—either *Rouen Cathedral* or *Water Lilies*. "Because of how broken up the surfaces of the paintings are," she said. "The Impressionists fascinate me," she continued, "because they're interested in representing not only an object, in this case a church or water lilies in a pond, but also the light and shadows on those objects. And while that changes what representation means, I think it's the truest form of it."

"Which inevitably leads to cubism," Nora added, but the museum had no examples of that.

"And Schuyler?" Molly asked, trying to draw him in. "What's your favorite?"

He responded that it was impossible for him to choose just one, then quickly named three, all of which had in common that they were violent seascapes: Turner's *Slave Ship*, Washington Allston's *Rising of a Thunderstorm at Sea,* and Copley's infamous *Watson and the Shark.*

"Because?" Nora asked.

"Because I like 'em," Schuyler said arrogantly. "Because they're exciting." And then he muttered, "Unlike this."

The group either didn't hear Schuyler's remark or decided to ignore it, as Davis chose two nearby paintings: Copley's *Nicholas Boylston*— because, he said quickly, remembering the rules, "it reminds me of Molly's portrait of *me,*" which Molly then said she could see, in the finery, perhaps the *excessive* finery, even, of the costume. But also Copley's

Boy with Squirrel, Davis added, not only because of the sweet nature of the subject matter (he was hoping for a son), but also because of how well the painter handled the different textures and surfaces in the painting. They all studied the boy's rosy complexion, his pink satin collar, the gold metal chain he dangled, the near-empty glass of water, and the squirrel's furry tail, and they agreed with the reasoning behind Davis's choice.

Nora said she was in a quiet, dreamy mood, and she, too, protested that she was incapable of choosing just one. "I find myself responding to the little Chardin still lifes," she said, "such as *Kitchen Table,*" and she pointed to it. But then later she came upon Rembrandt's hushed *Old Man in Prayer* and said, "That's it!"

"Because?" Molly asked with a smile.

Nora smiled back. She was tired. "Because I feel so humbled here, with all of this great art, and with all of you. Humbled and thankful and *blessed,*" she added. "And because I *adore* Rembrandt, especially the brave, late self-portraits." But they'd better move on, she suggested, deflecting attention; the museum would be closing soon, and Emily and Leo had yet to name *their* favorite works.

Emily surprised everyone with the simplicity of her choice, Dennis Miller Bunker's portrait *Jessica.* "Mostly just because of this," Emily said wistfully, pointing to the subject's elongated neck. "It's *so* beautiful and *graceful*—like a swan's." Emily was quiet for a moment, seemingly lost in thought. "And because I like red hair," she said, giggling.

"And Leo?" Nora asked as they walked on. Leo gestured as if he were saying "Who, me?" and laughed. He quickly pointed to a Japanese suit of armor from the Edo period that they happened to be passing at that moment; and then said that though he liked a great deal of what he saw, he could not honestly say he had found a favorite work. "At least not today. Tomorrow might be another story." (But it was not, in fact, until a similar visit in 1936, after the museum's acquisition of Gauguin's *Where Do We Come From? What Are We? Where Are We Going?* that Leo could honestly say he had a favorite painting at the Museum of Fine Arts: *The principal message of Gauguin's painting,* Leo would then think, *is the spirituality of nature's wholeness. The painting portrays the stages of life, from birth to fertility to old age and death. Gauguin may be saying that death happens only to the body and not to the soul. It's a very spiritual painting, but without a hint of religion.*)

By the time the seven of them got back to Park Street, it was dusk, and Nora pointed to the snow-covered Common and asked if they remembered the painting by Childe Hassam called *Boston Common at Twilight*. All said they did.

"Well, here we are," Nora announced. "*In* the painting!"

The Great Depression

Because Cape Cod was so isolated and self-contained, the Great Depression did not hit it as hard or as fast as it did most of the rest of the country. But hit it it eventually did, so that by late 1934, like most other Americans (though never quite as badly), the people of Cape Cod were suffering.

The inhabitants of True House gathered to discuss it.

"In the past, selling an occasional painting was enough to sustain me for a while," Molly said, "but art simply is not selling now, and my money supply is dwindling fast."

"It's not selling largely because tourism is off," Hortense offered. "People just can't afford to come to the Cape right now, much less buy paintings."

Austin was constantly reporting what it was like in Manhattan these days—so many storefronts boarded up; long bread lines of gray, sad-looking people stretching for blocks; dirty, undernourished and underclothed children standing on street corners and begging; people literally freezing to death. . . .

Through her connection with the Provincetown Art Association, Hortense learned about Ross Moffett's work for the federal Public Works of Art Project, painting murals in Provincetown's Town Hall. She and Molly were both hired immediately. (For Molly, a job meant the realization that she and Davis would have to put aside their plans to have a child for the time being—not that they had been having any luck anyway. But it also meant that she would *not* have to give up her studio anytime soon. Having time for it was another matter.)

And it was through Moffett, too, that Molly eventually learned of yet another WPA project, the building of an airfield out by Race Point.

Leo said he would try to sign on. Nora quickly offered to drive him there and pick him up every day. And before the end of the week, he had the job.

Now all of the adults were gainfully employed, Molly, Hortense, and Leo out in the world, Davis in the garden, and Nora and Lark inside the house, for the two of them agreed that since they did not have paying jobs, they would be responsible for making meals *and* for keeping True House clean, well stocked, and in good repair.

Morning Ritual

"Lark?" Nora called. She was sitting in the parlor and just happened to see him coming down the stairs with his mug, presumably on his way into the kitchen for more coffee. It was ten-thirty in the morning, and Davis was already outside working in the garden.

Lark peeked into the parlor. "Hi."

"Are you doing anything now?" Nora asked.

"Not really," Lark said with a shrug.

"Come sit with me, then, will you?"

He smiled and nodded. "I was just going to get more coffee. Can I bring you anything?"

"Sure, I'll take a cup."

When he returned, the two of them settled into what would become their morning ritual: sitting by the window in the parlor, looking out at the day through the frame of the window (as if it were a work of art), and talking. Because they did the household chores in stages, the few morning tasks were finished by now, and there would be nothing more until around one, when one or both of them would rise and go into the kitchen to make lunch. This was *their* time.

"How are you?" Nora asked.

Lark felt sheepish. He quickly considered all of his worries and insecurities about Austin and the fact that they weren't seeing each other as often, and then he went through the checklist of his disappointments with himself . . . but he sensed that Nora had something on her mind, something specific, and so he brushed his darker, more self-absorbed thoughts aside and answered, "I'm fine; how are *you?*"

And then it came out: "I'm worried about Schuyler."

Lark looked at her and felt that he knew *exactly* what she would say, what she was worried about; he waited for her to say it.

"He seems so restless and frustrated and . . . I don't know . . . rebellious all the time. I feel like he resents us, all of us, but especially *me.* . . ." Nora shook her head. "It's just terrible. Do you know at all what I'm talking about, have you seen it?"

Lark interrupted her, nodding. "I *do* know," he said. "I *have* seen it. But what I don't know is if it's behavior that's typical of young boys, boys growing into men, or if it's something that's specific to Schuyler." He stopped and looked at her. "I mean, I was like that, Nora. But then I had very different parents."

Nora went on: "He's fourteen now. I don't know what to do." Her face was contorted. "I don't want him to hate me."

Lark looked at her; she appeared to be on the verge of tears. Dare he say what he was thinking, what in fact he had been thinking for some time? "You know, Nora," he began, rousing her from some deep place, "I have been thinking about something, a possible solution, even before this conversation." He paused to look at her, trying to gauge whether or not he should say it, and if so, how. "But . . . I don't know quite how to say it. It's just a suggestion; one idea. . . ."

"Go ahead," Nora said, fixing him with her eyes. "Just say it."

Lark swallowed. He was nervous. He hated even admitting that he'd been thinking about it. Nora closed her eyes as he began to speak: "I've been thinking about, well, I've wondered if maybe, you know, if, well"—he cleared his throat—"OK, I'll just say it—if maybe sending Schuyler to live with Ben for a little while might not be a good thing to do, to let him get it out of his system."

Nora opened her eyes, took a deep breath, and said she *loved* that he'd expressed it in the negative, then added that she had been thinking the very same thing. "Although of course I *loathe* the idea," she almost hissed. "But maybe you're right; maybe it would be the best thing. For a while." She paused to look out the window, then she took another deep breath, and her eyes narrowed. "Of course Ben would just love it. *Not* having to take care of Schuy, I don't mean that—heaven forbid he should be any kind of a father to his son—but he would consider it some sort of a moral victory over me."

Lark shrugged. "We're talking about Schuyler here, Nora," he reminded her, "and what's best for *him*." He caught her gaze. "Maybe he'll appreciate you more, and what he has here at True House—*our values, and us*—if he lives with the opposite for a while."

Nora burst into tears. "You're right. I know you're right. It's just that . . ." And here she started to sob.

Lark set aside his mug and rose to his knees to embrace her, rocking her back and forth in his arms.

"It would only have to be for a little while," he said softly. "Not forever."

Nora sat up and wiped away her tears. "I know. It's just so . . . *hard.*

I mean, what if he wants to stay? Or what if Ben won't let him come back? And what will Emily think?" Nora started sobbing again, and again Lark held her, this time putting her head on his shoulder, rubbing her hair, and saying, "Shh, shh."

"I love our house," Nora said now, smiling through her tears and withdrawing from Lark's arms. "I love what we've made here—all of us. And it's just *terrible* to me, one of the worst possible things imaginable, that Schuyler doesn't appreciate it. It feels like such a blanket rejection of who I am and who we all are."

Lark smiled back at her to convey that she knew he loved it, too.

"But if it takes his having to go away to make him grateful for what he has," she said sadly, gathering herself up, "then I guess it is for the best, isn't it?"

Lark nodded and said quietly, "Yes."

Nora looked at her watch; she wiped her face with her hands and tucked her hair behind her ears. She would talk to Schuyler, she said, and assuming that he wanted to do it, then she would call Ben. She stood up now and looked at Lark. "Thank you," she said, hugging him.

"Thank *you*," Lark said in return, for he was glad that Nora had unburdened herself to him; it felt only right, for a change.

Davis in His Garden

■\\\\\\\\■

Davis was down on his knees, crouching in the vegetable garden, pulling up weeds. On the ground beside him were a small hand shovel and something that resembled a steel claw; towering above him was the rocking chair, now anchored by twisting, meandering vines. He was going for the weeds' roots and, once successful in isolating them, he tossed the whole into a large pail that he would later set fire to. He hoped this would put an end to the damned things once and for all.

Wearing overalls and a white T-shirt, he was humming—humming something low and somber, but feeling happy. *Damn, I am happy,* he thought. He looked up at the clear blue sky: *I've got work, Pops.* He often spoke to his father while he was gardening, or whenever he was alone. *I've got work, and it's not working for anybody else, either. It's my own garden, my own garden of Eden right here on Cape Cod.* He wished his father had lived to see it. *It's something I love. With some*one *I love. And then if all that isn't enough, I've got good friends, too. . . . I'm a rich man. Life is good.* That he was something of a captive on "the isle of Truro," as he called it, a slave of another kind, had become a given.

The morning sun was high but not hot; Davis had a straw hat for the hot days. He lowered his head to the ground now to smell the pungent earth and all of the fresh green life bursting out of it. He fingered the soil, sniffed it, then took a deep breath and extended his arms, wanting to embrace it all, to take it all in. Because not every day was like this. Oftentimes it was just day-to-day, business as usual: deadening habit. Or he felt confined and wanted to break out. And sometimes it was hard, or just plain frustrating. But there were plenty of days, too, when he did feel this way, when he just couldn't believe his good luck; and when those days came along, he tried to take full advantage of them, to praise and be thankful for them.

If only he and Molly could have a child, Davis thought, *then* everything would be complete. But that would have to wait now that Molly was working, he knew that. And he shouldn't be ungrateful for what he did have; he knew that, too. *I will simply be the father of this garden in the meantime.*

The Arrival of the Patriarch

"I just had to see for myself what it is my son is *leaving*," Ben Croft said, standing at the front door of True House.

Nora immediately wanted to block his way, as if his merely entering True House would somehow taint it. She had wanted to drive Schuyler to Boston herself; she had not wanted *this*. But Ben had insisted, just as he had insisted, throughout their marriage, that she do this or that. That was Ben: *insistent*.

"He's in his room, still packing," Nora said civilly. "Schuyler!" she called upstairs. "Your father's here!" She had resolved not to lose control, to be strong: this was too important.

Looking at Ben now, Nora noticed what so much exposure to the sun was doing to his skin (he was an avid sailor): his neck was stained with spots, and he had deep lines around his eyes. . . . Suddenly she felt sorry for him: he was going to die. And then in an instant, in the roominess of sympathy, she was able to recall *moments* in the marriage when things had been good between them, when she had still been happy. *They were in a sailboat on the Charles* . . .

She would have liked to linger there, felt she could have learned something. But suddenly everyone seemed to appear from out of nowhere (everyone, that is, except Emily). Lark emerged from the kitchen, wiping his hands on a dish towel so as to offer one in a handshake. Croft quickly shoved his hands into his pockets and nodded, saying, "Mr. Marin."

Instead of being put off by Croft's refusal to shake his hand, Lark made the quick decision to be amused by the pathetic, squirrelly white-blond mustache Croft had grown since he last saw him.

"Would you like something to drink after the long drive?" Nora asked Ben, ushering him into the parlor, where Molly and Davis waited.

Croft started at the sight of them, surprised by the contrast in their coloring. But ever invested in presenting a cool exterior, he crossed his arms and said hello.

"Molly, Davis, this is Ben Croft."

He's so . . . white, Davis thought.

And indeed it was the *visual* of Ben Croft that instantly impressed itself upon Molly—his unwrinkled three-piece light-blue seersucker suit and the fact that the sun-reddened part in his white-blond hair was as straight as an arrow.

"Where's his room?" Croft asked Nora, looking through the parlor doorway.

But before Nora could answer, Leo and Hortense waltzed into the room arm in arm.

"Leo, Hortense, this is Schuyler's father, Ben Croft. I'll go check on him," she told her former husband.

Croft nodded to Hortense and Leo. A stifled silence followed, permeating the room. "How many people live here?" he finally asked.

"This is all of us," Hortense said, fighting her natural urge to be naughty and instead merely smiling. "What?" She looked to the others, feigning casualness. "Eight?"

Molly nodded, then the oppressive silence resumed.

Ben Croft paced, looking down at the floor.

Nora came back. "He'll be right down," she said. *Oh, but this is awkward,* she thought. And she actually felt sorry for Ben, for his having to enter their *den* like this. She felt for him so much, in fact, that she found herself wishing Emily would come down, at least to say hello. But she daren't ask her: this was a point on which she knew Emily was intransigent.

There was Schuyler, carrying two suitcases; he looked ashen, having just said good-bye to his sister. He placed the suitcases next to two boxes of his things; a mostly blue globe of the world stuck out of one. He and his father shook hands. Then time, which had seemed to move so slowly before, suddenly quickened. Schuyler woodenly hugged his mother and waved a dismissive good-bye to the others, and he and his father were out the front door, followed by Nora, who had begun to weep.

"Poor Nora," Molly said, "being married to *that!*"

At last they had all met Ben Croft.

"Poor *Schuyler,*" Lark offered, to which Davis added a solemn, "Amen!"

Strange Interlude:
A Kiss in the Cupola

_{᠁᠁᠁}

"Is that you, Lark?"

Leo stood below, crouched, peering up into the cupola.

"It's me." Lark's voice. "Come on up."

Lark extended a hand to help Leo climb up and into the cupola, as the wood under him creaked with his weight.

A pair of binoculars hung around Lark's bare chest; he was wearing only a pair of shorts, which rode low about his waist. It was a hot summer day.

"Where is everyone?" Leo had just returned home.

Lark removed the binoculars from around his neck and handed them to Leo, then pointed. "They all went down to the beach."

Leo looked through the binoculars, found them in view, and laughed: "There they are!"

Lark said he was concerned about Nora and wondered how she was doing now, with Schuyler gone to live with his father.

"Mmm." Leo nodded sadly.

"Not that I was looking at *her*," Lark said, worried that Leo might think that. He took the binoculars back and trained them on a spot in the opposite direction. "There!" he cried, handing them to Leo again. "Here's what I was really looking at."

"What? Where?" Leo asked. "All I see is the ocean—in two lovely little round frames," he said in a British accent, laughing.

"Keep looking."

"Oh my God!" Leo suddenly exclaimed. "Is it—it's a whale!" He watched intently now as the huge black beast broke the surface of the blue water, rose up into the air in a graceful arc, and then fell with a splash back into the foam and spray and submerged itself again. "That's beautiful!" Leo cried.

"Isn't it?"

Leo continued looking. "I don't see him anymore," he said eventually. "I think he's gone."

"He *was* getting awfully close to shore," Lark said. "It's dangerous, you know?"

Leo nodded. But now, without the focus of the whale, Leo became aware of just how close and hot it was in the cupola. It was so close, in fact, that he and Lark were actually rubbing against one another on the little bench. He looked at Lark: beads of sweat were gathered around his neck and running down his chest. . . .

Leo put the binoculars to his eyes again and applied them directly to Lark's face.

Lark laughed and gently pushed away the hand that held the binoculars. Leo laughed, too, grabbing at Lark's hand and tickling him. And then, without even thinking, he leaned over and kissed Lark on the lips.

The little room suddenly became silent and still. Lark seemed frozen but not rejecting. Time was frozen. Leo leaned over and kissed Lark again, this time using his tongue, and Lark opened his mouth to receive Leo's tongue, took it in, sucked it, and gave Leo his tongue in return.

Leo's hand slid out of control across Lark's sweaty torso. Lark's arms hung limp at his sides. The kiss went on for at least a minute, their eyes tightly shut all the while.

But then—mutually, somehow—Leo and Lark stopped kissing at the same time and rested their foreheads against each other's, keeping their eyes closed.

Lark opened his eyes first and sat up. Leo did the same. They looked at each other. They both smiled and blushed. "That was nice," Lark said, kissing Leo on the cheek, remembering that it was in the cupola that Austin had kissed him for the first time.

"Thank you." Leo kissed Lark on the cheek. "I've wanted to do that for a very long time," he said, and he laughed.

Lark nodded. "I know," he said, adding, in a whisper, "I'm sorry," and the two embraced. Lark shrugged and then abruptly changed the subject, saying that they *must* replace the windows in the cupola soon with the kind that could be opened and closed.

Disappointed, Leo simply nodded in agreement.

After Schuyler

After Schuyler had been gone for a month, Nora had a telephone installed in True House. This way he would be able to call her whenever he liked, she told him. Dutifully, then, like the well-trained little soldier he was becoming, Schuyler called from Boston once a week, always on a Sunday.

While Emily missed her brother and lifelong playmate, she was also mature enough to realize that Schuyler's absence was a direct result of his own actions and that, in short, he had got what he wanted: to live with his father; to be away from *them*. Whereas she decidedly did *not* want to go and live with, or even visit, her father; she was happy where she was. Like her mother, however, Emily could not help but feel rejected by Schuyler, as to a lesser extent did Lark and Hortense and Molly and Davis and Leo. But life at True House went on, with Nora quietly missing Schuyler. It was a loss, she thought, a little death, and one that she was responsible for: it was all her fault.

Schuyler did not visit for several months, and when he did finally return to True House, on Thanksgiving weekend, Nora was horrified to see that all of his hair had been chopped off. But just as she began to comment on it and to accuse Ben, Schuyler warned her not to blame his father, saying that it had been *his* idea, that *he* had wanted it; Nora suddenly felt as though she no longer knew him, her little boy, her son. He was fifteen, Schuyler went on, swilling a Moxie and sounding too much like his father (and probably echoing him), and it was high time he began the hard work of becoming a man.

Everyone was eager to please Schuyler that weekend, and no one did. Nora cheerfully suggested a walk on the beach, and Lark a drive into Provincetown, whereas Molly invited them all to visit her studio—a first. Leo thought Schuyler might enjoy ghost stories by the fire (as he once had), and Davis said he wanted to show him what remained of the garden in late November. But moping about True House, Schuyler refused to allow himself to be interested (he was still too close to it).

"Well, the hell with him!" Hortense said to herself under her breath, furious at the way he was treating everyone, particularly Nora and Emily. Nor could Emily, either, bring herself to reach out to this stranger she had once called Brother, for Schuyler, she thought now, held his hardening little heart close and closed, as a boxer nursed a sore fist. (Increasingly, she was thinking in similes and metaphors.)

And then there was the argument at the dinner table, chiefly between Schuyler and Lark, about the Great War and serving one's country and patriotism (with Schuyler championing all three and Lark, less enthusiastic, holding out for pacifism).

"Austin served in the war," Lark told Schuyler. "Why don't you ask him about it?"

It was an escalatingly nasty encounter that concluded with Schuyler's calling Lark a fairy. Overheated, overwrought, and certain that this was an expression Schuyler had got—along with the rest of his mixed-up ideas—directly from Ben, Nora impulsively popped her son on the mouth with the palm of her hand. He immediately jumped up from the table, knocking over his chair, and walked out the front door.

In short, the weekend was not a success, and at the end of it Nora was bereft to realize that she had driven Schuyler even further away: how long would it be now before he visited again?

Nora Sends Her Brother, Michael, a Postcard
Upon Learning He Is Contemplating a Visit

■⟍⟍⟍⟍⟍⟍■

17 December 1935

True House

Dear Michael,

Mother tells me you may visit: how can I entice you? It has been *too* long. You have not seen the children since—was it '27 when you last came to Boston? I can help financially. My friends are wonderful and want to meet you. And it *is* beautiful. Thoreau wrote to a friend from Truro, "Come by all means, for it is the best place to see the ocean in these States." Come, by all means! And bring Mother if she will.

Love,

Nora

The Bed That Michael Made

■\\\\\\\\■

But Mother would *not* come, not by any means, Michael wrote Nora. "She simply will not leave Charleston"—"Never have!" she announced proudly—"and I can't leave her," he concluded.

And that was *that.*

The Men of True House

Work with the WPA ended for Molly and Hortense that fall, and when it did, both women decided that they had done their duty *and* made enough money to last them for a while; it was high time they got back to their own work. Leo, however, continued going to his job out by Race Point building the airfield, still driven most days by Nora. He almost liked it, he told her one morning on the ride out—"for now"— adding that he especially enjoyed the camaraderie among the men. "Besides," he said, laughing, "I get a lot of thinking done."

As for Molly, over the past two years, because she'd been working, she had been able to afford to keep her studio, the catch being that she didn't have much time to use it. Now that she was free again, she was resolved on maintaining the same schedule in the studio that she'd had working for the WPA; and she was equally determined to earn money through her painting.

Hortense also moved in a new direction, invigorated. While she continued to prefer to work *en plein air,* she moved her easel down by the ocean: she wanted to capture the sea in paint, she said; she had been inspired by the Impressionists. This would be her first attempt at pure landscape. She would paint the ocean over and over again, and in fact she wouldn't stop painting it, she told Molly, until she got it right, at least once—that was her challenge. Her ultimate goal was to learn to be able to paint more loosely and more freely and more boldly. And so now every morning she woke early and carried her supplies out across the backyard, down the hill, and onto the beach, and it was there that she set up for the day.

Molly, meanwhile, had had another vision: *The Men of True House*, she called it. She wanted to paint Davis, Lark, Austin, and Leo (it was too bad Schuyler was no longer there, though she would be careful not to say this around Nora); she would pose the four of them in profile, with their heads turned to the left but their torsos straight on. Furthermore, she would paint them, from the waist up, against a black background, and all four would be wearing black shirts (meant to blend in with the background), unbuttoned and falling off their shoulders so that they resembled capes or shawls, thus revealing the men's necks, their shoulders, and part of their chests.

Once again Molly was standing tradition on its ear, posing men in a way that only women had been posed, particularly and frequently during the latter half of the nineteenth century (the portrait that Emily had loved so much on their visit to the Museum of Fine Arts in Boston, Dennis Miller Bunker's *Jessica*, was a good example). Molly did not upend tradition for controversy's sake, however; she did it because she knew it would yield interesting results.

The studio sessions were a logistical nightmare; simply getting all four men there at the same time was an ordeal. First of all it had to be done on a weekend, since Leo worked weekdays; and it had to be a weekend when Austin was in town. Molly's other primary dilemma was keeping all four men still and straight-faced for very long, since

Leo said he felt silly with the shirt falling off of him; he kept cracking them up. Sucking in his cheeks, he would swiftly cross his legs, quickly posing, and say "Jean Harlow!" Finally, at the end of the single two-hour session that Molly got with the four of them (which she did spend sketching), she decided also to photograph them and try to work from the results, and so she took not only group shots, but several close-ups of all four men as well.

It is a large work, four feet by eight, Davis, Lark, Austin, and Leo, in profile and in that order, seemingly spotlit, only their faces and part of their torsos showing as their black shirts disappear into the black backdrop. Molly has had to work particularly hard with Davis because of his dark skin, so that his face and torso don't get lost against the black; to do this she has manipulated the lighting, giving him highlights in all the right places, and she has succeeded wonderfully. (She has also had to resist bejeweling him, not an easy thing for her.) All four men are easily recognizable as themselves, but even more, Molly has captured their character, perhaps even their very essence.

Once again, Molly had had her vision.

"But what about the women of True House?" Hortense cried once the painting was finished and everyone had been invited to see it.

"Yes, what about the women, indeed?" Nora echoed, smiling mischievously.

Suddenly Molly had another painting to do.

The Women of True House

How different in tone these studio sessions were from those with the men.

"The knowledge that women have been *objects* for thousands of years, in art and in life," Nora was saying, sitting stiffly in Molly's studio on a cold December morning, "I think it inevitably creates a self-consciousness in a female *subject*. Don't you all agree?"

"Well, I know how you *both* feel," Hortense said laughingly to Nora and Molly, "the paint*er* and the paint*ed*."

And whereas Molly *should* have told Nora to try to relax, she was preoccupied, and said nothing. There they all were—they had gathered, *for her*—and still she had had no vision. She had always worked from inspiration, from visions and dreams; now she simply did not know what she was going to do. She had been racking her brain for days; she had done research—art books were spread open all over the studio—but nothing had leapt out at her, nothing had come: there was little to no historical precedent. Should she have canceled the session? she wondered.

"I just know it's going to be splendid!" Emily almost sang, as if sensing Molly's dilemma and offering rescue.

And with that, somehow, the idea came to Molly in an instant; it was as if a blinding flash had gone off and she had seen it, as if it had been there all along, hovering just beyond her line of sight. She'd seen white at the end of Emily's sentence—"splendid!"—and then she'd had her vision. She hoped it wasn't too obvious, or didn't seem a mere reaction to her painting of the men. But they would all have to come back for another session, dressed appropriately, Molly told them apologetically.

At that second session, Molly once again took several photographs, of each of them individually and as a group. Because she had painted many self-portraits over the years, she was not worried about herself: by now she felt sure that she could paint herself blindfolded, if necessary. Her sitters were serious, but they were not grim. Almost a month later, then, just after Christmas, the painting was finished.

It is even larger than the painting of the men, five by ten. Nora, Emily, Hortense, and Molly sit facing front, in that order. All four are dressed in white against a white background, so that their faces shine out and come to the fore like sunflowers, which, in fact, was the very image Molly had eventually arrived at. They are souls, spirits, characters, intellects, what have you— but by God, they are not objects!

Davis's Dream

Davis had a recurring dream in which he was running, naked and free, all over Cape Cod. Chasing him, or racing him—he was unsure which, though he thought it was the latter—were a group of men, white men, including the three who had accosted him. But the feeling that accompanied the dream was *not* one of fear or danger; this was not a nightmare. Instead, as he ran, Davis had a confident, unfettered, and victorious feeling. In the dream he was much taller than he actually was, his feet were oversized, and his stride was superhuman; the views, as he ran, were phenomenal from up there. It was like a children's story, or a folktale—everything was exaggerated, and the morality of it was simple.

After the dream, Davis always woke up feeling happy and confident and . . . aroused. And so he turned to Molly. It was, he told her again and again, the perfect time to try to make a baby. Pleased that Davis's unconscious world was such a happy one, Molly agreed.

Daily Life

That winter Lark spent all of January in Manhattan with Austin, who had arranged his schedule so that there was nothing he had to do, and nowhere he had to go, for a full month. Lark was in his glory; this was what he had wanted: daily life with Austin. A mere few days into their first week, Lark felt strong and secure in Austin's love for him once again; there was little to no pressure, the days were theirs. This was an oasis, time out of time.

Austin lived on the seventh floor, in a small but well-apportioned apartment on the Upper East Side, only twelve blocks from the Metropolitan Museum of Art. His drafting table dominated the crowded living room just as it had done in Provincetown, covered now with drawings, parallel rules, T-squares, photographs, and an assortment of pencils, pens, and erasers. His bedroom, however, was almost completely empty, even monastic, save for the bed and a small reading lamp.

That first week Austin and Lark mostly stayed in, getting reacquainted; a heavy snow fell for most of those days. At night, after a bottle of wine and one of Austin's sumptuous dinners, they would turn out the lights and lie in bed, wrapped in each other's arms and talking while they watched the snowfall and the sparkling lights of the city out the window. Austin's apartment was so well heated that they could comfortably walk around naked, something Lark had always enjoyed doing.

They made love almost daily now, sometimes twice a day, and that, too, had a new intensity; it was almost as if, Lark said to Austin on one of those dark, snowed-in evenings, almost as if they had just met and fallen in love all over again. "But we have, Mr. Marin," Austin said with a wink, doing his best Cary Grant.

Later in the week Lark ventured out to the market some afternoons to shop for dinner. He loved being able to live this way, buying fresh meat, vegetables, fruit, and even bread on a daily basis; it was very European, and a style of life that was impossible in Truro, unless one was willing to eat nothing but fish seven days a week. He tried to make sure that Austin always had fresh flowers, too, and so he frequently arrived back at the apartment with a bouquet. Together they reached that sublime height which longtime lovers only rarely recover: the plateau of playfulness.

Perhaps as a direct result of having rediscovered this level of intimacy, during the remaining three weeks they went out more and more. Austin took Lark on a long and meandering architectural tour of Manhattan, pointing out some lesser-known buildings that were among his favorites. Starting downtown and walking northward, he first showed Lark the Federal Hall National Memorial on Nassau Street, near the intersection of Wall and Broad Streets. "It's a simplified version of the Parthenon," Austin said. "An example of Greek Revival."

Then came Delmonico's Restaurant on Beaver Street, with Austin pointing out its elegant, rounded portico. Lark responded that he would like to eat there sometime, and Austin assured him they would.

Austin also liked the Potter Building at Beekman and Nassau—"New York's first introduction to the ornamental possibilities of terra cotta," he explained. "Designed by N. Y. Starkweather."

And there was so much more!—the decorative columns of the James S. White building at Broadway and Franklin; the Condict Building, designed by Louis Sullivan, on Bleecker; and a rather ornate apartment building on St. Mark's Place, whose architect Austin could not identify.

"And at the opposite end of the spectrum," Austin said, pointing up, "the Flatiron Building," which he admired for its simple but dramatic form.

What Lark enjoyed most about the tour, besides the buildings themselves, was Austin's passion for them, his knowledge of and excitement about them.

"Sometime I'll take you to the chapel at Columbia," Austin told Lark at the end of the day, "my alma mater—that's another favorite. And then there's the whole city of Chicago!"

During those third and fourth weeks they also took in *Grand Illusion,* perused bookstores and galleries, and decided to "do the Met," which, for them, meant going to the Metropolitan Museum every day for four full days, until they had seen everything they wanted to see. There they both saw, for the first time, among many other wonders, John Singer Sargent's splendid and by now infamous portrait *Madame X.*

That night, snuggling in Austin's bed, they wrote a combined letter to Nora:

Dear Nora,

Austin & I come to you here breathless, having just returned from day number two at the Met: we are determined to continue going until we have seen *everything* we want to see—*at our own pace*. But not only that: today we came upon your beloved Sargent's masterpiece *Madame X*. Do you know it? Have you seen her? I'm not sure you could have, as I noticed the painting was acquired only last year. Oh, it is glorious, Nora (the real woman dusted her skin with lavender powder!); she is a rapture—& a raptor! We've also been to the Museum of Modern Art, where we saw (among many other things) something by Charles Demuth, who lived in Provincetown for a time. Here's Austin:

Greetings, Nora. Lark and I are having the best time; I wish you could see us—and I mean that literally: it would be swell if you and Emily could come for a visit while Lark is here. Why not?

Indeed, why not, Nora? (Me again.) How about next weekend? Write & let us know. Or even better, call! We'll be waiting. Love to everyone, but especially to you & Em.

Lark & Austin

But Nora could *not* come, she said, reaching them by telephone that Saturday evening—what with Emily being in school, and her duties at True House. . . . But she was delighted to hear that they were enjoying themselves *and each other* so much. And though neither Austin nor (especially) Lark thought hard enough to see through such poor excuses, the truth was that Nora had decided it was best that the two of them have this time alone together, uninterrupted.

As they talked into the night, Austin playfully asked Lark if he would ever consider moving to Manhattan. Instead of being moved by the question, as Austin had hoped he would be, Lark turned grim-faced and shook his head. "You know I wouldn't. I lived here, remember? And I had some terrible experiences," he huffed. "Things I'm trying to forget." He got up from the bed and walked to the window.

"OK, I'm sorry," Austin said. "I was just asking."

And then there was silence.

"It was an insensitive question," Lark said, still angry. "Would you consider moving to Truro, or at least back to Provincetown?" he asked provocatively, knowing the answer.

"No," Austin responded. "I am not ready to move back to Province-town. Or to Truro. *Or* to True House, for that matter."

That did it: Lark went into the front room and slept on the sofa, and by morning he was gone. He knew he was being unreasonable, walking away from Austin's apartment; knew with every step he took that he was wrong. He knew it, but he could not help himself.

A Midwinter Night's Dream

Dearest,

Although we see each other in one season only (but then every night—secretly, privately, *you are my lover*), there have now been nine of those seasons. How I have changed in that time. How life around me has changed, too (Schuy gone)! But you have remained the same, always the same—just as you were before I was alive, and as you will be long after I am dead. You are a constant.

But then I ask myself, what are you? Nothing but a shaft of light, a mere beam, a projection, and all that is caught in it (dust motes). . . . You are not solid but transparent, and yet there is something solid in your constancy (shall I call you Constance?), or so I experience you. In you, through you, and perhaps because of you, I have found my . . . can I really call it genius? You have illuminated the way for me. I cannot begin to tell you how, though I know it has something to do with solitude, with confidence, and with keeping secrets.

Shh! I hear a rustle. Footsteps. Someone is coming to my room. They are nearing my door. Quick: I must pull the shade, jump into bed, and feign sleep, lest they discover you. Away!

Your Emily

P.S. I shall never write an aubade!

III *The Beat of the Years*

—Yes for a time they held as well
Together, as the criss-cross'd shelly cup
Sucks close the acorn; as the hand and glove;
As water moulded to the duct it runs in;
As keel locks close to kelson—

　　　　Let me now
Jolt and unset your morticed metaphors.
The hand draws off the glove; the acorn-cup
Drops the fruit out; the duct runs dry or breaks;
The stranded keel and kelson warp apart;
And your two etc.

　　Gerard Manley Hopkins, "*—Yes for a time*"

Snapshots

That spring was a tentative one (*a tentative spring,* Lark thought; the phrase haunted him so much that he wrote it down in his notebook because he felt it in his very bones). Although he and Austin were back together again, they were seeing each other less and less frequently—about once a month now. It was a decision that Austin had made alone and that Lark could do little to change.

———

Nora took to driving alone around the Cape that fall: up to Wellfleet, then reentering Truro by way of Pamet Point Road, heading west, down-valley, toward Old County Road, into Paradise Valley, and on and on—past Coast Guard Beach, the Salt Meadow, and Pilgrim Lake—until she was in the Province Lands, where she often parked, then sat listening to the silence. On one of her drives, near dusk, she happened upon a tall, older man hunched over an easel set up outside of the Mobil station. It was a haunting, indelible image, like the sudden burst and illumination of a lit match in pitch darkness, and it stayed with her. (But it was not until several years later, after the Museum of Modern Art purchased *Gas* and she saw it there, that Nora realized the man she'd seen that day was none other than Truro resident Edward Hopper.)

Like most of Hopper's paintings, True House had a pervasive melancholy air that fall for Nora. Lark was not there as much as she was used to (and when he *was* there, he was frequently sullen, or in his room, or both); but also her boy, Schuyler, was very much on her mind: it was two years since he had gone to live with his father. She could count on her two hands the number of times she had seen him in the interim, and when they were together now, it was almost as if they were strangers: they were both exceedingly polite. Physically, Schuyler was scarcely recognizable: his round, friendly face had been transformed into something lean and fierce and muscular, and his jaw was hard and set. Far worse was that his grades were just barely above average; Nora worried about where, how, *and when* it would all end.

For Emily, too, there was a deep well of sorrow about her lost brother, though she was wise enough to realize that it could never be as deep for her as it was for her mother. Also, she had her writing, for by age fifteen Emily had chosen her art form: poetry. (Or as she would later say, *it* had chosen *her.*) She practiced her art regularly now, unbeknownst to anyone except, perhaps, her mother, whom she had asked for a rolltop desk for her fifteenth birthday; it was in this desk that she now carefully and painstakingly hid all of her work. (In the process she also learned—yet another mystery solved—how rolltops were made: slats of wood applied to canvas!) She had said nothing about *why* she wanted the desk (she was still in school, after all, so it was not such an unusual request), and her mother had not asked. But that winter Emily was especially prolific (as she would be every winter for many years to come, a fact that became apparent only over time; she would eventually bind together her first fifty poems and call the manuscript *Constance,* but she was not especially interested in publication). Meanwhile, she was also intensely studying that other poet named Emily.

———

By the spring of 1938 Molly was finally pregnant, and the following winter she gave birth to Henry Davis Munroe, only to lose him within a week's time. Both Molly and Davis took the loss extremely hard; Molly couldn't even bring herself to attend the infant's burial, leaving it to Davis and the others.

The two stayed shut up inside all winter long, trying to console each other. The inhabitants of True House rallied, acting as a fire brigade of support: meals were brought to Molly and Davis's room; outings were planned in an attempt to cheer them; Nora's ministrations were replaced by Lark's, which would be taken over by Hortense, who would then relinquish the task to Leo (the airfield was built, his job over), who, when tired or feeling ineffective, would let Emily take the reins for a brief time before she handed them back to Nora. . . . By winter's end, the fire was out, the emergency over. Although newly broken, knowing they would try to have another child, Davis went back to work in the garden, fingering new green, and Molly returned to her studio to face a blank canvas. While both of them remained haunted for some time—Molly seeing her baby's face in the canvas, Davis feeling his little boy's fingers in the garden—they knew that in time the wound would if not heal, then at the very least close up and not hurt quite so much.

Leo remained alone and unattached, but only by default: he was still waiting and hoping and pining away for Lark. (All those years he had lived on his fantasies.) Occasionally, now, especially when the house was empty, he would climb up into the cupola, leaving the "door" into the room aloft so that it would be clear to *anyone* who happened to come home and pass by that *someone* was in there. He was obviously hoping for a reprisal of the kiss he had shared with Lark that summer day (and he had decided that *this time* he would go further), but he was not so pathetic as to sit in the cupola waiting without a writing pad, a book, *and* a pair of binoculars—Leo was always prepared.

Hortense was finding the winters particularly hard to get through now, given her predilection for working *en plein air* and her inability to do so during the harsh months of January, February, and March, at the very least. She tried to weather some days on both sides of those worst of the winter months, bundling up and heading out on frosty December afternoons and chilly April mornings; but still it was frustrating, and not enough, and she knew she had to find a solution if she was ever going to see any improvement in her work. She tried painting from photographs (which she quickly learned would not do, for unlike the ocean, photographs were still!); she even tried painting the sea from *inside* the cupola, but it was so cramped in there that she had no elbow room, not to mention the fact that, inevitably, she would steam up the windows (which they still had not replaced with the

kind that opened) with the breath of her own effort. Besides, she concluded, the ocean was simply too far away for her to be able to come
anywhere even close to getting it right from in there. Clearly, something else was needed.

Museum Haunting

And so it was that Hortense and Leo began making twice-monthly train trips into Boston together. If she wasn't working from nature, Hortense announced, she could at the very least be studying paintings that were; and so in Boston, whether at the Museum of Fine Arts, at Mrs. Gardner's house, or at one of the many galleries on Newbury Street, she and Leo would make the rounds, often sweeping in arm in arm, always an impressive and imposing twosome. Hortense had taken to wearing a floor-length purple cape on these occasions, and Leo, who had maintained his shaved head over the years, now frequently sported an impressive five-o'clock shadow *and* a black beret. Inspired by these forays, Hortense even had the idea of their going to Paris together—they could go to the Louvre, and to Montmartre, where they could at least walk past 27 rue de Fleurus and perhaps get a glimpse of the famous Misses Stein and Toklas (and perhaps more!). But Leo convinced Hortense, she who was completely oblivious to the news of the day, that it was no time to be in Europe; they would have to wait until things calmed down there, and *then* he would be more than thrilled to accompany her. Hortense said that she would settle for an occasional trip to the museums in New York City; she *so* wanted to see Picasso's *Les Demoiselles d'Avignon*, not to mention the master's infamous portrait of Gertrude Stein, and both were at the Museum of Modern Art, which Austin told them had recently moved to a handsome new building on West Fifty-third.

That Private, Dark Place of His

Spring turned into summer, which burned into fall, and Lark and Austin still had not got the rhythm back.

"Maybe you just don't want things to be the way they were," Lark said defensively one weekend when they were together in Truro. They were walking along the beach; it was a cold and windy day, but the sun was out.

Austin turned to Lark, put a hand on his shoulder, and in a pleading voice said, "*Please* don't let's fight."

But Lark had already split off and gone to that private, dark place of his, and he took off running down the beach.

Austin knew that he was supposed to run after him, to follow—that *that* was what Lark wanted and expected. But he just couldn't do it: he was tired of it, completely worn out, *worn down,* and weary. Instead, he walked back to True House alone. And by the end of the day, when Lark still had not come back, Austin packed his bags and returned to Manhattan a day early. (It was, Lark thought much later, the beginning of the end.)

Stoking the Fires of Friendship

Nora got up out of bed that November morning, immediately descended the stairs, and walked to Molly's room. Without even putting her ear to the door first to check for sounds of movement or states of awakeness, she knocked forcefully.

"Just a minute!" Molly's sleepy voice called from inside.

So what that it's just after seven! Nora thought. *Some things are more important than sleep.* She and Molly *had* to talk. She had dreamed about them, or daydreamed, she wasn't sure which: she had remembered their first meeting, and then their ensuing days together, how exciting and exhilarating it had all been. She missed that, realized they'd let it slip through their fingers, as most people did—people settled. But they weren't most people. And she simply wouldn't stand for it; she couldn't. She wanted more and was sure that Molly did, too.

"Who is it?" Molly whispered, just before she opened the door. And then there she was, in all her fresh, midwestern blond loveliness, with no makeup on.

It almost took Nora's breath away, and she immediately pictured fields of golden wheat blowing in the wind. Stunned, she could say only, "I miss you."

Molly looked puzzled at first, her head tilted slightly.

"I mean, I miss *us*," Nora tried to go on, now whispering but still barely able to articulate her feelings and suddenly worried that she might cry. She took Molly's hand and gently pulled her out of the room and into the hallway. Molly closed the door behind her. It was a cold morning: Nora blew on Molly's hand as she waited for the words to come to her, and then she rubbed it between her own hands.

"I was remembering the first time we met, at the Parker House," Nora said. "And our talk late that night . . . and the colors of the tulips during our walk through the Public Garden the next morning, and your saying you'd like to bite their heads off." Both women smiled at this. "And then you took me to see *Boys in the Grass*," Nora continued. "How overwhelmed I was by it! And from there we went to Mrs. Gardner's house and saw *Madame Gautreau* and then talked about art over tea. I realized then that you were someone I wanted to join us here, a soul mate. . . . And here we are!" Nora was out of breath. She paused, searching Molly's face for some sign of understanding.

Molly smiled and took Nora's other hand. "I know," she said. "It's been a long time since we've had that, hasn't it—just the two of us?"

Nora nodded.

"I miss you, too," Molly said, embracing Nora.

"The days just pass too quickly," Nora said. "But what are we going to do about it? Can we plan something now, just the two of us together?"

Molly nodded. "I think we must." And she said she thought she knew just the thing, too; it was something she'd been thinking about anyway. "Can we drive into Provincetown and have breakfast first?" Molly asked. "We can talk more there."

Nora said she'd go get ready and write a note to leave on the kitchen table.

Molly said she could be ready in fifteen minutes or so: she just needed to throw on some clothes, put on her makeup, and let Davis know where she was going.

———

"I'm so glad we're doing this," Molly said as Nora maneuvered the winding, hilly roads of Truro on the drive into Provincetown. Although cold, it was a sunny day.

Nora smiled.

"Thank you for coming to my room this morning: I think this is just what I needed . . . and I *have* been thinking along the same lines, Nora; it's just a question of balancing everything. . . ."

Nora nodded, but then a silence settled between them; it was as if there were not enough space, as if things were too close and contained in the car and their intensity were somehow a peril. So it wasn't until after they were seated in the Surfside Café, one of the few Provincetown restaurants that remained open throughout the winter, and had ordered, that Nora resumed the conversation.

"I guess I've just realized that friendships take a certain vigilance," Nora said now. "It's something Lark is very good at—when he's not preoccupied," she added. "And it's something that I want to learn." She paused to take a sip of her coffee and wait for Molly, then she went on. "Yes, I have Lark. And I have Emily. And of course I do love Davis and Hortense and Leo, too. But it's not the same, Molly. From the very moment you and I first met I felt that something new, a new dimension, had come into my life—and I was very aware of that and of your being beneficial to me. And what made it doubly wonderful was that it seemed mutual."

Molly smiled, but she was struck and saddened by the fact that Nora had not mentioned Schuyler; she did not have him, then. "Oh, Nora. . . . It *is* mutual. You know I feel the same way, don't you? You've brought so much into my life!"

But then Molly's attention was diverted by the sight of Hortense and several of her women friends walking into the restaurant. Nora turned to see what had distracted Molly. Three of the four other women were variously overweight, and they all wore their hair short; but they were of all ages. There was Abigail, whom they had met when they painted True House and she lent them her ladders; she'd told them at the time that she was sixty-two, and that was—how many years ago? Two of the women appeared to be somewhere in middle age, but the fourth had to be only in her early twenties.

Nora called to Hortense, who came over and introduced everyone quickly, then hurried off, saying she didn't want to "interrupt."

"Well, well, well," Molly said under her breath but with a smile, once she and Nora were alone again. "The other side of Hortense's life! Which one do you think she's sleeping with?" Molly whispered jokingly.

"All of them," Nora replied, and then both women laughed.

"I wouldn't be surprised!" Molly said admiringly. But she had lost her train of thought. She scooped up the yolk from her poached egg with a piece of toast and regarded Nora, who was looking back at her over the rim of her coffee cup. Then Molly remembered her original idea:

"Do you want to go to my studio?" she asked. "I could show you what I've been working on."

"I'd love it!" Nora exclaimed.

And so once the two women had finished their breakfast and paid the check, they were back in the car and on their way.

———

Meanwhile, at Hortense's table, Madge, the youngest of the women, was boldly telling the others about her painting teacher, Hans Hofmann.

"He makes alterations *directly on your work,*" she said. "Just walks right up, takes your paintbrush, and does whatever he wants to do, right on your canvas."

"I don't know that I'd like that," Hortense said. "Do you?"

Madge said that at first she hadn't, but that then she had actually come to find it helpful. "He does it to show alternative compositions."

"Typical man," Abigail said. "I'd probably haul off and slap him one if it was me," she added, at which all four women laughed.

Celeste, whose hair was white despite her youthful face and body, said that while she knew Hofmann's school was controversial, she *loved* his work. "I find the surfaces of his paintings *so* sensuous."

"Oh, girls!" Abigail said, fanning herself and batting her eyelashes. "It's getting warm in here."

Hortense leaned over and kissed Abigail on the cheek. "Darling!" she said.

Once inside her studio, Molly immediately set to stuffing logs and a few rolled-up newspapers into the wood-burning stove and lighting them with a match. Turning back to Nora, she pointed to a canvas leaning against the wall beside the sofa. "This is what I've been working on—a self-portrait, obviously. I've been concentrating on nudes for some time now. . . ."

Nora oohed and ahhed, as much at the painting as at the sight of Molly's form. She suddenly realized it had been years since they all went to the nude beach: how time stole away! (In the painting, Molly stands facing the viewer, her feet apart, with a paintbrush in her hand as if it were a weapon. She is heavily, exaggeratedly made up, as if wearing war paint. Perhaps a direct reference and challenge to Molly's inability to leave even her room without first putting on makeup? Nora wondered.)

"And over here"—Molly pointed toward another, larger canvas on the other side of the room—"is another recent one." It was of Davis, lying on his side in bed, against white sheets, propped up on one elbow (his head in that hand), one foot flat on the bed so that his knee is bent and points toward the top of the canvas, the other leg extended, with his penis lolling over it.

"They're beautiful!" Nora exclaimed. "Both because and *in spite of* their subjects."

Molly smiled, then showed a few other paintings, all nudes of people Nora did not know. "Models," Molly said.

"But why nudes?" Nora asked.

"Mmm, I'm glad you asked," Molly said. "Because I think the nude is an art form in and of itself; not the subject but the object."

Nora nodded.

"But also," Molly went on, "and I know everyone doesn't share this opinion, I think a really good nude is the closest you can get to a person's soul, to his or her very essence; it is, or at least it can be, very pure. Some people think it's just the opposite. Are you getting warm yet?" she asked suddenly, gesturing toward the stove.

"Yes," Nora said brightly.

"Good," Molly said. "Because I'd like you to pose for me."

"Now?" Nora said with a laugh. And then she added, "Naked?"

"No, *nude*." Molly laughed, too. "If you would."

Nora smiled nervously. "I guess I should say yes and be flattered."

"You should!" Molly cried.

"All right, then," Nora said. "Where would you like me?"

"Mmm, let's see. Well, let's talk about it while you're getting ready. I'll set things up."

Nora began taking off her clothes while Molly assembled what she would need: a blank canvas, stretched and primed, that was already attached to the easel; her paints, brushes, and other supplies, all on a cart, which she now wheeled over. "Do you have a favorite nude, or nudes?" she asked.

"Good question!" Nora replied, removing her skirt. "Let's see—I've always liked Manet's *Olympia,* how bold she is in her nudity. And I love Ingres's *Odalisques,* with those beautiful, elongated porcelain backs and backsides."

"I agree!" Molly said resoundingly. "Anything else?"

Now Nora was removing her underclothes. "Well, the classical nudes, of course."

"Lovely," Molly said, smiling, once Nora was free of all clothing. "I know just the thing."

She positioned Nora half sitting up, half lying on the sofa on her side—cradling her breasts, her body turned in profile—then she went to her easel and looked. "Nice!" she exclaimed, continuing to study the pose. "Just one more thing," she said, and she walked over to her desk, foraged through a drawer, and picked up several hairpins, then stuck them between her teeth to hold them and returned to where Nora sat. Now Molly scooped Nora's hair up off her neck (that was what she wanted to see, that long, graceful line of her neck) and loosely fastened it with the pins. Then she stepped back to her easel. "There," she said. "Perfect!"

And so it was.

————

"OK," Molly said about an hour later, signaling to Nora that she could break the pose. "That's probably enough for today. But of course we'll have to do several sittings."

Nora rolled her head around and massaged her shoulders, smiling warmly at Molly. And then she said all she needed to say—"Good," because it was a way for them to be alone together.

Embracing the Good

Schuyler came for Christmas that year, and somehow—miraculously, it seemed—it was almost like old times. He arrived on Christmas Eve and stayed two nights. And once there, he actually joined in, making decorations and hanging them on the tree (they had one this year), singing carols, and telling stories around the fireplace. Schuyler was nineteen now, and though he had *not* gone directly on to college (to Nora's profound disappointment), he *did* have a job—working at Bethlehem Steel on the waterfront in East Boston. He also seemed somewhat surer of himself; thus (Nora mused) he could be less guarded around her, less defensive and more open. Her eyes filled with tears and the room became a beautiful, amber, candlelit blur when she saw Emily and Schuyler sitting in the corner, talking and laughing together, just as they had done when they were children. In that one moment ten years might have passed and nothing have changed; how she wished that were true, knowing all the while it was wrong: to wish things to remain the same was against nature, and she quickly chased the idea from her mind. She was happy for the moment, she told herself, and that had to be enough.

In January Nora's mother fell and broke her hip; less than a month later she would be dead, at the age of only sixty-eight. Before the end, at Michael's urging, Nora went to Charleston to see her mother; she stayed on to help bury her and to console Michael.

Before Nora left Truro, Emily had insisted that she be allowed to stay at True House (after all, this was *her* season), and after talking with Lark and Molly, who assured her that her daughter would be fine and that they would do all they could for her, Nora agreed and left for Charleston alone.

She arrived to find Michael not doing at all well, and things only got worse after their mother died. He had lived with her for all forty-four years of his life; she had been his best friend; how was he supposed to go on living? That was the question for Michael now, Nora realized, Lark's question: *How to live?* But she couldn't tell him, or Lark, or anyone. . . . She believed it was a question one had to find the answer to for oneself, a question she herself no longer even felt compelled to ask, because she was living the answer—*for her.* What she *could* do was encourage and cajole Michael.

"Remember the dreams you told me about?" she asked him. Looking at him was so much like looking into a mirror. Michael nodded.

"You said you wanted to open your own nursery and eventually settle down with someone. Do it, Michael, and do it *now!* You're forty-four; the house is yours. . . ."

Although Nora had adored her mother, she had always felt that Michael's relationship with her was unhealthy, that he was always, to some extent, under her thumb; it was, after all, because of their mother that Michael hadn't joined them all at True House. "This is *your* time," she added, "your chance."

And so it was that Nora's planned two-week stay in Charleston extended beyond one month. Of course she was in frequent contact with True House, where Emily sounded just fine, a fact that Molly happily confirmed. Nora was pleased with the deep knowledge that Emily could do so well without her, that she had her own wings and could fly. But Lark was another story altogether. By the end of the fourth week of life without Nora (and without Austin, too, for that matter), he could contain himself no further and sent her the following letter:

11 February 1940
True House

Dear Nora,

How are you holding up? & how is Michael? We miss you here, but Emily is doing fine—much better than me, actually. I know you would be proud of her.

You will be glad, too, to hear that I have been reading Chekhov in your absence. This, from Epihodoff in *The Cherry Orchard* (who, as you may remember, is a clerk), spoke to me: "I am a cultured man. I read all kinds of remarkable books, but the trouble is I cannot discover my own inclinations, whether to live or to shoot myself, but nevertheless, I always carry a revolver on me. . . ."

But not to worry—I don't carry a revolver, & I am still trying to answer the big questions (as opposed to having given up). Just hurry back to True House as soon as you can, which doesn't feel as true without you.

Your/Lark

Nora called Lark immediately upon receiving his letter and told him she missed him and hoped to be home within a week or so; she just wanted to be sure that Michael was all right before she left. She said that it was good to hear his voice, that it reassured her, and he told her that hearing *her* voice—and just the fact that she'd called—did the same for him, and then he thanked her.

Two days later, while still in Charleston, Nora received a rare letter from Schuyler.

Feb. 13, 1940

Boston

Dear Mother,

I was very sorry to hear about Grandma Hartley. I hope you and Uncle Mike are OK.

I have been meaning to write to you since Christmas to tell you what a swell time I had. Also, I have some news: I have joined the army! I know you won't be happy about this, but everyone says that I would have been drafted anyway, that a draft is inevitable, and Father and I agree that this is the more honorable way to go. Besides, I am anxious to serve my country and see the world.

Please say hello to Uncle Mike, and the same to the gang at True House when you return. I will write again as soon as I have my orders. Love to you and little Emily.

Schuyler

Nora was amused that Schuyler should feel the need to diminutize Emily, since the Emily she knew, while delicate in appearance, perhaps, was actually quite strong, even rather fierce (*fierce* in her intelligence, independence, courage, and resolve), much more so than her brother. But the news that Schuyler had enlisted in the army was like a blow to the stomach, leaving her gasping for breath—for many reasons. It worried her terribly, of course, particularly because of what was going on in the world, but also because she knew that like so much else having to do with Schuyler these days, it was completely out of her hands, and she was resigned to and had finally accepted that fact. She scarcely had time to digest that bad news before learning the very good news that Molly was pregnant again. (From this point on and for the rest of her life, Nora would always make the conscious, philosophical decision to embrace the good news and, as best she could, ignore the bad.)

Trompe l'Oeil

■\\\\\\\■

In addition to reading Chekhov *for Nora*, in her absence, Lark had also spent a lot of time thinking about her and about their friendship. How much he owed her! He thought about their first meeting, in Boston, and about the plan they had eventually hatched for what would become True House. . . . But he also worried: had he let her down? Disappointed her?

How to express his love for her, his gratitude *to* her? he wondered. He didn't want to do anything as impersonal as merely buying her something. He thought about asking Molly or Hortense or Leo to make something for her but quickly dismissed that. He wanted this to be from him, *of* him. But what could he do? He had no talents. So he thought. What would it be? He wanted it to be something big, some-thing grand—something that fully expressed the *size* of his feelings. He racked his brain for several days until he finally came up with an idea: he would re-create *A Cup of Tea* for her. Or try to, anyway. But how? The task seemed daunting. Should he ask for help? No, he wanted to do this himself, both to prove to himself that he could do it *and* to show Nora the depth of his love for her.

Where to do it? was his next question. *In his room*, he quickly decided. And so, over the ensuing weeks, he set about gathering what he would need. The red-and-white-striped wallpaper was easy, though instead of actually applying it, he merely tacked it to a bare wall in his room. The table was also simple: he found an old, somewhat beat-up coffee table and painted it red. Even the sofa came along surprisingly easily, as he discovered a remarkable likeness to the one in the painting in a Provincetown antique shop that had recently opened, then somehow convinced the owner to lend it to him. But he was having no luck whatsoever with the silver tea service, so finally, using Nora's car, he drove up to Boston, where he knew of a place he could rent one.

Now, what else? he asked himself. The white cups and saucers they had. But the fireplace with the white mantel, he would have to let that go: Nora would get the picture without it.

With two days left before Nora was scheduled to arrive home, Lark assembled everything, comparing his simulation to a print he had of the actual painting. *Not bad,* he thought. At last he showed his creation to his housemates, all of whom, in one way or another, said that they were impressed. Lark was pleased. He asked them to keep it a secret, and then he waited.

Finally, Nora came home. Molly and Davis and Emily and Hortense and Leo were all there at the front door to greet her. Hugs and kisses all around and then, "Where's Lark?" Nora asked.

"I think he's in his room," Emily said on cue, for they had planned it, and she, it had been decided, could keep the best straight face.

"Up here, Nora," Lark called sheepishly.

Finding it slightly odd that Lark would not come down to greet her, especially after such a long absence, Nora—not without dread—began climbing the stairs.

Hearing her footsteps, Lark quickly prepared himself: he positioned himself on the sofa, picked up the saucer and held it in one hand and with the other hand lifted the cup to his lips.

Nora walked into the room, saw him, and stopped in her tracks. Her mouth opened. Her eyes widened. For a moment she felt displaced, disoriented.

"Welcome to our world," Lark said.

Nora smiled. "Lark!" she cried, then she ran and threw her arms around him.

There, he thought.

She stood back and looked again, taking it all in. "It's beautiful. Incredible! I can't believe it!" And then she started laughing. "We *must* get a photograph!"

Lark beamed at her.

Fruition

All that spring and summer Molly was especially careful; having consulted with her doctor, she knew that she could not afford to lose another baby and that this could very well be her and Davis's last chance. She stopped going to the studio in her fifth month, stayed home, and, as much as she was capable of doing, rested.

That summer, too, the churches and women's groups of Truro and Provincetown were sewing for the British. Little did they know that within two years, they would be working to defend *themselves.*

Toward the end of August, when it was no longer too hot and when so many Manhattanites were out of town at their summer homes on Long Island, Lark and Austin spent two surprisingly idyllic weekends in Manhattan—with Hortense and Leo. None of the four of them was sure quite how it had happened: the first time they simply ran into one another, completely by accident, on a rainy Saturday afternoon, on the great steps outside of the Metropolitan Museum of Art. One thing led to another, and before they knew it, Sunday evening was upon them and the foursome was enjoying a late dinner in Austin's apartment. This time having gone so well and been so refreshingly pleasurable, they decided to actually *plan* a second weekend together two weeks hence, and that time, too—they spent all of Saturday at Coney Island; on Sunday they went to the Cloisters in Tryon Park—was enjoyable.

It was something about the mix, Austin reasoned, the chemistry among the four of them: as in a great recipe, thoughts of the individual ingredients put together might not immediately set the mouth to watering, but together, combined, those ingredients somehow made for a delectable dish.

———

Nora and Michael were in frequent contact that September about a possible visit one way or the other. Although always close, they had grown closer in the months since their mother's death, largely because Michael finally felt free, or so Nora surmised. But by October it had become apparent that a visit anytime soon was not to be: Michael told Nora that he was seeing someone special and wanted to devote himself to it. Nora said she understood.

———

Having finished high school in June, Emily that fall had time to read every volume of poetry she could get her hands on. And what she couldn't get from Cobb Library in Truro Center or from the Provincetown library, she mail-ordered from the Grolier Bookshop in Cambridge; she hoped to be able to go there one day soon, perhaps in the spring. Nora had to limit Emily to buying four books per month because otherwise her passion could render her voracious, and the costs did add up. And while Emily had read a great deal already, there was still so much more to read. The pile currently stacked on her desk revealed volumes by the poets she called her grandparents, Emily Dickinson and Walt Whitman, as well as books by Robert Frost, Muriel Rukeyser, Louise Bogan, and Constantine Cavafy. She had read, knew well, and loved the Romantics, and she had read Shakespeare's sonnets, but what Emily said she wanted now was to familiarize herself with the work that was being done in her own time, which was what had led her, specifically, to the verse of Frost, Rukeyser, and Bogan (Cavafy was already a favorite). She had also picked up a volume by Edna St. Vincent Millay at Cobb Library, but perusing the book under the ornate brass green-shaded lamp that sat atop one of the two round oak tables in the Cobb's reading room, she had quickly realized that the verse was not to her liking—it was too sweet—and thus she returned it to its proper place, saving herself the task of checking it out and carrying it home. It would not be long now (she thought, pausing and looking at the trees out the library windows) before all the branches were bare again and her nightly communing with the lighthouse would resume.

But there were still some flaming beauties on the trees when, just before Thanksgiving, Molly gave birth to a strappingly healthy eleven-pound, two-ounce boy; she and Davis named him simply Will, Will Munroe—no middle name.

While working in the garden that fall, Davis had, as an act of faith, fashioned simulated, homemade cigars for the occasion (weeds wrapped in corn husks and dried), and after the first couple of weeks, when it became clear that Baby Will was fine and would not only survive but thrive ("failure to thrive" had been little Henry's diagnosed fate), Davis gleefully and proudly passed them out to all the inhabitants of True House, much to the surprise and delight of everyone, particularly Leo, who was inspired by Davis's ingenuity. (And in the spring after Will's birth, Davis also planted something especially for him: a whole cluster of Sweet William. Also known as *Dianthus barbatus,* Leo said proudly.)

While Nora, Emily, Lark, and Austin all saved their cigars as mementos of Will's birth, Hortense and Leo actually "smoked" theirs. Sitting in the parlor wearing one of her purple dresses, her legs spread and her sandaled feet planted firmly on the floor, Hortense said she felt just like Gertrude Stein, even though—she said, laughing—she actually had no good idea whether Stein smoked cigars or not. It would *seem* that she did, Hortense added: "It feels right." Leo laughed and made up an identity for himself, as her chauffeur and occasional stud, whose name was Max. How Hortense chortled!

Already little Will was a beautiful, bright, and charismatic baby— the very best of Molly and Davis, Nora said, with light-brown skin, dark, curly hair, a wide face, big, bright brown eyes, and a fetching smile.

There was much to be celebrated at True House at Christmastime this year. Austin came up from Manhattan, and Schuyler, just home from boot camp in Georgia, took the train down from Boston for the day.

The atmosphere was one of frenzied merriment, especially on Lark's part. It was at his instigation that they made a *papier-mâché piñata,* filled it with candy, and hung it from the ceiling, then took turns striking at it with a broomstick, blindfolded. Hortense and Molly laughed as they watched Davis and Nora swing wildly at the *piñata*—and completely miss each time. Leo had strung colored lights all about the house, and the champagne was flowing freely. At midnight everyone but Will was still wide awake, slightly tipsy, and in a celebratory mood. It was Schuyler who finally burst the *piñata,* to cheers and the rabid scrambling for its fallout. Once the floor was cleaned of candy, Nora suggested that they gather around the fireplace and sing carols, to which Emily quickly appended, "and recite poems."

"'I have desired to go,'" Lark began dramatically and eloquently, immediately silencing the room:

> I have desired to go
> Where springs not fail
> To fields where flies no sharp and sided hail.
> And a few lilies blow.

"That's true!" Davis said.

Lark nodded. "That desire is what brought me here," he said. "It's from 'Heaven-Haven.'"

"That's beautiful, Lark," Nora said. "It's what brought me here, too. Along with you, of course." She hugged him.

"The name of the poet, please?" Leo asked, reaching in his shirt pocket for the small pad of paper and pen that he always kept handy.

"Hopkins, *of course,*" Lark quipped. And then noting that Leo was writing it down, he added, "Gerard Manley: eighteen forty-four to eighteen eighty-nine."

"Lark's favorite poet," Austin said, putting an arm around his beloved. But of course Leo knew that.

Emily seemed filled up and aglow with Hopkins's language, but she kept her mouth shut; she would have to borrow a volume of his work.

"Who's next?" Lark asked, wanting to deflect attention away from himself.

Inspired, Emily raised her hand, and once again the room quieted. She stood in the middle of the room, not shy but poised and confident, and recited:

> We play at Paste—
> Till qualified, for Pearl—
> Then, drop the Paste—
> And deem ourselves a fool—
>
> The Shapes—though—were similar—
> And our new Hands
> Learned *Gem*—Tactics
> Practicing *Sands*—

"The unmistakable voice of Miss Emily Dickinson," Leo said, applauding along with the others.

Emily nodded and smiled. "Number three hundred twenty," she announced (she was memorizing them), and then she sat down.

Nora was struck by her daughter's choice; it was certainly not one of Dickinson's better-known poems. How she admired her own Emily; and in that moment, too, the truth was suddenly revealed to her, and she somehow knew in her heart what she had only guessed at for so long: Emily *was* writing poetry! Nora turned to her daughter now, smiled at her, cupped her face in her hands, and looked into her eyes, as if to say *I know your secret and it is safe with me. I am so proud of you.* And then she herself began to sing her favorite carol: "Silent night, Holy night. . . ."

At first everyone else was silent, enjoying Nora's sweet voice; but then, at Nora's prodding, Austin joined in, harmonizing with her in his rich baritone. The room was now completely quiet; the two of them together were quite enough, and everyone knew it—for none of the rest of them could sing nearly as well. While Lark's ears were trained on their voices, he couldn't keep his eyes off Austin's Adam's apple, which almost seemed to be a part of the music as it rose and fell, an accompanying musical instrument, and an aphrodisiac.

Molly and Davis followed with a spontaneous but rousing rendition of "I've Got My Love to Keep Me Warm." While not a Christmas or even a holiday song per se, as Davis admitted before they began, it *was* appropriate for the season. Once Molly and Davis had finished and collapsed to the floor amid applause and laughter, Leo and Hortense stood up together and shared in reading several things from a book of Sappho. The festivities continued until three in the morning, at which point everyone—wearily but happily—kissed one another good night and went to bed.

Roses in December

Lark,

I could not talk to you tonight after you recited those lines from Hopkins: I felt too much. I feel too much still—I am on fire with Hopkins's words—which is why I write. The desire behind his words, *your* desire, and those chosen words are all so *terribly* beautiful. Although I have been aware of your love of Hopkins, I had not befriended "Heaven-Haven," nor had I known that it was *those lines* that brought you here to True House. I feel as though I know you in a whole new way now, more deeply.

Thank you, Lark. Because of you, and because of Hopkins, I am glowing and growing. I am,

Your Emily

And then the light from the lighthouse swung around, and Emily set to work for the night.

Waking up the following morning, Lark spotted Emily's note on the floor just inside his door. He read it and wrote back immediately, slipping his note under her door, as Emily did not usually emerge from her room until well after noon.

Dear Emily,

No one has responded to those lines of Hopkins's as intensely as you have—*no one!* & so of course your note means *everything* to me. & you are so right about the words: there *is* a terrible beauty behind them, isn't there? The speaker of the poem is a beaten man, one who isn't asking for much in this world. I was that man, Emily. But in so many ways I have found that haven, here, at True House, with your mother & you & the others. & I am so very impressed that you, at your age, understand the lines as keenly as you do. Thanks for writing.

X Lark

Lark,

Can we meet and talk? I feel we must and hope you feel the same; I am close to bursting with the need.

E

Dear Emily,

By all means let's talk. Shall we say a walk on the beach tomorrow at four? The light should be beautiful then. I'll meet you there unless I hear otherwise.

X Lark

And so they met, Lark and Emily—the same two people who had lived in the same house together for over twelve years, and yet now everything was different; *they* were different.

Lark got there first and paced, wearing down a small strip of beach. When Emily arrived, he embraced her. She seemed dazed.

The day was cold and the sea was rough, roiling and rolling in as the two walked along the shore, but the light was a pearly lavender.

"I sense something," Lark said, looking at Emily and smiling. "Something . . . I don't know quite . . . what it is." He waited, hoping she would jump in, but she just looked at him expectantly. "Something with you," he went on. "It's as if you wanted to tell me something."

Emily continued to look at him, her eyes fierce and hungry. She couldn't speak, at least not yet.

Was he supposed to guess? Lark wondered. And then he changed course.

"I want you to know that I have *always* admired you, Emily"—his voice was choked with emotion—"for your self-knowledge, your self-possession (you know who you are), your otherworldliness. I'm sorry I haven't conveyed this before now; I know I can be selfish—I have my demons, you know?"

Emily nodded. *Demons,* she thought, because she had them as well, though she had not named them. Nothing specific; just a dark shape, always there. But she smiled at Lark. "I *have* felt it," she said. "Thank you." And then she thrust a folded sheet of paper into his hand and ran off.

Lark was stunned. He looked after her and opened his mouth to call her name, but stopped himself, his eye having been caught by the glitter of white sand kicked up by her feet; then she was out of his line of vision. He slowly unfolded the sheet of paper. It was a poem, a poem she had written. And it was good. He would tell her so.

——

Dear Emily,

Thank you for entrusting me with your words; I am so very moved &
honored. You are what I could not be—a poet. You are the future.

X Lark

High Notes

∎\\\\\\\∎

The new year, 1941, began on one long, suspended high note, as everyone sat around the parlor sharing plans and resolutions: Lark announced that he and Austin would be going to Key West for two weeks at the beginning of February; Nora said she was pondering a springtime trip to visit Michael in Charleston (and here she pictured the dogwoods in blossom), this time with Emily, she continued (who was mute on the subject of both plans and resolutions).

Hortense touted that since she and Leo could not go to Paris, they thought they might take the train to Montreal or to Old Quebec City—"The closest thing to Paris around here as far as I know" (Nora mentioned New Orleans). Hortense said she also was hoping to receive an invitation to Yaddo, the artists' colony in Saratoga Springs, New York.

Leo took the floor, boldly pronouncing that in addition to all Hortense had said, he hoped to find a man. Then he giggled.

Davis quietly said that he would be more than happy just to stay at home, taking care of little Will so that Molly could get back to the studio, and tending to the garden once the weather improved. Molly kissed him gratefully, nodded, and said she agreed, adding that she hoped to get solidly back to work in the studio.

"Is that everyone?" Molly asked once she had finished.

"Schuyler," Nora said, lowering her head. The room fell silent.

He had left the day after Christmas and was now off serving his country, sent to God only knew where (Nora didn't even know yet). And so because he was not there with them, Nora spoke for him and said that wherever he was and whatever he was doing, she wished him safety, to which the group of them, *en masse,* said "Amen!"

"And Your Two Etc."

But high notes can be held for only so long before the voice catches and breaks, and Lark's broke in Key West; it was in the middle of his and Austin's two-week vacation. During their first week they rented bicycles and rode down Duval Street, seemingly wafting on the tropical air, which smelled of fruits and flowers. They swam off the beach at the southernmost point in the United States, and from there they could see Cuba. With other revelers, they partied on a boat and watched the sun set, and they went for the first time together to a twenty-four-hour bar for homosexuals, where they danced close and slow. They lodged in a small, cozy bungalow on Caroline Street, and it was from their room there, snuggling in bed, that they witnessed one of the South's great treasures: a prototypical late-afternoon thunderstorm, replete with deafening thunder, blinding lightning, and drenching rains that seemed to come down in sheets.

They were having a wonder time until . . . on the first day of their second week, with six potentially glorious days still dangling in front of them, Lark went and spoiled it. It was a Monday morning, and they were getting a late start on the day, not that *that* much mattered to either of them since in Key West just about everything, it seemed— waking up in February without any clothes on, drinking coffee and eating breakfast on the terrace—was enjoyable: *Laziness is all* was their motto. Austin bathed first and said that while Lark was taking a bath he wanted to run an errand; he would be back soon.

After bathing, Lark sat on the terrace, waiting for Austin to return. The air was thick and heavy, humid. After about half an hour he grew suspicious and began pacing: *what could this errand be?* By the time Austin had been gone for forty-five minutes, Lark was in a state. But then there Austin was, riding up on the bicycle, smiling and waving. Lark scowled (his face red) and turned his back on Austin, walking inside their room and slamming the door behind him. The jalousie windows shook in their frames.

"What the hell is going on?" Austin asked when he came in.

"You've been gone for almost an hour," Lark said, looking at his watch. "Just long enough to—" But then he stopped himself.

"To what?" Austin asked. And when Lark wouldn't answer him, he repeated the question, this time screaming it: "TO WHAT?"

"YOU KNOW WHAT!" Lark screamed back, his eyes burning with unreason. "To go back to that bar, or to meet someone on the street and go to his place. . . ."

Austin laughed. "Right." Breathing heavily now, he was so incensed that he was unsure of what he was going to say or do next. "Right," he went on. "But it wasn't only one, Lark—I had ten men in those fifty minutes! 'Line up, fellows, you've got five minutes each!'" And with that, Austin stormed out the door.

Lark and Austin did not see each other again in Key West, or in Miami, which was where their flight back to New York departed from: Austin wasn't even on the flight. And it was only then that Lark began fully to understand what he had done.

Back at True House, he tried calling Austin incessantly in the ensuing days, always to no answer. Then he sent countless postcards and letters, *pleading* for a response. But March came and went with no word.

Lark sat at True House, unresponsive to everything and everyone around him, looking at his watch: the second hand seemed to be pursuing the minute hand, and the minute hand the hour hand, and all three were pursuing him and Austin, for time had run out on them, he knew that now: it was over, it was over and he was responsible.

The rest of True House's inhabitants tried to go on with their lives, but it was not easy, seeing Lark so disconsolate. March gave way to April, and the days began to lengthen and lighten and grow warmer. Nora implored and cajoled Lark; Emily wrote him several notes; Hortense joked with him; Leo offered frequent hugs; and Molly and Davis held out to him their beautiful Will, whom Davis had nicknamed Little Green. But all of it was of no use to Lark.

And so Nora and Emily and Hortense and Leo and Molly and Davis all resumed their business, seemingly holding their breath until, early in May, Lark received a brief note from Austin: "I will be in Provincetown in two weeks," he wrote. "I hope we can meet." They had not seen each other in three months.

Of course they could meet, Lark wrote back. "Just name the time and the place and I'll be there." He said he was looking forward to it. He also said again that he was sorry.

They met at the very end of the cape, on the Provincetown breakwater, and sat down on the rocks. Austin was thinner, unshaven, his hair unkempt; and yet somehow he had never looked better, Lark thought. But Lark could not help but notice, too, the grim expression on Austin's face, and the fact that he had shrugged out of their embrace.

"I'm sorry," Lark said, tears immediately rolling down his cheeks.

"I had gone to look into renting a boat so that we could take a sunset cruise alone together," Austin said in a controlled monotone. "It took longer than I thought." He fished around in his pants pocket: "Here's the receipt."

"Oh God!" Lark gasped, covering his mouth. "I'm sorry," he said again, taking the slip of paper but not looking at it, unable to see it.

Austin shook his head slowly, wearily. Lark could see his jaw muscles working, clenching; he was trying to keep control, to steel himself. And then it came.

"I'm sorry too," Austin said tightly. "I can't go on with you."

Lark caught his breath. Suddenly the horizon was a blue blur. "No!" he gulped.

Austin took Lark's face in his hands and chastely kissed him on the lips. His green eyes flashed, as he, too, was crying now, and again he said that he was sorry. "I hope we can be friends . . . eventually," he added. Then he stood up and said, in a shaky voice, "I've got to go."

"NO!" Lark screamed, trying to grab hold of Austin's pants as he walked away. And then, like the wounded animal that he was, Lark began howling. Austin just kept walking and didn't look back; he couldn't.

———

It was pitch dark when Lark finally arrived home that night, his clothes still damp from his having "fallen" into the water; he was also drunk. Nora had been keeping vigil for him, watching and waiting, worried sick. She rushed to him when he came in the front door and could see, immediately, that the news was not good. Lark fell into her arms and began sobbing. "It's over," he said. "I've ruined it. I can't believe it. Austin was the one. All I ever wanted. I've killed it. I can't believe it. . . ."

All Nora could do was hold him and say, "Shh, shh." She led him into the parlor, sat him down on the sofa, and continued to hold him and to stroke his hair and the back of his neck and say, "Shh." Before long he fell asleep in her arms, and she stayed there with him, holding him, nodding asleep on and off herself, throughout the night.

For several days after the breakup Lark appeared numb, didn't eat, and barely stirred from his room; and when he did move about the house, he did so slowly and methodically, as if merely walking through life. Alone in his room, he covered Molly's painting with a bedsheet; it reminded him too much of Austin.

Comings and Goings

Now Nora hung on Lark's every move, his every word, but she had other things to think and worry about as well. There was Schuyler, of course; she had finally heard from him: he was stationed in Dover, England. But more pressing and immediate was the fact that she had been unable to reach Michael by telephone for a full week, and she had not heard from him in two. She had been concerned about him before this, because when they had last spoken he had alluded to the fact that he was no longer seeing the man he had been seeing, and suggested that it had ended badly. After trying to call him at many different times of day, she stayed up late one night and dialed his number at three in the morning: *still* there was no answer. Now she knew in her gut that something was wrong. She called the Charleston police. They went to the house but found no sign of Michael, and no sign of anything's being amiss. And then she began calling around to Charleston hospitals, and it was in one of them that she found him. He was gravely ill, a nurse told her; they had been trying to locate a family member. If she was his sister, she should come soon if she wanted to see him alive.

Nora flew into action and was in Charleston and at Michael's bedside within twenty-four hours. From his doctor she learned that Michael had a "social disease," compounded by pneumonia.

"But thankfully, we now have penicillin," the doctor told her. Nora had read about this new antibiotic.

For several days Michael slipped in and out of consciousness; when conscious, he was aware of Nora's presence and asked her to hold his hand.

In Nora's absence, Lark resumed going to the dunes. In his notebook, under the date 30 May 1941, he wrote, "Feasting with panthers," a phrase of Oscar Wilde's.

As the days turned into weeks and the weeks passed, it seemed to the others at True House that Lark was slowly getting better. He and Nora kept in close touch by telephone and by mail. After Nora had been in Charleston for two weeks, she sent for Emily. Although Michael's condition was improving, Nora could see that her presence would be required for some time to come. Besides, it just felt like the right time for her and Emily to be in Charleston together and for Emily finally to see her hometown. Because it still felt like home— another home—and she wanted Emily to know it, to experience it. Spring had not been completely taken over by summer yet: there were a few magnolia blossoms left on the trees, and a warm, sea-salt air blew through the streets, now thriving with crowds of *friendly* people (*that* was different from the Northeast). And the quality of the light! It was, Nora thought, an Impressionist painting come to life.

Also that summer, one of Hortense's dreams came true: she was invited to Yaddo, and she left for Saratoga Springs for two months at the beginning of July. Standing on the front lawn that dewy July morning before driving her to the train station, Leo promised that he would visit her there.

Now it was only him, Lark, Molly, Davis, and Will left at True House, Leo thought as he returned home: it had not been this empty since he first moved in.

The day after Hortense left, Nora called from Charleston and talked to Molly (Lark wasn't there). They would be taking Michael home from the hospital that afternoon, she said, but he probably would still need her and Emily to stay with him for another two to four weeks. Molly told Nora about Lark and little Will and the rest of them, and she gave her Hortense's address at Yaddo. Then she told her she missed her and said good-bye.

By mid-July, with Will now well over six months old, Molly and Davis decided that they were finally ready to take that long-anticipated trip to Boston so their relatives could meet Will. Using Nora's car, they left on a Thursday, telling Leo and Lark that they hoped to be back by Monday; they were just going for a long weekend.

Late that same night, a hot July night, not long after Leo had turned out his reading lamp, he heard a faint knock on his door. "Come in," he called quietly from his bed. Lark walked in, and though the room was dark, Leo could see that he was naked. He was also crying.

"Can I sleep in here with you?" Lark asked, sniffling.

Also naked, Leo stood up from the bed and embraced Lark, soothing him in just the same way that Nora had soothed him, by holding him and rubbing him and saying, "Shh, shh."

"I was up in the cupola, trapped with a hummingbird," Lark said. "It was horrible—he was flying about, his wings like a motor, crashing against the windows, against me. All around my face I could hear his little heart beating." Lark buried his face in Leo's shoulder. "It was a horrible nightmare; I tried to get back to sleep, but I couldn't."

"Shh," Leo said, thinking that Lark *felt* like a bird: he could feel his ribs as he hugged him. As they lay down on his bed, he pulled the sheet over them. Lark continued to whimper, and so Leo held him close and kissed his head and wrapped his body around him.

Before long they were both blissfully asleep, and that was how daylight found them, their bodies entangled under a thin white sheet.

Lark woke first, kissed Leo on the cheek, and then got out of bed and tiptoed out of the room. Awakened, Leo watched. He was shaken by what had taken place during the night, shaken and worried. Was this the beginning of what he had been wanting and waiting for for such a long time? Or was Lark simply seeking temporary solace and comfort? The latter was more probable, he knew. And yet . . . ? And yet they would have three more days and nights alone, Leo reasoned; *anything* could happen. Anything *could* happen, but should it? he asked himself, knowing the answer: it was too soon for Lark; it would be a mistake. And yet, because he had wanted this love with Lark for so long now, he didn't know if he would have the self-control to stop it. *It seems to have a life of its own,* he thought.

Both men stayed in their rooms for most of that morning, Lark haphazardly filing through his notebook and Leo reading. Worried that they might *appear* to be avoiding each other, both made noisy trips to the kitchen, each wanting to give the other the opportunity to come down and join him. Neither did. The two finally met up for a hastily thrown together lunch—apples and cheese and carrots and bread and coffee—that they took on the front porch. Sitting there talking, they skirted the obvious, choosing instead to discuss Nora and Emily and when they might return from Charleston, Molly and Davis and Will and how their trip might be going, and Hortense's stay at Yaddo, with Leo mentioning his promise to visit her there—might Lark be interested in going with him?

No, Lark said, he thought not; he felt like staying close to home.

After lunch, Lark told Leo he was going for a long walk. When Leo asked if he could join him, Lark apologetically explained that he would prefer to be alone. (He was going to the dunes.)

While Lark was gone, Leo wandered about the yard, checking on Davis's garden, visiting the rocking chair (*his* rocking chair), and ruminating. He hoped that night would be a repetition of the previous one, and to that end he thought he would prepare a nice dinner for them.

First, the menu: he would have to see what was on hand (he went into the kitchen and poked around). He could make an omelet. They had potatoes. And asparagus. A bottle of red wine: that would do it. He spread a tablecloth over the table and set two candlesticks on top. In true Leo fashion, he also readied all of the utensils and ingredients that he would need once he began the preparations. Then he went into his room and took a nap.

When he awoke it was dusk, and Lark had not yet returned home. And when at seven Lark had not come home, Leo decided to start preparing dinner, thinking surely he would be home by eight. He filled a large pot with water and four potatoes and turned on the stove. He peeled the asparagus—it was tenderer peeled—then put it in a shallow saucepan of water. He opened the wine and put bread on the table. And last he began assembling the omelet.

At eight Lark still was not there, and now Leo began to worry. But he pressed on, thinking Lark should be home *any moment now;* he would start the omelet and everything would be ready by the time he walked in the front door.

But at eight-thirty Leo could wait no longer: he was worried, he was angry, *and* he was starving. He ate his share of the dinner and drank half the bottle of wine, and when he was finished, he covered Lark's dinner and went up to his room.

Lark came home shortly after nine; Leo heard him. And while his impulse was to rush out of his room and down the stairs to greet Lark and warm up his dinner, he didn't stir. He listened, suffering silently and thinking that he might at the very least have the pleasure of hearing Lark eat the dinner he had prepared. But no: Lark immediately ascended the stairs, took a bath, and then went straight to his own room. Leo waited; surely *now* Lark would come to him. But again he was wrong. *It's going to be a long night,* Leo thought to himself then.

And about that he was right. He couldn't sleep, nor could he read or concentrate on much of anything. Lark was so close, and yet still so far. And Leo felt used. And angry. This was no good. And so he hatched a plan: he would go visit Hortense at Yaddo for the weekend. He had promised her. And the timing was right. Couldn't be better, in fact. He slept for a couple of hours, then got up and checked the train schedule. He wrote Lark a brief, breezy note to tell him where he was going, and then he left at seven.

Ironically, but unbeknownst to Leo, Lark had already left the house that morning, too—never to return.

How to Live?

■\\\\\\\\■

I had gone out on Pilgrim Lake in the little boat early that morning. It was predawn and there was still a lot of fog coming off the lake; I found myself thinking about how it might as well be the moon. I went there with thoughts of killing myself. I wasn't sure that I was going to do it, or that I could do it, but I left these lines from Hopkins out on my desk just in case:

So I go out: my little sweet is done:
I have drawn heat from this contagious sun:
To not ungentle death now forth I run.

It seemed the best thing to do at that point, with Austin gone. I had despaired for months—years, really, if you count all the worrying in advance—I had despaired for all that time about the day I knew would eventually come. It had finally come. Austin had to leave me, and I couldn't blame him. I had ruined it. It was all my fault. I was of no use to anyone. I could think of no reason to live, and every reason not to; I didn't know how to live anymore. That is, until I managed to think of Nora: I actually pictured her sitting down on the floor (in one of her long skirts) in front of Emily, and Schuyler was there, too; Nora was trying to explain my death to them. And then I saw Leo crying; Leo, who suffered so much all those years on account of me; and I thought about Hortense, and about Davis and Molly and little Will; and of course I thought about my beloved Austin, because I still hoped, hoped against hope. Thinking of my friends saved me. At least temporarily. I took the boat out of the water, tied it to a tree, and began the long walk home. I thought I smelled rain in the air; I even felt relief and some joy.

It was on the walk back that I encountered a tall man coming toward me on the same path in the woods. He had a rifle. It was hunting season. He looked at me. I looked at him; our eyes met. There was a recognition between us, a familiarity. I didn't immediately know what it was. I bid him good day and kept walking, because something was in the air—a disturbance of some kind. I felt a profound sense of unease. Just after I passed him I heard his voice. It seemed a feigned voice, a high-pitched voice attempting to be low and deep: "Wait a minute, boy."

I stopped and turned around. He was looking me right in the eyes, squinting.

"I seen you in the dunes, ain't I?" The sound of his voice was dry and metallic.

And then, in a rush, everything fell into place. That was why his face was familiar. And that was why I sensed trouble. Because what he really meant was, I had seen him in the dunes, hadn't I? I shook my head. I looked at the rifle: I should have taken off running right then and there, but I didn't.

"Deer," he said, shaking the rifle slightly. His mouth seemed to turn up at the ends in a sick smile, out of nervousness. He might as well have said "Lark."

I clenched my jaw, hoping not to show fear; I stiffened myself and proceeded to walk on, slowly.

But in the back of my head, as I walked away, I could just see him raise the gun to his shoulder, put his eye in line with that long, cold, metal barrel, and lift the rifle a final time, checking his aim. Then he fired—right into the center of the back of my head.

My skull probably exploded; I fell face down on the ground and must have died instantly. I don't recall anything after that. Especially not the recognition that I had, in a fashion, committed suicide after all, against my own better wishes.

By the time I was found, come upon by some hapless hunters, it had been raining for quite some time; I must have looked a sight. . . .

———

There is a tradition among poets reading their work aloud to repeat a poem or lines from a poem. I would like to honor that tradition now by repeating these lines from Hopkins:

So I go out: my little sweet is done:
I have drawn heat from this contagious sun:
To not ungentle death now forth I run.

Adieu.

How to Die

Leo, Molly, Davis, and Will were all back at True House for several days before learning what had happened to Lark. Although they reported him missing on Tuesday, it took until Thursday for the authorities to find his body. And then once he was located, he had to be identified, a grim task that Leo and Davis carried out together, Davis offering rocklike support to Leo, who almost passed out at the sight of Lark's dead body.

Gathered in the parlor later that afternoon, Molly, Davis, and Leo sat in shock, completely empty and out of tears. But perhaps the hardest work had yet to be done. "Somebody has to call Nora," Molly said, sniffling. They were all quiet, still. "*And* Hortense," she added.

"I can call Hortense," Leo said solemnly.

"And I guess we've got to tell his family, too," Davis offered.

But then Molly said that she wanted Nora to know first, and that she supposed she should be the one to call her, because she was probably closest to her—they had known one another the longest, anyway. But how she dreaded it.

"Oh my God, and Austin!" Leo gasped, suddenly covering his mouth and beginning to cry all over again. "We *have* to let Austin know."

The notifications, particularly of Nora and Austin, were wrenching. Nora apparently collapsed—her end of the telephone line went dead—and Austin, after considerable silence, simply said, his voice trembling, that he would be there as soon as he could.

Within half an hour the telephone rang; it was Nora, recovered enough to place the call, but still sobbing. She wanted to know if Lark's parents had been notified, and when Molly said no, Nora asked her to keep it that way for the time being, because only she knew what Lark had wanted, and she did not want them to interfere.

As she hung up the telephone, Nora was already recalling a conversation she'd had with Lark only a couple of years before: they were walking on the beach together; it was a cool, sunny day, probably in September; they were both wearing sweaters. Lark was the one who brought it up: "How would you like to die, Nora?" he asked her. She thought for a few seconds, the wind blowing through her hair as they walked (how happy and far away from death she had felt at that moment), and then she turned to him and said with a smile, "Quickly. And peacefully: in my sleep." And though in truth she wasn't particularly enjoying this little game, she cooperated by asking how *he* would like to die. Lark's answer was immediate: "Dramatically," he said, giving as an example Gerald's death, buried in the snow, in D. H. Lawrence's *Women in Love*.

Well, he had got his wish, Nora couldn't help thinking now, though when she did think it she also immediately answered that *that* was not at all what he had meant: he did not have a death wish; she refused to accept that. And she was determined that his funeral should be exactly what he'd wanted. The conversation that day had in fact moved on to funerals, and Lark had said that he wanted his kept as simple and inexpensive as possible: "A pine box carried out the back door of True House and buried in the nearby graveyard. A poem or two—Hopkins, of course, and perhaps Dickinson. And music, something simple and beautiful, maybe 'Danny Boy' played on a flute"—he had always loved the melody. And then he had stopped walking, taken Nora by the shoulders, and looked at her intently. "And I want my friends to have a party afterward, with good food and plenty of wine. . . ."

She had smiled at Lark through her tears that day. But she would also take her cue from him: he'd been saying that he wanted her, wanted all of them, to go on, to celebrate life. . . . And so she orchestrated the funeral just the way he'd wanted it. It was a Saturday morning. Hortense had returned from Yaddo. Austin was there and, more than anyone, he understood. He read those few lines from Hopkins that Lark had left on his desk the day he was killed. Emily recited "Heaven-Haven" as they lowered Lark's casket into the hole in the ground, choking back the words that now Lark was "finally there." Then they all hummed "Danny Boy" as best they could.

Afterward, at Nora's urging, Austin agreed to stay overnight at True House; she found his presence a comfort and told him so. For one thing, he had known Lark better than anyone—besides her.

Austin slept in Lark's bed that night. Although other sleeping arrangements were offered him, this was what he wanted, he said. And as he lay there, with Molly's painting directly in front of him, reminding him of the boyish, exuberant side of Lark, he thought: *Everything will remind me of Lark. Now and for a long time to come.* And then, covering his face with Lark's pillow so as to be as quiet as possible, he cried himself to sleep: there was nothing else to do, nowhere else to go, but *through it.*

That same night, in his reading, Leo came upon the following quote: "He who has a *why* to live can bear with almost any *how.*" It was Nietzsche. He recorded it in his notebook, and then he added the following: "Found for Lark—too late—28 July 1941." Unable to sleep, Leo crept into Hortense's room and, at her urging, climbed into bed with her.

Nora lay in her bed alone, thinking about Austin and how both of them now had a huge hole in their lives. She could still feel his warm arm around her as they'd stood around Lark's grave, his massive hand caressing, kneading, her upper arm, both offering and seeking comfort. Her mind stayed there for a time, lingering on and contemplating his touch, until that brought another thought to mind—that of Lark in his casket, alone; six feet under ground, dead. But she did not want to think of that; she knew it, and it was all too real to her. Nora had always found her mind to be fairly malleable and at her will, and so she turned it now to thinking about Schuyler. The last time she'd heard from him he was near Dover Beach; she had received a letter and thought of the Matthew Arnold poem of the same name. *"Ignorant armies,"* she mused, and shuddered. She would have to tell Schuyler about Lark, but how? In a letter? And what, she wondered, would his response be? He and Lark had not been on the best of terms since he moved out. Unfairly so, Nora thought: just because Lark was her closest friend, he had come to symbolize for Schuyler what he liked least about her. But then she remembered last Christmas, just before Schuy had gone away; things had seemed fine between them then. She had an image of them in her mind from that time: they were holding glasses of wine, talking together cheerfully. Yes, that was it. Now she could sleep. She would wire Schuyler in the morning.

Austin left for Manhattan and Hortense returned to Yaddo on Sunday; Nora drove them both to the train station, and Leo rode with her. There they all said their sad good-byes. Hortense would be returning to True House at the end of August, of course. "And you, Austin?" Nora asked him. "When will we see you again?" He hugged Leo, then kissed Nora good-bye, saying he would be up again soon: he wanted to stay on top of Lark's murder, wanted whoever had done it caught and punished. He said he would be in touch with the authorities and keep them up to date.

Nora thanked him, knowing it was a task she simply was not up to. She and Leo stood with their arms around each other and watched as Austin boarded and the train pulled away. As they got back in her car, Leo broke down. "I loved him, too, you know."

Nora nodded and bit her lip. "So did I," she said.

Leo looked at her and shook his head. "But I mean I was *in love* with him."

"I know." Nora hung her head and began to weep.

Then Leo told her about how, in Virgil, as a result of Pan's invention of the panpipe, even the mountains could be made to cry for man's sorrows.

Nora looked up and around, as if expecting to see those mountains; she smiled at him through her tears.

He embraced her, and they held each other for a time. Then Leo started laughing: "We were rivals!" he said.

Nora smiled and looked at him. She had often felt puzzled and even slightly offended by Leo's easy and sometimes inappropriate-seeming laughter, but now she thought she finally understood: it was an internal mechanism that triggered comic relief, a healthy thing.

"What do you say we pick up some coffee and pastries from the bakery and drive out to the breakwater?" he asked.

"I'd love it," Nora said, and she started the car.

After Lark

The rest of the summer dragged; Nora did not know quite what to do with herself now without Lark, but she knew she had to do *something.* Emily was completely independent, but that was nothing new; Schuyler was far away; and Michael was fully recovered now and getting on with his life—that was a relief. So Nora could turn her mind to this question of how to go on, to enjoy life, without Lark. *How to live?* She whispered the words to herself as she walked through the days. And what she realized, what she came up with, after much contemplation, was this: Lark, of course, could not be replaced. There could be no substitution. The only solution, therefore, was to love again and to love even more, for it to be bigger. And she thought of this as a life lesson—always to take the risk, make the plunge. . . .

Leo kept his promise and again visited Hortense at Yaddo late in August. After artists' work hours, at four o'clock, Hortense showed him around the grounds. They toured the rose and rock gardens and the four ponds, and she told him how each was named after one of the children of Spencer and Katrina Trask, the founders of Yaddo, all of whom had died in childhood. "The name Yaddo comes from one of the Trask children's attempts to say 'shadow,'" Hortense informed him.

Completely taken by the dark, elegant beauty of the place (it *was* shadowy), Leo said he wished *he* could spend two months there. That night they went to the famous horse track, just up Union Avenue.

Late that fall, Nora and the others received a letter from Austin asking if he might spend Thanksgiving with them at True House.

"Of course!" Nora wrote back, two words on a postcard—for fun. But then, immediately concerned that those two words hadn't been enough, she called him.

By Thanksgiving Day, little Will had turned one and was now tottering about True House on his own two feet. It was unusually warm for late November, and the windows of the house were thrown open to the sea breezes. Austin arrived that afternoon, bearing gifts—several bottles of red wine for dinner, preparations for which were already well under way.

At first the atmosphere seemed light and festive, but when Austin immediately opened one of the bottles of wine, poured a glass for everyone, and then proposed a toast (as they all stood around the dining room table), as if the light had abruptly changed and the room suddenly darkened, the group became somber: the *fact* of Lark's absence was all too apparent. Nora and Emily broke down first, followed by the others; finally Austin himself began to cry.

"And they *still* haven't caught the bastard," Austin said, clenching his jaw, both hands gripping the table. "They found the shell and know what kind of gun it was—some kind of rifle." Now he was almost mumbling: "They told me the name."

There was silence around the table, then Nora held out her glass: "To Lark," she said solemnly.

"To Lark," the others chimed in, clinking glasses.

"And to all of you," Austin added.

Again the glasses were clinked.

"To you, Austin," Nora threw in, extending her arm.

(In that moment, looking at Nora, Molly was reminded of *Madame Gautreau Drinking a Toast*. Nora winked at her knowingly.)

And then little Will in his highchair, who had seen and heard his parents toast time and time again and who was told the meaning of *everything* they said in front of him, touched his bottle to Molly's wine glass and said something that sounded like "Cheers!"

Dinner went off smoothly, with everyone successfully avoiding the subject of Lark's absence. Before they began eating, however, Nora requested a moment of silence, asking everyone to hold a good thought for Schuyler.

After dinner all of them, save for Emily and Will, decided to make the most of the unusually warm weather and take in a moonlit stroll along the beach. For a while the six of them walked together, but gradually they paired off in what seemed a natural fashion: Molly and Davis; Hortense and Leo; Nora and Austin. (Back at True House, Emily had begun reading poetry to Will.)

Molly and Davis leaned against each other, not talking much but simply holding hands and enjoying the peace and quiet.

Hortense and Leo were all animation, as usual.

And Nora and Austin surprised one another by *not* doing what they both feared they would do (even as they dreaded it): they did *not* talk about Lark—at least not at first. Instead, Austin told Nora how unhappy he was in Manhattan; he said he was thinking of giving it up altogether and moving back to the Cape. But he had commitments for another full year, he told her—through December of '42—and he wasn't sure how he was going to get from here to there.

Nora listened, encouraging him along, because in her experience it was unusual to hear Austin talk so much about himself. She offered that he would simply have to visit True House more often during the coming year, and that they would all be more than happy to do what they could to help him.

He said he would like that. And then his conversation began to roam widely, from his passion for the sea and his love of the works of Joseph Conrad (he said he'd read *everything*) to his admiration for the architecture of Frank Lloyd Wright, which Nora said she shared— perhaps they could visit Fallingwater together sometime soon.

But then the seemingly inevitable subject came up, and it was Austin who broached it: he said he *needed* to talk about Lark, would Nora mind?

She shook her head. Because in truth, she felt the need to discuss Lark, too. It seemed to just come over them both.

"It's all right," Nora said softly, meaning to soothe him. She looked up at his face and then continued, saying that she thought it was understandable.

Austin nodded his head. "I feel so guilty, Nora." There, he had said it! And he felt not so much like crying as like letting out air—the stale, fetid air that had built up inside him since Lark's death. "If I hadn't broken things off," he went on, "what happened to Lark never would have happened. I should have been more patient with him. . . ."

"No!" Nora cut him off coldly. She said she would not hear it; she couldn't. He should *not* feel guilty; she wouldn't have it. He *had* been patient, *had* been kind—she had seen it. And he was *not* to blame. She had realized there was a certain . . . *inevitability* . . . about what had happened to Lark, she said. She hated to say it, but there it was: Lark was on a course.

Austin was fighting back tears now; he thought he had cried enough. "Lark was like a motherless fawn, wasn't he, Nora? Always lost in the woods."

Nora thought about the question, but not for long, because she saw that it was true: there was about Lark, always, a *lost* quality. She nodded. "I think I was in love with him," she said carefully.

Austin smiled. "I know."

"Did *he* know?" she asked.

"He never said as much to me, but I think he did."

Nora looked up the beach at Leo and Hortense, then gestured in that direction with her head. "Leo was in love with him, too."

Austin nodded, then laughed. "We should form a club."

Nora smiled, raising her eyebrows, and said, "I think we have."

Later that same night, when the house was dark and quiet, Nora and Austin, dressed in their pajamas, ran into each other in the hallway outside their rooms; much to their and everyone else's surprise (the following morning), they wound up in her room, in her bed, without their pajamas and in each other's arms.

Another Bird Falls from the Sky

After that weekend it became possible for some semblance of normalcy to return to True House—as normal as things could be without Lark. Austin returned to Manhattan but took to calling almost every week, usually speaking with Nora.

The next year, 1942, would bring gas rationing to the Cape and to most of the country; the war in Europe was now in high gear. Nora grew increasingly worried about Schuyler, though he swore to her in his infrequent letters that, driving an ambulance, he was about as safe and far removed from the action as possible.

That winter, the first without Lark, seemed endless; suddenly it was as if True House were too small, with everybody getting on everybody else's nerves. One night at dinner, Molly and Emily had an argument: what in the world, Molly wanted to know, had Emily been doing up there in her room, one floor above, at all hours of the night before? It had sounded like she was pacing, Molly said, or dragging something back and forth across the floor.

That's a good metaphor for what I'm doing, Emily thought.

Regardless, Molly said she and Davis had heard her—and it wasn't the first time. They had hardly slept because of it.

Emily grew defensive, feeling guilty because she had accidentally dropped her dictionary on the floor the night before. But all she would say was that she liked that time of night, and besides, she couldn't sleep.

As always, Nora tried to smooth things over: it was the war, she said; their nerves were frayed. As a diversion, she suggested another trip to the Museum of Fine Arts in Boston. She knew it would be difficult for her—after all, it was where she and Lark had first met. But she wanted to face it down.

"That's a *marvelous* idea," Hortense said, clapping her hands together.

"I'll second that," Leo threw in.

"Let's *all* go," Nora pleaded, casting a smile around the table. "Even little Will—his first trip to a museum!"

"OK," Molly said.

Emily acquiesced, nodding.

"When?" Davis asked.

"Two weeks from Saturday," Nora said off the top of her head.

The week before they were to go, Nora happened to mention the trip to Austin over the telephone; he immediately asked if he might accompany them.

"Of course, Austin!" Nora exclaimed. Then she laughed. "But why would you want to travel all the way to Boston when the Metropolitan and the Museum of Modern Art are right there in your own backyard?"

"I miss you all," was his simple response. He would meet them there, he said.

———

At the museum, they took turns carrying little Will, who knew paintings from having seen so many of them around True House *and* in his mother's studio. He was excited to be amid so many different-sized squares and rectangles of color, wanting to be held close to them, to point and say "pain-ing" again and again.

They didn't play the same game they had played on the last group visit, naming their favorite painting for that day, though everyone did agree that Monet was undoubtedly a master of light; and Nora, noticing Cassatt's *A Cup of Tea* out of the corner of her eye, had an overwhelming desire both to avoid it and to go up close to it, to touch it, even. She fought the impulse and moved on, again admiring Rembrandt's *Old Man in Prayer;* but this time it was Constable's landscape of Weymouth Bay that called to her: Nora said it made her long to *be there.* Austin had always been drawn to El Greco and said that *Fray Hortensio Felix Paravicino* was one of his greatest works—they were lucky the museum owned it.

Leo and Hortense bemoaned the museum's poor showing in contemporary art, but Nora quickly changed the subject, asking if everyone remembered Schuyler on their last visit and his love for the dramatic seascapes of Copley and Turner.

Increasingly, Nora noticed that she simply did not have the time, the mind, or the energy for negativity of any sort; she wanted everything to be fine and for things to run smoothly, as far as possible. She wanted to float, and she felt she deserved it, too. (*And after all, such a desire was, at least in part, the original inspiration behind True House, wasn't it?* She recalled the lines from Hopkins that Lark had always quoted.)

And so she turned her mind from listening to Leo and Hortense's complaints about the museum's lackings to thinking about Schuyler, which was always a positive for her now; for as long as she could picture him, imagine him in a particular setting (amid the white cliffs of Dover, say), she felt that she could somehow protect him and that he would be safe.

But she was wrong. For on that very same day in February when the inhabitants of True House were touring the Museum of Fine Arts in Boston, the airplane Schuyler was flying (he had told his mother nothing about piloting planes) was shot down over Germany, and he was unable to parachute to safety.

———

A loud, metallic boom up in the wild blue; a tearing; a shattering; then a gaping hole, and Schuyler knocked unconscious; his copilot, Matthew Brande, killed instantly. That, followed by a vacuum—the sound and feel of air suddenly sucked out in a roaring whoosh; a cold blast; air seemingly pushing and pulling simultaneously; a vortex. And all the while the machine falls and spins—blue-white, blue-white—sky, turning and droning, spinning and falling, silver cartwheels (resembling a child's jack), a blur of silver metal trailing thick black smoke, until suddenly the ground appears to be rushing toward it, pushing up, rushing to meet it, until, inevitably, there is contact.

———

Notification took several weeks, and over the following month or so, as Nora lay in bed or sat in the parlor window, bereft, unable to move, she was consumed with wondering what *exactly* she and the others had been doing in the museum, what they had been looking at or talking about, *at the very moment* when Schuyler was killed. The thought haunted her. She hoped it had been something worthwhile, something meaningful. Perhaps it was the same moment in which she had pictured him amid the white cliffs of Dover. (*"Ignorant armies," indeed: Damn them, killing the young!*) Of course she was angry, angry many times over—at Schuyler's death, at the army, at a world in which older men sent younger men off to fight their battles, and, most difficult of all, at Schuyler himself, for having lied to her, for not having told her that he was flying airplanes. Perhaps the lesson in this for her, she thought, was that she could protect no one—not Schuyler, not Lark, not Emily; no one. But if only she could know what she had been doing *the very moment* Schuyler was killed. She tried to learn his time of death, but the most she could get out of the army was that it was in the afternoon of February 11, 1942.

But then, Nora had not learned of Schuyler's death in real time. It wasn't until March 3 that the army officer had come to the door of True House and knocked. Molly had answered, taken one look at the uniformed officer, guessed his message immediately, before he delivered it, and crumpled. Davis had been standing just behind her and caught her in his arms, saying in his deep baritone, "No! Oh Lord, no!" And then both of them had turned to look behind as Nora walked toward them—Nora walking toward them simply wanting to know who was at the door, and the two of them wanting desperately to stop her, to freeze the moment, to put it in reverse, to prevent her from having to know this, for it *not* to be true. But Nora, too, once she saw the uniform, had known immediately, and collapsed on her way to the door.

Although a telegram was the usual means of notification, the officer told her that because he was a neighbor (from Wellfleet), and because the boy was so young, he had wanted to do it himself, in person. They had been unable to reach the father, he added.

The next several weeks were a blur for Nora as she mostly lay in bed, tended to by the others. From that horizontal station she requested that Schuyler's body be delivered to her so that she could bury him in the nearby graveyard, as they had done with Lark. After his body finally arrived late in March, a second funeral service was held at True House. It was very simple: Beethoven's *Grosse Fugue* played on the recently acquired phonograph as Nora's friends assisted in carrying the casket out the back door and through the field to the neighboring cemetery.

Ben showed up, completely broken down, saying he felt responsible, shaking and sobbing the entire time. But Nora, coldly and to her confusion (her heart constricted), resented his presence (it surprised her; and she resented his grief, too), so much so that she could not go to him, could not comfort him or absolve him, much less seek solace from him, the father of her son. And so it was Hortense who tried to comfort Ben Croft, putting her arm around him and letting him rest his head on her shoulder when he seemed incapable of holding it up any longer.

And Austin, of course, was there, literally supporting Nora, holding her up on one side; Emily was on the other. Nora was grateful. She had asked in advance that nothing formal be written for the occasion, but she said that if anyone wished to speak spontaneously, that would be fine. But then when the time came, no one said a word. Silence hung in the cold air, as noiseless as a plane falling from the sky must be noisy. And that was fine with Nora, for what was there to say? *What could possibly be said that would make a difference? Nothing,* she thought. *Absolutely nothing.* There were times when words simply did not do it, were not enough; she had long known that.

Emily was too young and inexperienced to know anything about the limitations and ultimate failure of words; she still believed in them—fervently. Today, however, she was not talking, though she *was* writing: "I have lost two brothers," she penned on a scrap of paper at her desk, "one of the flesh, and one of the spirit." Now she sat on the sofa with her head on her mother's shoulder (Ben having left immediately after the service), clutching a bundle of letters from Schuyler, Nora's hand brushing the hair off her forehead again and again in a repetitive, seemingly mechanical rhythm.

Nora knew that she should rise and demonstrate a "life goes on" attitude. It was what Schuyler would have wanted, she told herself. And so she tried, tried to get up, to participate, to put one foot in front of the other and to feel that tomorrow would come and then the next day, and then the next, and that it all mattered. . . . But she couldn't do it. She was flattened, limp, wasted; like Hamlet, she felt "weary, stale, flat and unprofitable"; she was completely hopeless.

Amid it all she saw the faces of her friends: Molly and Davis and little Will, Hortense and Leo. And Austin. His was the only voice she could really make out, deep and resonant and with appropriate— what?—*gravitas* (how she had always loved that word!). They had slept together again, and sex was a revelation to her now, after all those years: she felt newly awakened, if also raw. But after the weekend Austin returned to Manhattan. He had work to finish up, but he said he would keep in close touch.

And so Nora returned to her bed, and the days and weeks passed. But then spring came. And as Nora lay in her bed, she could not help but notice the stronger quality of sunlight that played, filigreed, across the wall, the sweet sounds of birds chirping in the trees, and, eventually, little Will's voice as he played outside while his father worked in the garden. And in Will's voice Nora couldn't help but hear her own son's young voice, Schuyler's voice. She had always been a forward-looking person, and she was not going to give up on that now.

So Nora climbed out of bed, through the cobwebs, and back into life; a passionate woman, she *threw* herself back into it. It was May when she finally noticed, fourteen years to the month since she, Emily, and Schuyler had first joined Lark at True House. Walking outside now, she found that everything seemed beautiful and sacred to her: the sky was endlessly blue; the forsythia and lilac bushes were so vividly colorful that it almost stung her eyes to look at them; and there was the blessed apple tree. It all looked much the same as it had when they first arrived, in 1928. Save for Davis's lovely garden. And the house having been painted sky blue. And Leo's rocking chair. . . . My, they had done a lot with the place over the years! A lot, but perhaps not enough. (And looking back on this moment over a year later, Nora would recognize it as the seed of inspiration for something they could all do together, something permanent that would last, something immortal.)

Emily, Molly, Davis, Hortense, and Leo all gathered around Nora now as water surrounds and envelops whatever is tossed into it—relations at True House were *that* natural. They had had, all of them, their ups and downs over the years, times of feeling close, times of feeling less close; but that, too, was natural and true.

Nora's time spent in bed grieving for Schuyler (and Lark, too, for that matter) had not been completely fallow, wasted time, for lying there hour after hour, day after day, and night after night, she had become keenly aware of the passage of time and how illusory it could be. "For in a minute there are many days," Nora recalled Juliet's line. To which she might add, *And a year can take place in a week.* Where had the past fourteen years gone, for example? She remembered them well; they had been rich; but they had *flown* by (whereas the relatively few years of her marriage to Ben had felt endless, an eternity). It seemed only yesterday that Schuyler and Emily were children and she herself was only thirty-three. But suddenly she was forty-seven, and soon she would be fifty, giving her (she guessed) another fifteen or twenty years. Maybe. It was not long. Time was running out. Then and there Nora made a conscious decision to try to live even more fully in the present and to go more passionately after whatever she wanted. At the moment, for instance, she missed Austin, and so she simply called him and told him so; she also said that she hoped she would see him soon.

Austin visited often that summer. "Less than six months now," he said to Nora as they walked along the beach one day in July.

"Until what?" Nora asked. It was a softly sunny morning; cool.

"Remember I told you that I had commitments through December of this year?"

Nora nodded.

"After that I'm giving it up. Leaving Manhattan for good."

"And?" Nora looked at him quizzically.

"I'm thinking about moving back to Provincetown."

Nora smiled. "Good," was all she said for the moment. But as they continued walking, a gentle breeze blowing in their faces and the surf ebbing around their bare feet, Nora took Austin's hand, looked up at him, and said, "You're welcome to live with us at True House; I hope you know that."

Austin smiled and nodded shyly, but "Thank you" was all he said.

Both of them seemed to have made a decision *not* to discuss the new intimacy that had developed between them, as if somehow knowing, and embarrassed by the fact, that it was temporary.

That night in the parlor, Nora, Austin, and Leo all sat on the edge of their chairs discussing the war. Davis sat on the sofa reading a copy of the *New York Times* that Austin had brought with him (so what if it was several days old?), and Molly sat on the floor, playing with Will. Hortense was walking back and forth from the kitchen, where she was making something chocolate—Davis said he could smell it.

"Speaking of the war," Hortense said, "Max Ernst has been expelled from Provincetown! Madge just told me on the telephone. The officials were nervous that he would signal submarines from his seaside window." She laughed. "Isn't that ridiculous?"

"Typical American xenophobia," Leo said, also laughing.

"She also told me about some wild goings-on at a party she'd been to at Hans Hofmann's," Hortense went on. "A fellow named Pollock and his wife were staying with the Hofmanns. Pollock was jealous, got drunk, and threw Hofmann's easel off the balcony at him, but he missed."

"Artists!" Leo sighed, rolling his eyes, and Hortense returned to the kitchen, still laughing.

When Emily happened to walk through the room, Nora looked up and asked her to stay. Then she called to Hortense. She'd had an idea, she said, standing up and announcing it. She wanted them all to participate by saying what they wanted from the future. She would start them off.

"First, I want long and healthy lives for all of us," Nora said. "I want True House to go on and on, so that Emily and Will and whoever else will still be living here forty years from now, even into the twenty-first century." She smiled. "And I'd like for there to be some kind of memorial here to Lark and Schuyler," Nora continued soberly. "Something *we* make." Then she paused and took a deep breath, for this last thing was perhaps the most difficult for her to say. "And finally"—she cleared her throat—"I'd like to find someone—not a husband, I don't want to get married again—but just *someone* to be with . . . ," and here her voice trailed off. She looked around the room now, and everyone was beaming at her. "Who's next?" she asked.

Hortense stood up, planting her feet wide apart. "I want to go to Paris!" she crowed. "I want to have a one-woman show in Manhattan before I die! And finally, I want to learn how to make *crêpes suzette!*"

Everyone applauded and laughed, then Leo took the floor. "I only want what I've always wanted," he said. "To do the great work." And then he laughed.

Molly volunteered to go next. Looking at Will, then at Davis, she said she wanted to see her little boy grow up to be a good and gentle man, like his father; she wanted to enjoy life with Davis and with all of them at True House. "And of course I want to continue to paint— and to have a good time!" she added.

Davis was ready as soon as Molly sat down. He said he wanted the same things Molly did, for her, for Will, and for all of them. And then he looked at Molly. He was slightly worried, for he had never told her or anyone else about this wish, but it was a strong one, and a story he'd just read in the *Times* had made it fresh; it was something that was growing inside of him, and he wanted to be bold: "I'd like to travel to Africa someday, somehow—to see my native land."

*Ooh*s and *ahh*s swept around the room, and Leo slapped Davis on the back, congratulating him on his far-reaching vision.

"Make it happen," Austin said, putting one arm over Davis's shoulder.

Now only Emily and Austin were left. Emily got up shyly and shrugged. She knew that what she wanted would be neither popular nor understood, but it was the only thing she could think of: "I'd like a year of winter," she said, blushing and quickly sitting down. The room was suddenly buzzing and humming: "Winter! Why winter?" they all wanted to know. But Emily had already sat down. She shrugged again. "Because I like it," was all she would say.

Which left Austin. He stood up and looked around the room. "I don't suppose I can wish Lark and Schuyler back," he said, hanging his head. And then he immediately apologized for saying it: "I'm sorry." He shook his head as if to clear it; then he cleared his throat. "I look forward to being out of Manhattan in December and then to moving back to the Cape." He stopped and looked to Nora for her approval of what he was about to say; she smiled at him. "And to living with all of you here at True House, which Nora has invited me to do." At this line, everyone broke out into applause and welcomed him. "Thank you," he said, "I accept," giving a slight bow from the waist. "That's about as far as I can see at the moment," he added, and then he sat down.

Davis Hitches His Wagon to a Star

Because of the dream I announced to everyone, Nora has given me two books: one is called *The Souls of Black Folk,* and the other one begins, "I had a farm in Africa, at the foot of the Ngong Hills." Molly and I are reading this one aloud in our room at night with little Will, before he falls asleep—all of us absorbing the words, which are beautiful and powerful.

And while I have never heard of the Ngong Hills, I will learn of them, and I will see them—I am determined to go to Africa, with my son, and with Molly, before I die. I feel a duty to have a bigger life than my father had.

Emily Realized . . .

. . . that she no longer needed the lighthouse to create. *I can now work without her,* she thought (though of course she still loved it—preferred it, even—when the light was with her).

A new poem:

The temporal

for Lark

At rain fall, the ground remembers being in water.

Animals underground listen and remember too,
collecting light.

Night mists rise from cooling branches;
a trail.

The spirit moves, intangible to the senses.

Hortense Paints the Perfect Seascape

Hortense dug the heels of her bare feet into the soft beach sand, a feeling she had always loved. *Dammit!* she thought, *I will not cry*—not now! She would refuse, would will herself not to cry. As she moved her eyes from the sea depicted on her canvas to the real thing just beyond the easel, both seas appeared to her—in something of a runny wash—to be one and the same, the sea on the easel *a part of* the larger, moving sea. But she knew that her vision was blurry now and that she would have to see her painting clearly if she was to know whether or not the reason for the tears was true: had she, in fact, got it at last?

For years, days, hours, minutes, and sometimes interminable seconds she had struggled, looking at the ocean, studying works by the masters, and then once more staring at the thing itself. She had stood out there *en plein air,* in the blistering hot sun, in cold, biting air: she had done her time. She had dipped her brush into the many shades of blue, of green, of white, even of gray and, on rare occasions, yellow; she had applied the brush here and there. She had mastered new brushstrokes, here something small and subtle, almost pointillistic, there something bigger and wilder, sweeping, more brushlike.

Her eyes now clear, she stood back and looked at the painting, turned away, and then looked at it again. And again. And again! Then she looked at the real sea. Yes, she was happy with it; yes, she thought that at last she *had* got it! She couldn't wait to tell the others.

Slowly she began gathering her supplies together, but as she did so a calm feeling overtook her, and instead of rushing back to True House to tell Leo and Molly and Nora and Davis and Emily, she lay down on the beach with her head in her hands. Then Hortense closed her eyes and smiled the smile of a woman at peace with herself. It was a quiet thing, this success.

Leo in His Room, Alone

■\\\\\\\\■

Leo lay on his bed looking through a book of Leonardo da Vinci's anatomical drawings, something he had done time and again since he was a child. Because his parents were first-generation Italian immigrants, he had made it a point, early on, to acquaint himself with their country (especially its art, history, and geography) and some of its great men: Dante, Michelangelo, and especially da Vinci. Back then Leo had tried to imagine *being* da Vinci, because he knew the man was unique (*a genius,* people said), just as he knew, deeply, that he, too, was somehow special. Although where this feeling came from, he couldn't say. Certainly not from his parents or his schoolmates. Perhaps from his teachers, then? One or two of them *had* seemed to *recognize* him. Or maybe it was simply something inside, something he had been born with. It had remained with him, this feeling of potential greatness, all of his life and to this day. *And yet,* he had to ask himself now, *what have I done?* He knew the answer all too well, because he lived with it, thought of it, almost every day. *Nothing.* Or very little, anyway. He'd built an oversized rocking chair. He'd read a lot and kept a journal. . . . But these thoughts were getting him nowhere. He returned to his reading: "Leonardo's study of anatomy was helped along by the fact that he dissected corpses in the mortuary of the Santa Maria Nuova hospital, in secret." *In secret. . . .*

Before long, Leo had fallen asleep and was dreaming: onstage at La Scala, an opera singer opened her mouth to sing. He saw her lips, her teeth, and the darkness within her mouth in close-up; he was practically peering down her throat. Finally she began to sing, in a lovely, soaring soprano. It was not words that came tumbling out of her mouth, however, but buildings, architectural wonders (in miniature), one after another—accompanied by mathematical equations. A smile came to Leo's face. . . .

A Will-full Chapter

"Mama! Mama! Mama!"

(Pointing) "Pain-ing."

"Red."

"Blue."

"Puh-ple."

"Yellow."

"Grrrreeeeeeeeeeeeen."

"Ornge."

"Leo: read book."

"Papa, Papa: Baby go to garden." (And often little Will would sit there while his father worked, propped up in the rocking chair—Davis kept the vines *off* the seat—like a little buddha.)

(Pointing) "Sweet Will-yum."

"Brrrrrrrrrrrrr."

"Blue choo-choo."

In Memoriam

▪◟◟◟◟◟◟◟▪

The new year, 1943, brought the war ever closer. A typical newspaper headline of the day screamed: "PROVINCETOWN TO REHEARSE EVACUATION OF WOMEN AND CHILDREN BY SEA." Hortense would not, it was clear, be going to Paris anytime soon.

Early on in the winter, one January evening after dinner when they were all gathered in the parlor, Nora announced the plan that she only now fully realized she'd had during those months in bed, grieving for Schuyler and Lark. Looking around the room at Austin, Leo, Molly, Davis, Hortense, and Emily, she said she would like all of them to work together, to collaborate, on some kind of permanent memorial to Schuyler and Lark. She wasn't sure what—they would have to talk about it—but for some reason, she said, she envisioned a work of sculpture in the backyard. She hoped they could finish it before summer.

All that winter, then, there were frequent house meetings. Although the others were always consulted and involved, Austin and Leo seemed to take the lead in the project, in February traveling to Manhattan together to peruse (or *pillage,* as Leo joked) the galleries and museums for ideas and inspiration. The name most frequently on their lips after this visit was that of a young sculptor named David Smith. (The finished piece, Leo would always say later, was a marriage of David Smith and Brancusi.)

Much of March was spent in Molly's studio, with Austin, Leo, Molly, and Hortense hovering over and comparing sketches and designs at the end of the day. It was then that Austin and Leo realized they would need outside help—someone who knew something about welding, for example.

"I know just the fellow," Hortense said, snapping her fingers. "Billy Smithin." And then she winked at Leo and Austin. "He's a sculptor. Originally from Alabama. Knows his business."

And so Hortense arranged for Billy Smithin to meet them.

A compact man with blue eyes and curly black hair showed up at Molly's studio on the designated evening; he walked through the door smiling. Although short and small, he was also strong and powerful-looking; his clothes were spattered with plaster and paint. Hortense introduced him all around (Leo giggled), and then Austin described the project to him.

Sure, he'd be happy to help them, he said in his southern accent. And while he wished he could do it for free, he added, times were hard, and he would have to ask them for *some* pay—for his time.

They could do that, Austin said. "How's a hundred?"

"Sounds like it'll be less than a week's work." Billy nodded. "That's fine with me—if you're sure it's all right with you all?"

Austin nodded.

By early April, myriad supplies were constantly arriving at True House, and the work began in earnest. In the weeks that followed, stainless steel was delivered in sheets and tubes. And then once they were ready for him, Billy came over with his welding tools.

At most times during the week when Billy was around True House, he worked alone; he said he preferred it that way. Nora would go out to him now and then with food or something to drink. Their shared southern background was a comfort, and like a lot of southerners, Billy was a lively conversationalist. He was especially interested in Eastern religions, he told her.

———

It was by torchlight, aided by a full moon, that in late May the memorial work to Schuyler and Lark was unveiled. Its title, Leo announced, was *Sky/Lark,* Emily's contribution; that brought immediate applause.

"I'm just sorry Billy can't be here," Nora said; he had gone south for the month.

Standing approximately one hundred feet from the back door, Austin and Leo had covered the work with a sheet. As Nora and the others stood around, Austin ascended the steps of the footstool and pulled the sheet aside, to immediate *ooh*s and *ahh*s. There it was, shining in the light, constructed and mounted in such a way that it moved with the wind—curved arcs of polished stainless steel *signifying* a bird, *conveying* flight, *reaching* skyward. . . .

Nora glanced around at the dimly lit faces of Emily, Austin, Molly, little Will, Davis, Hortense, and Leo as they formed a circle, all of them looking up, their faces like bright coins. This seemed to her just right.

Curtain

That summer Truro, Provincetown, and Wellfleet were blacked out at night, and sirens for practice air-raid alarms were frequent.

So this is war, Nora thought: *night succeeding night; a profusion of darkness.* Was the world as they knew it coming to an end? Was it the end of humanity? Would men become savages once again? That was how it *felt* sometimes. It was like the wing of a great black bird (or, fittingly, of an airplane)—the black wing of war, forever blocking out the sun. It smelled like fire, or sulfur. And it tasted like metal. As for what it *sounded like?* Nora asked herself: a cello, or several cellos, moaning mournfully in unison, or dissonantly sawing, carving up one's peace of mind, tearing apart flesh, eating away at one's very soul.

As Nora lay in her bed at night all that summer, when—more often than not, it seemed—rain drummed on the roof and she could not sleep, her mind, inevitably, turned to thoughts of Schuyler and Lark.

And so it rained; so darkness prevailed. . . .

IV *The Swept Azure*

The vex'd elm-heads are pale with the view
Of a mastering heaven utterly blue;
Swoll'n is the wind that in argent billows
Rolls across the labouring willows;
The chestnut-fans are loosely flirting,
And bared is the aspen's silky skirting;
The sapphire pools are smit with white
And silver-shot with gusty light;
While the breeze by rank and measure
Paves the clouds on the swept azure.

Gerard Manley Hopkins, "A windy day in summer"

The Freshness of New Beginnings
(After Rain)

I am beginning this journey, this journal, taking up pen and paper, in an effort to—what? Express myself? Expose myself? Discover myself? Probably none of these (or perhaps a little of each); but more likely, and simply, toward a recording of daily life, *my* daily life—thoughts, feelings, events (personal and historical). . . . Toward an autobiography, perhaps? I suppose that would be possible, though it is not my intention at the moment, as I am not especially interested in going back in time and putting it all down here (verbatim and *ad nauseam*), except of course at those junctures where the past plays into the present, as it so often does. But no ancestral musings, no chronological disburdening of biographical details for me, please; no *My name is Nora Hartley and I was born in 1895 in Charleston, South Carolina!*

No. Instead, what I want is to make note, for example, of how vivid colors were to me that spring after Schuyler's death two years ago, and why that was (or perhaps more truthfully expressed, why it *seemed*), and then to try to understand how one might maintain that state of *aliveness*.

I want to think—out loud, so to speak—about Emily's writing, for she has finally shown me a poem! Dedicated to Lark, it is called "The temporal," a very confident, subtle, and knowing piece of work, *very* Emily; I am so proud of her.

Or I may want to remember Lark—*happy thoughts!*—and ponder what he would be like today if he were alive, what his life would be and, dare I say it, what he would think of what has transpired between Austin and me. Do I feel guilty? Should I? No to both! (But I decidedly do *not* want to think about the fact that Lark's killer has never been found.)

Or in thinking about Schuyler, I may feel like railing against the masculine machine of war, which still rages on as I write (Lark's killer being but one soldier in an army of murderers, for in my eyes it is more or less the same, the reason being irrelevant).

Or I may want to muse on Michael's flowering since Mother's death—Michael and his new and seemingly constant love.

Also, I want to record news that is significant to me, such as the miraculous cave paintings at Lascaux, which fascinate me, which I can't get enough of, and which I hope someday to visit. I've taken some notes:

> Found by children, the Lascaux cave paintings are an inexplicable and miraculous reality that compels us to look and consider them. It is an overwhelming discovery: paintings some twenty thousand years old that have the freshness and vividness of youth. . . .
>
> Never, before the discovery of the caves, were we able to obtain a reflection of that interior life of which art alone assumes the communication. . . .

Or I may write about whatever I am reading at the moment, currently *Let Us Now Praise Famous Men:* I find myself weeping at the beauty of James Agee's prose and Walker Evans's photographs. Just this morning I noted (thinking of Lark):

> I could not wish of any of them that they should have had the "advantages" I have had: a Harvard education is by no means an unqualified advantage.

He would have appreciated that.

Last, but perhaps most important, I simply want to get down on paper *something* of this life we have been living for over fifteen years now, as it is clearly not the ordinary life nor the life that most people have (or want).

And that, I think, is good enough for a beginning.

"The Look of Experience":
Portrait of a Lady

Several weeks ago Molly surprised me with the news that she wanted to paint me—again, for the third time. She said that she had something very specific in mind and wanted me to wear a simple black dress when I came to the studio.

That something specific, she has told me just today (after the fact), was a portrait of me *inspired by* a painting of Sargent's—*Mme Allouard-Jouan, ca. 1882* is its title. (I looked at her, moved—thinking this was so appropriate after *Madame Gautreau*.) Molly says her painting is a tribute to me and to all I have been through. She says she believes those experiences have changed me, even changed how I look, and she wanted to document that.

And so now that the sittings are over and the painting has been completed, Molly has shown me this, which Henry James wrote about the Sargent painting; she says she will affix it to the back of my portrait:

> I should like to commemorate the portrait of a lady of a certain age, and of an equally certain interest of appearance—a lady in black . . . which was displayed at that entertaining little annual exhibition of the "Mirlitons," in the Place Vendôme. With the exquisite modeling of its face (no one better than Mr. Sargent understands the beauty

that resides in exceeding fineness), this head remains in my mind as a masterly rendering of *the look of experience*—such experience as may be attributed to a woman slightly faded and eminently sensitive and distinguished. Subject and treatment in this valuable piece are of equal interest, and in the latter there is an element of positive sympathy which is not always in a high degree the sign of Mr. Sargent's work.

—Henry James, *Harper's New Monthly,* October 1887

"It is beautiful!" I cried. And Molly said that now—putting the three portraits of me she's done together—she felt she'd finally "captured" me, "the Nora I know and love."

Another Day . . .

I don't know that I even want to bother to date these entries, which I think assumes a significance, a posterior view, that I am not particularly interested in. For what I want is to make up my way as I go along; I want to *use* this forum (instead of being used by it). I want *process* to be all! Of course I may very well change my mind later on, and I will feel perfectly free to do so—that is one of the many wonderful things about being *here* (and this being mine . . .).

But the subject of the day, the hour, the moment, is *sex*. Didn't someone say that death is a great aphrodisiac? Well, I believe it, because I have noticed that since Lark's death, since Schuyler's death, and even since Mother's death, more & more, my sexuality, my desire—seemingly dormant & buried for so many years—have suddenly come alive, come to the fore: *I want*. . . . Perhaps it has to do with what has transpired between Austin & me (that he has reawakened me), or with the fact that I married Ben so young (too young) & arrested that natural sowing, just as most women do; or maybe it is that in relation to those deaths the value of life has been magnified. . . . But more likely, as is so often the case, it is probably a combination of these things, along with other elements that I don't even know, that remain submerged, subconscious. . . . Often now I feel this incredible, seemingly insatiable hunger, this longing. . . . Austin & I have talked. He says he can't just suddenly stop the feelings he has for men—or acting upon those feelings. And of course I understand & respect that. But it leaves me still . . . wanting. Just the other day, out in the garden with Davis . . . he was wearing overalls with no shirt on underneath, & I found myself stealing glances at him & thinking . . . wondering . . . (I am embarrassed to admit it.) He is *such* an appealing man, so . . . well, beautiful, really, is what he is. But such thinking is ludicrous! I could never interfere between Davis & Molly, not that I think he'd allow it—thankfully, he is totally devoted to her. I suppose the only solution is that I must venture out more, meet new people. Specifically, men. Yes, I think it is probably time for some new blood.

Like Mrs. Dalloway . . .

■⟍⟍⟍⟍⟍⟍■

. . . I have decided to give a party, war be damned! Molly & I have talked it over & we both agree that it is; or at least it could be, a good way to meet people (she says she ought to know).

As for whom we shall invite—a guest list—well, both Molly & Hortense are acquainted with plenty of artists through the Art Association, through their work with the WPA, & other venues—and artists are almost always interesting, one way or another. Hortense throws out names: "Mary Hackett and her husband, Chauncey; Stuart Davis; Ben Shahn. . . ." I don't know them but say the more the merrier, & I know Austin is still familiar with a lot of people from when he first lived in Provincetown, & Leo tells me that he has kept in touch with a few of the men he worked with out at the airfield. (Davis jokes that he knows "no one but us chickens," a comment that makes me sad because it gives voice to how circumscribed his life here has been, simply, stupidly, because of the color of his skin.) And Billy says he has a sculptor friend he'd like me to meet. And then there are those people one has encountered frequently over the years & always exchanged pleasantries with & perhaps even wondered about, such as the mailman, for example, whom I have always liked: I heard from someone, I can't remember who, that he writes novels. We shall attempt to compile a guest list of approximately fifty people so that even if only half of them show up, it will still be a good-sized & lively party.

And then Molly asks what *kind* of party it should be: should it have a *theme?*

I say I think not, not this first time, anyway.

Perhaps at least masks, then? she asks hopefully.

Maybe at a future party, I say—let's keep this one simple.

She is disappointed, but I tell her that the party is fraught enough for me as it is, without adding extra factors—such as disguises—to worry over. (Besides, I laugh, I *want* to be seen: that is the point!)

So we are all set. We must still decide on a date & time. Molly & Hortense say they will make the invitations.

Hortense asks if we need an occasion, if we should give a reason for the party?

Molly laughs & says "No!" I second her opinion: why must there be a reason? "Just because," as Schuyler used to say.

Emily says she will hide in her room, a comment I must immediately let go.

We decide to have the party late in September, over a month away.

In the evening, I suggest. 9:00 P.M.

The house will be filled with lit candles.

And flowers.

And there will be wine, lots of wine (flowing wine) & cheese & fruit & sweets. . . .

And we must have music somehow—for dancing! The phonograph? Or do I hire musicians?

And I will wear—what? I must buy a new dress, something rich in texture & color; burgundy, or forest green, perhaps velvet (it will be cool by then). With long, crystal earrings that catch the candlelight (& perhaps I'll wear my hair up).

Leo says he will rent a tuxedo. Davis & Austin both agree to follow suit. Davis asks if we think we could find one in little Will's size, too. Probably in Boston. Or New York.

Molly, Hortense & I all agree to go shopping together for new outfits. I'd like to buy some new shoes, too, something silver or gold, I think, with a thin strap around the ankle.

(My, but it is fun to write this out here, whether it goes off or not.)

And then I ask Emily if she won't reconsider. She smiles pacifically and says that instead she will walk the beach (and immediately I picture her walking up and down, perpendicular to the rolling, roiling waves, into the wind, in moonlight, the proud figurehead at the prow of a ship, talking or reciting poems, inaudible even to herself because of the pounding surf).

And then that pounding causes me to think of Schuyler, & of Lark (*war; death*), & I grow sad. I think about the fact that we never had a party, not like this—inviting people who *don't* live at True House—while they were alive, & I wonder why. And I suppose the shortest & simplest answer is this: because we didn't think of it! And if we didn't think of it then, we must not have needed it, or wanted it, in the way that we—or at least some of us, specifically *I*—seem to need and want it now. These are such different times—Schuyler, Lark & Mama all dead. There is the war now. And then there is my burgeoning sexuality. . . .

I have just caught myself out using ampersands, those pretty, fanciful little signs, instead of the word itself, as Lark always used to do (ah Lark, you are still with me—*&* in so many ways). Looking back in these pages, I see that it started a few entries ago, without my even consciously knowing it. Lark *&* I did seem to merge at times . . . where *I* became *we,* and *mine* became *ours.* . . .

The Party

■\\\\\\\■

I have not written here for a while because I have been busy. Is that the true reason? I ask myself, looking at the sentence I have just written (for I want, above all, to be truthful here). Yes & no. I *have* been busy, that is true, but also . . . well, let me back up: the party went off without a hitch, at least as far as I know. & Molly, Austin, Hortense, Leo, & Davis all agree (true to form, Emily indeed stayed hidden from sight the entire time). The candles glowed. The flowers sang their colors; the music, too, added color. There were more than forty people, talking & some occasionally dancing. It was beautiful.

But most important for me was the fact that I met someone—Billy's friend, the sculptor. His name is Theo—Theodore Schloss. We talked. We danced. But before I go on, let me describe him. He is around my age, or perhaps a few years younger. He is long & lean. His hair—& beard—are a shaggy strawberry blond, & his eyes cornflower blue; a sharp nose, a blade slicing down the center of his thin face, saves it from perfection. His big hands & long fingers are beautiful. There is a fierceness, an intensity about him that I find enormously appealing. At one point during the party, late, many hours into it (I know it was after midnight), while we were dancing, somehow—in the smoothest of segues—he swept me out of the room & into a closet, where— in the pitch dark—he kissed me passionately & deeply. . . . It was thrilling!—something I have not known before. The behavior of a much younger man (& of a much younger woman, for that matter).

He is a sculptor, & I cannot wait to see his work. Everything he does involves texts, in one way or another. He says he loves words (& here I think of Emily, though they have yet to meet) & always incorporates them into his work. He tells me that from a very early age he had a fondness for letters—A's & B's & C's; he had the alphabet on little painted wooden blocks. & he loved constructing things—such as small containers, boxes. . . . In his teens, his love of letters naturally led him to calligraphy . . . & he sees his work now as an outgrowth of all that.

But I don't mean to give the party short shrift because of Theo (& he wouldn't want that, either), for it, too, was a work of art.

All looked their best—Molly all in bright colors, squired by Davis, stunning in his tuxedo, along with little Will, who looked like a flower himself. Hortense—always a delight, even more so now that she has painted a seascape to her satisfaction (& it *is* lovely)—wore her traditional flowing purple, & Leo—Leo was nothing less than a revelation, the tuxedo gave him something I had not seen before, but what to call it? Stature? Presence? He looked so very handsome. I think there is a dormant greatness in him, & I know he feels this, too—frustratingly so. Only how to uncover it, cultivate it, and expose it to the light? (And on this note, he told me he'd met a retired classics scholar who lives in Provincetown, and with whom he has arranged to take Greek lessons: I sense that Leo is on his way!) & Austin looked so dignified—more & more like Abraham Lincoln as he gets older. (After the party he came to my room & we talked until four.) But there were also many people there from *outside* of True House: the mailman, whose name is Red, does indeed write novels! An interesting fellow. & I was especially glad to see Billy again; he came with another man—a fellow southerner and a playwright, was how he introduced him, though I'm not sure of his name (could it really have been Tennessee?). Ah, Billy—it was you who very well may have been responsible for the party! & it was because of you, too, that I met Theo!

As for me, I felt as though I had never looked more beautiful, which is exactly what Billy said when he introduced me to Theo. In short, I think the party was everything a party should be: it brought together a myriad group of people in a beautiful setting (amid light & color & food & wine & flowers & music), & for just a little while they all forgot about their private worries & the troubles of the world & became part of something bigger, had a collective good time. . . .

A Ripeness

Something is happening between Theo & me—something very real. I know I must sound like the silliest of schoolgirls, but it has taken me so completely by surprise: never did I expect to find love like this so late in life, at age forty-nine! I feel so full, & so fully loved. There is a fire between us, but we can also talk—easily & freely. What will happen? There is room for him in the house (my room!). But we have yet to discuss that. I know he loves his freedom. As do I.

My mind is flying. . . . Let me try to anchor it.

Austin tells me that he has been reading Lark's diary—he has at last felt able to do so. He says he will share it with me once he has finished. How will that be? Too painful? No, to feel is to be alive! (He also told me that he's happy for me about Theo, that he understands the attraction.)

Watching little Will totter about in the garden today with his father, I found myself wishing that Theo & I could have a child together. The urge was so strong & powerful that I actually felt it in my belly.

I see that I am back on the subject of Theo once again. Well, then, let me give it—give him—free rein.

We walked to the lighthouse yesterday. It was the first time I had been since Lark's death, & because, I believe, I was with Theo, it was fine (indeed, I had a moment where, hugging him amid the buffeting winds, he became for me, briefly, the lighthouse itself . . .).

But I will paste in this letter from him & leave off for the day:

Dearest Nora,

The animals are calling to me tonight as I sleep out under the stars in the back of the truck. I came out here because I could not sleep in my own bed: knowing that we had been in it together made me restless; I could smell your hair on the pillow. Even now it is all I can do to resist jumping into the driver's seat and tearing my way over to you.

I know that what is happening between us is taking us both by surprise. Such passion is not supposed to take place at our age. But it is something deeper than mere passion—a true kinship, too. We owe Billy a lot for introducing us.

Thank you for the poem by G. M. Hopkins and for telling me that he was Lark's favorite; the man has quite a way with words. I hope to use the poem in a piece someday, a piece for you.

I am writing this by the light of a candle—a soft light that reminds me of you, your softness, your glow. Good night for now.

Your,

Theo

A Page from Lark's Diary

15 May 1928: Here I am in Truro on Cape Cod, sitting in my room in the house that Nora & I have bought together—*our House*. I am waiting for her, Schuyler & Emily to arrive from Boston *for good*, which will happen in but a very few days. *For good*, indeed!

Who am I writing to here? To myself & myself alone: I am enough. This new diary will be a song that I sing of, for, & to myself, & I will sing it—when I can—at the top of my lungs. Or I will whisper it—whatever (and whenever) I wish; whatever I deem appropriate (only *I* define "appropriate"). It is *mine*—what is that Emily Dickinson poem? "Mine—by the Right of the White Election! Mine—by the Royal Seal!"

Oh, how I wish I could write poetry—*good* poetry, I mean, of course (I wish I could write it *well*). But I am slowly adjusting to the fact that I am not & never will be a poet. What is it? Am I too concrete? Or not concrete enough (too abstract?)? I am not even sure, that is how stupid I am. But let me not dwell *there*. Instead let me think about . . . *this:* that perhaps I can become a poet of life instead! That is, live life poetically—vivid & alive—from moment to moment. Yes, that is what I want. *Yes. Mine. Yes. Mine*—two favorite words. But Nora and the children are coming, arriving any day now, & *ours* is also a favorite word: *Our* house. *Our* yard. *Our* boat. *Our* . . . arcadia.

The Swept Azure

I dream, vividly, that the war is over & we are all meeting in the south of France—me, Theo, Emily, Molly, Davis, Will, Austin, Hortense, & Leo. Theo & I will arrive first & open the house we have let for the summer, an old stone farmhouse in the country with plenty of room for the lot of us. We are just outside Montignac, & the Lascaux caves are not far.

Gradually the others will trickle in—first Emily, with Molly & Davis & Will, then Austin, who will come by way of London, & finally Hortense & Leo, who have stopped off in Paris for a few days on their way (& they will have spotted the Misses Stein & Toklas walking out of 27 rue de Fleurus). Those arrivals (oh, and Billy, too, if he likes), again & again, will be exhilarating—just as they were in the beginning at True House.

There will be a journey, perhaps several journeys, to the caves at Lascaux, but otherwise we will mostly stay put, happy as cows. I see us—eight once again—sans clothes, bathing in a sapphire pool. We come & go through fields of shoulder-high sunflowers (all of us wearing straw hats), picnicking on the grass in the shade of a willow tree, lolling in hammocks—wine sparkling in the sunlight. & of course there will be a view; I see a vast & beckoning & utterly blue sky. . . .

All the days of summer, that summer, will be like this.

Acknowledgments

My heartfelt thanks to beloved Yaddo, where much of this book was written during autumn residencies in 1997 and 1998.

Special thanks to Lee Salkovitz. I am also grateful to Sena Jeter Naslund, Steve Bauer, and Kirkby Tittle (aka Kirby Gann), my critical readers and friends; to Angelo Monaco, for poetry; to Martha Corazon and Neela Vaswani, for their belief, encouragement, and support; to Bruce Aufhammer, for driving me around "rural Truro" so memorably; to Jennifer Hagar, for help with research; to my agent, the aptly named Joy (Harris), who lifted me up—also to Leslie Daniels; to Dorothy Straight; to Kate Griggs; to Carla Bolte, for her beautiful design; and to my dream editor, Ray Roberts at Viking.

Thanks also to Ellen Balber, Bonnie Barber, Gaynor Blandford, the Honorable Joseph Caldwell, Michael Carroll, Art Corriveau, Eileen Fitzpatrick, Peter Gardner, Anne Hoppe, Bob O'Handley, Rick Reinkraut, Louise Riemer, and Jamie Sieger.

Many books were helpful in my effort to portray Truro and Provincetown in the years 1928–1943, among them *Time and the Town: A Provincetown Chronicle*, by Mary Heaton Vorse; *My Pamet: Cape Cod Chronicle*, by Tom Kane; *Art in Narrow Streets*, by Ross Moffett; *Provincetown: The Art Colony*, by Nyla Ahrens; *The Outermost House*, by Henry Beston; and *Cape Cod*, by Henry David Thoreau. Several issues of the fine journal *Provincetown Arts* were also of great value and interest.

The poem on page 287 is by Angelo Monaco and is printed with his permission.

An excerpt of this book appeared previously in the *Louisville Review.*

2011